Pride Publishing books by AE Lister

Persuasions
Various Persuasions

I0681014

Persuasions

VARIOUS PERSUASIONS

AE LISTER

VARIOUS
PERSUASIONS

Dedication

To those who know who they are.

Prologue

My fingers holding the photograph were pale with the effort not to crumple the damn thing up and be done with it, with *him*. My nails were rough and jagged from my gnawing on them. I didn't know why the 'breakup' had caused me such anger, except that I felt used and cheated.

It had been months, but I still couldn't think about Zane without anger and feelings of betrayal.

He'd said he would teach me. He'd said he would show me how to be a good Dom. I'd been so thrilled that a male Dominant would take me under his wing that I hadn't questioned his reasons. I'd figured he'd seen something promising in me and wanted to refine it.

I knew I was unique. I knew I was different. I was proud of it. I had never expected someone to use that uniqueness to their own advantage.

I felt like his circus pony. He'd trotted me out to his subs like a fancy treat to be enjoyed for its flavor then tossed aside.

He hadn't cared for me the way I'd cared for him — the way I'd *thought* he'd cared for me.

I stared at the blurred outlines of the man who'd taken my heart and trampled it and vowed never to care so much about anyone again.

Chapter One

Two months later

The call came in near midnight that Friday.

I was sitting down with a beer and my remote to watch *The Great British Baking Show* when my phone started playing *Sympathy for the Devil* – Daphne's ringtone.

What could she possibly want from me at this hour? She should have been working. I *knew* she was working. It was Friday night, for fuck's sake. But the curiosity got to me.

"Hey, doll." My standard greeting for Daphne.

"My lovely Nic. Are you busy?"

"Never too busy for you, Daphne. What's up?"

She giggled. I pictured her face, its pixy-like innocence that belied a very dark soul. "I have this client—"

"No," I said without thinking. I knew what she wanted, and the answer was no. It was always no.

"But, Nic, I haven't even told you—"

"You know I don't do that anymore."

She sighed. "Just listen, okay? Just listen to what I have to say."

My jaw tightened and I wanted to hang up, but I wouldn't do that to Daphne. We'd been friends for too long. She'd known me, like…forever.

"Fine. But the answer is still no."

Not to be deterred, Daphne continued. "This client… His name is Vincent."

I snorted with derision. "A *guy*, Daphne?"

"Yes, Nic, a guy. Get over it. *You*, of all people, shouldn't get hung up on gender."

I mean, she was right. But…still. "I don't have experience with guys, Daphne. You know that."

"Look… Hear me out. Please, Nic."

I looked at the clock above my flatscreen. It was twelve-oh-four. "You have five minutes."

She giggled. "Okay. So, he just left. And our session was…interesting."

"Really." I tried to sound remotely engaged.

"I don't think he's into women like me," she said with a pout in her voice.

"Huh."

"I mean, he's into submitting. That's for sure. And he *did* submit for me. And he *liked* submitting for me. But…"

"But?" I picked up a pen from the coffee table and started pushing the button with my thumb. It made a comforting *clicking* sound.

"I think he needs something else. I think he'd respond better to something else."

I closed my eyes. *Click.* "To what?"

"To you."

"Are you fucking kidding me, Daphne?"

"No."

I didn't want to do this. I didn't want to be reeled in. "I don't do that anymore."

"Well, that's a damn shame, Nic, because you were the best at it."

I snorted again. "That's debatable."

"Not by anyone I've ever spoken to about you."

I held my breath. "*Who* have you spoken to?"

She hesitated and I knew the answer.

"Fuck you." *Click, click, click.*

"I mean, I know a lot of people who knew you when you—"

"Daphne," I said and closed my eyes, leaning my head back against the wall. "Did you talk to Zane?"

She hesitated again and I *knew* she had. "He misses you."

My heart shattered a little bit, but I put it back together with sheer will. "It doesn't matter."

"Nic, he didn't mean to treat you badly."

"Doesn't matter. He did."

"But you don't have to stop doing what you're good at."

My voice, when I found it, sounded small. "I'm only good at it…because of him."

"I know he taught you. I know he mentored you. But you surpassed him a long time ago."

"Daphne, that's not true."

"It *is* true. And *he* told me that."

That surprised me…and didn't. Zane had never been one to hand out compliments directly. It figured this would be how I found out.

"He did?"

"You know I wouldn't lie about this, Nic."

"I know." My voice was barely above a whisper.

She continued in a soft voice. "Can I please just tell you about Vincent? Please?"

Maybe it was because she was such a good friend. Maybe it was because we'd known each other for so long. Maybe it was because what she'd just told me about Zane was something I'd wanted to hear for so long.

"Fine. Tell me."

"Okay. Well, he's twenty-four and cute as shit. You know I only agree to the cute ones."

I couldn't help but laugh. Daphne had high standards when it came to physical attractiveness. I'd never cared about that as much as she had. Still…

"Twenty-four? That's way too young, Daphne."

"Too young for him to know what he wants?"

"I thought you said he's not working out."

"Yes, but that's my fault, not his."

"Why is it your fault?"

She giggled again and I heard her self-deprecating sigh. "I'm too girly."

"Fuck, Daphne."

Honestly, she *was* girly. She was fucking high heels and corsets and ribbons, doling out praise and punishment with crops and paddles and rulers. Most of her clients dug that. *Maybe not this one?*

"It's true. He needs something else."

"Um, like a guy maybe?"

"Not exactly. Like you, Nic."

"Is he gay?" He might have been gay and closeted — trying to get off on a Dominatrix when he really wanted a Dom.

"I don't think so. Maybe bi. He likes lady parts. I mean *really* likes lady parts." She paused. "I think he's attracted to the masculine but not necessarily to men."

"So, what am *I*, Daphne?" That was the question I'd been trying to answer my whole life.

"You are my Nic. You're a guy, a man for all intents and purposes. Except you have that unique element…"

I couldn't help but laugh. "A pussy?"

She laughed too. "Well, yes."

Honestly, I didn't feel like a man *or* a woman and I didn't feel like I had to choose between those two things. I was myself. I was Nic Walker.

My name had been Nicole, but people had started calling me Nicky, then Nic. That was probably because I'd never really looked like a girl — and I'd never really acted like a girl and I'd never really felt like a girl. But I'd never questioned what I was.

Physically, I was female. I had a pussy and I had boobs, albeit really small ones — small enough that I could ignore them for the most part, which I generally did. I didn't need a bra or a binder. If I had been stereotypically female, their size would have been a problem. I could pass as male most of the time. I *did* pass as male most of the time and I had no problem with that, except romantic relationships could be tricky.

I had predominantly dated women. I was predominantly attracted to women. There had been the occasional man — like Zane — and I'd always regretted those experiences. But Zane *had* taught me to embrace my Dominant side, and he'd taught me the practical skills to do it — not with him, but with women. Daphne had helped too. She had helped me to accept who I was and what I liked to do.

When Zane and I had 'broken up', for lack of a better term, I had turned my back on all that. And here was Daphne bringing it back up when it was really the *last* thing I wanted.

"What's his story?"

"He's lost, Nic. He's shy and he's ashamed of himself and what he wants. But he's at a point that he can't deny himself anymore. So, he came to me. But I think he needs *you*."

"How do you figure?" *Click.*

"He's not looking for stereotypes. I don't…do it for him."

I leaned my head back against the wall and propped one bare foot on the sofa. It was small, perhaps the most feminine part of me and the reason I generally wore boots and clunky shoes. I didn't deny I dressed like a guy. I *looked* like a guy. I *felt* like a guy most of the time. But I didn't hide the fact that I had female parts. It simply didn't come up in conversation. I wasn't ashamed to be atypical. To be honest, I liked it. I strived after uniqueness. I didn't want to be like everyone else, and I wasn't.

"You're not a stereotype, Daphne." I felt like I had to say that, even though if you looked up 'Dominatrix' on Google, you'd see Daphne or someone who looked a lot like her.

She laughed again. "I kind of am."

"Okay, you kind of are, but you're lovely." The truth of this choked me up and I realized I'd missed her. "I don't think I can compete with you."

"I'm not asking you to compete with me. I'm just asking you to meet with Vincent and see what happens."

"Have you told him anything about me?" *Click.*

"No. I feel like he should make up his own mind." She said this with confidence.

Daphne was perceptive and smart. "Good."

I heard a squeal on the end of the phone. "Then you'll meet him?"

What am I doing? "Okay. Sure."

"Yes! Even if it doesn't work out the way I think it will, thank you for agreeing to do this, Nic. It means everything to me."

"Sure. I know."

She cleared her throat. "I should mention that he's not a paying client. I took him on as a favor to someone."

"That's fine. You know I don't monetize this sort of thing."

"I know, and you're nuts. Do you know how much money you could make?"

"Yes, Daphne, I know. I've really got to go."

"Listen… He's really sweet. You're going to like him."

"We'll see."

"Love you, Nic."

"Love you, Daphne."

* * * *

I met the guy the following week. Daphne gave him my number and he called me pretty quickly. He seemed nice on the phone—a little hesitant, a little lost. Nice tenor voice. A bit of a stutter but it wasn't really obvious. Just shy. Seemed too deferential—a bit too *weak*. I liked my subs to have backbone. I didn't want it to be easy. Natural for them to submit, yes, but not necessarily easy.

We agreed to meet at the Starbucks near me. I made sure to get there first since I wanted to observe him as he arrived. I needed to get a read on this guy.

Daphne had said she'd shown him an older photo of me. I hadn't changed much. I'd been too skinny back then but I wasn't much more filled out now. My muscles were more defined because I made a point to work out. I had short hair now, while in the photo she had shown him my hair was long and I'd worn it in a tight ponytail at the base of my neck. It was a little more feminine, although not that much. I had no idea what he thought or expected of me.

We'd told each other what we'd be wearing. I was in my usual jeans, T-shirt and leather jacket. Combat boots. At only five foot seven, I stood taller than average for a woman. It wasn't tall enough for me. If I could have changed anything about me, that would have been it. Anyway, I looked taller in my boots and jacket. At least I *felt* taller, and that was the important thing.

He showed up about fifteen minutes after the agreed-upon time, which ticked me off. I *hated* waiting, and I'd arrived early so I could get a table and watch him walk in. I'd been there awhile.

He was cute, I couldn't deny that—more attractive than I'd expected, which also pissed me off. I'd seen enough cute white boys who thought they were the shit, even if they started off with a humble act. Then again, Daphne would have flogged that out of him pretty quickly.

He looked around at the other patrons then he found me. His eyes widened, flitted down to the floor then back up. He started toward me.

I sat up straighter, feeling a visceral reaction from a place deep inside me as he approached. I'd seen him before, *somewhere*. I was sure of it.

"Hi," he said when he got close. "Nic?"

I gestured to the chair opposite. "Sit."

He did, without question. The denim jacket looked big on him, his jeans a little loose. His runners were scuffed and dirty. He was supposed to be twenty-four—he'd better be twenty-four—but he seemed younger. *Dangerously* younger. I felt like asking for ID but I was sure Daphne had done that already. She knew what she was about, that girl.

"You're late," I said to Vincent while sipping my black coffee and appraising him. He was slight but he had some lean muscles and a decent build. His brown hair peeked out from under a black beanie.

I was wearing a dark green beanie. That didn't signify anything except that we liked to keep our heads warm.

He smiled, as if to disarm me, but I kept my expression neutral. This seemed to unsettle him and he shifted in his chair, dissembling. "I'm sorry. I misjudged the time."

"Strike one."

"Pardon?"

"That's strike one against you already. I hate waiting."

He stared at me. I held his gaze until he looked down, blushing, and uttered an apology. "Sorry. I'm sorry I made you wait."

"Good. That's better." I tried to relax but his looks and his appeal made me nervous. I didn't want to be attracted to Vincent but I was.

He shifted in his chair again, clearing his throat. "Daphne said you didn't want to meet me at first."

"What?" *Why would she tell him that?*

"She said you didn't really want to meet anyone right now but that you did her a favor by agreeing to meet with me."

I looked him up and down, seeing exactly what Daphne had described to me — a shy, handsome young guy who seemed lost and unsure. That was not without its appeal, if I were honest.

"What else did she tell you?"

He smiled again, and I had to admit that he *was* cute — really cute, with a dimple in his cheek and those brown locks sweeping his forehead. Blue eyes…my weakness. *Fuck it.*

"That your name is Nic. That you two have been friends since you were teenagers. That you might be more what I'm looking for."

"What *are* you looking for, Vincent?"

He swallowed. "I mean…well, you know…someone to —"

I fixed him with a stare. "Dominate you."

His blushed deepened. "Yeah."

"Sexually?"

He looked around to see if anyone had heard me. "Pardon?"

"You want to be dominated sexually? Or just dominated? There's a difference." I was making him uncomfortable. I knew that and I liked it.

"Okay, sure. Yeah. I mean, yes. I mean, I don't really know."

Okay, I'd make this simple. "Has Daphne made you come?"

He looked around again. I honestly didn't give a fuck if anyone heard me. The place was filled with people having their own conversations.

"Yes," he said very quietly.

"So, *yes*, then. But also, maybe, just *dominated*?"

He nodded.

I liked the way he looked and the way he seemed to defer to me, even though I was almost a complete stranger. It surprised me, really, because I hadn't expected him to be anything much. I hadn't expected to be *tempted*.

"What do you want in a Dominant, Vincent?" I asked because I wanted to hear it from him. *Rules, punishment, praise?* I could give him all those things. Or was it something more specific?

He stared at me, his eyes wide, as if he couldn't believe we were having this conversation in a coffee shop. But if he wanted to do this, he needed to know I didn't play games. I was straightforward and demanding. I was also fair, and yeah, this was kind of a test. If he couldn't handle talking about this in public, he wouldn't be able to handle what I'd want to do to him in private…if we even got that far. I was tempted. I hadn't thought I would be.

"I think I want *you*," he said softly, his eyes downcast.

"Sorry?"

His blue eyes flitted to mine and they were blown full of desire and trepidation and a blunt, brutal honesty.

"I think I want *you* as my Dominant."

I blinked. I didn't say anything. I held his gaze and sipped my coffee, focusing on the bitter, strong brew and chocolate undertones. His answer seemed at once the height of presumption and incredibly daring. So, he *did* have a backbone. *Hmm-m.*

He frowned. "I'm sorry," he said, and it seemed like he wanted to get up and leave. I'd made him uncomfortable again. *Good.*

"Why? You answered my question...in a way." I gave him the benefit of a small smile. A quirk of my lip really, to settle him.

He responded with a bigger smile, and it lit him up. *Jeez.* He was *gorgeous.* And I was truly *fucked.*

I leaned back in my chair. "Why don't you get something to drink, and we'll talk."

"Oh, I'm not really—" he began but saw my eyebrows shoot up. "Oh. Yes...um..." And I could see him running over forms of address in his head. He didn't have a handle on my gender yet. And I liked that he didn't presume.

"You can call me 'Sir'," I said, not giving him an answer to the question but letting him know what to call me.

"Yes, Sir." He whispered it, so no one else would hear. Then he got up slowly from the chair.

"Vincent," I said.

"Yes?"

I pulled a fiver out of my pocket and passed it to him. "I would like a chocolate chip muffin, please."

He took the money with a smile, his eyes downcast. That made me happier than it should have.

"Yes, Sir."

I could barely hear him, but he'd said it. I watched him walk to the counter. He was tallish, probably around six foot or so, with long arms and legs. *Rangy.* I could work with that.

What the fuck am I thinking?

Honestly? I was thinking that he was incredibly cute and responsive, and maybe I could work with him.

I couldn't believe I was going to give him a chance.

Chapter Two

As he placed his order, I caught him surreptitiously glancing my way a couple of times. I watched him closely but kept my expression neutral when he looked over. I knew I made him uncomfortable but I liked it. I thought he did too.

I also noticed he had a spectacular ass, which I would make plenty use of if we ended up doing this...*thing*. Even if we only got as far as domestic discipline with no sexual play, I would spank that thing into next week.

Unless, of course, he wasn't into it. I desperately hoped he was, and I was pissed at myself for thinking that far ahead. But I had my weaknesses, and spectacular asses were one of them.

I was determined to start slowly. We needed to get to know each other before we did anything remotely hardcore, and I didn't know if I wanted any of this to be sexual. In fact, I was thinking at this point I *didn't*. Even though I did find him attractive, it would be so much simpler if it was just about Dominance and service, at least for the moment. That would be a safer place to start, anyway.

He returned to the table and placed the muffin in front of me before putting down his vanilla latté. Then he sat and wrapped his long fingers around the cup.

"Drink," I said as I began to slowly peel the wrapper from the muffin. I mean, he was probably planning to drink, right? But now I'd made it into something he had to do *for me*. I was devious that way. Might as well let him know how this would go.

He blinked at me and I suspected I'd made him hard just by telling him what to do. There was a tell-tale flush to his cheeks and a shift in his posture. His pupils had darkened. I knew the signs. They were pretty much the same in both genders. Clits got hard, too.

All that meant I was doomed. He was fucking perfect. I told myself it didn't matter, that I would *not* fall for him. I'd do this favor, maybe, for Daphne...for Vincent. There would be a defined time limit—maybe a month, maybe two—and that would be it. He'd have to find someone else.

He lifted the cup to his mouth and took a small sip. It was probably too hot to take a bigger one.

"*If* we are going to consider this," I began, "I need some answers."

"Yes, Sir." Barely above a whisper again. I allowed it, since we were in public.

"How old are you, Vincent? Daphne told me but I want to hear it from you."

"Twenty-four. Sir."

"I won't ask you for ID, but if I were to ask to see some, I assume it would validate your answer?"

"Yes, Sir."

"I'm *thirty*-four. That's a ten-year age difference. Does that bother you?"

He shook his head. "No, Sir." His eyes flitted from the table to the floor, to the lineup at the cashier, then back to the table.

On a hunch, I said, "Does it turn you on?"

A tiny smile, then he schooled himself. "Yes. Yes, Sir."

"I know Daphne didn't really tell you anything about me. I want you to know that I don't conform to gender stereotypes, but I was born female and I haven't transitioned, nor do I feel the need to do so."

He glanced at me with those blue eyes and I forced him to hold my gaze.

"I am the way I am. I enjoy being called 'Sir' and many other things that might not be typical of a person of my sex. I prefer 'he' and 'him' from people who know me well. It's too exhausting to correct everyone else. I would say that eighty percent of the time, the general public uses 'he' and 'him' for me anyway, because of how I appear."

He observed me calmly, as if none of that information was a surprise.

"Problems with any of that?" I asked, waiting for something to be wrong with him or wrong with *us*.

He shook his head. "God no. I mean, no, Sir."

"And your pronouns are?"

"He and him," he replied, taking another sip of his latté. "But I don't necessarily conform to gender stereotypes either," he offered.

This information intrigued me. For all intents and purposes he looked and acted like a man. Of course, he wanted to be submissive to me, which already took him out of the gender norm. If there were more hidden layers to him, all the better—except now I wanted to find out what they were.

"Meaning? Be specific."

He blushed even more. "I, uh, like wearing lingerie. Skirts. Not heels really but other…ahem, feminine garments."

I liked the way he said 'garments', like a nineteenth-century dandy.

"I can work with that."

He cleared his throat. "Thank you, Sir."

His polite gratitude surprised and pleased me, but I needed to proceed cautiously—more so because I could feel my natural defenses weakening in the face of it.

"How do you make a living, Vincent?"

"I'm a financial advisor at Scotiabank," he said quietly, "for now."

"Long-term goals?"

He shrugged. "Not really sure at this point."

"Fair enough. You're very young."

He glanced at me and frowned. "Too young?" It seemed like his every hope hung on my answer.

"I'm not sure yet."

"Okay, Sir."

"If we go ahead with this…arrangement…for lack of a better word, we need to start slowly. I need to get to know you a little and you need to get to know me *a lot*. We need to see if this even has the potential of working out."

I already knew it did. But it was a big leap from potential to certainty, and we needed to tread carefully.

"I'm fine with that, Sir. It…makes sense."

"How are you with an Allen key?"

He blinked. "What? I mean, I beg your pardon, Sir?" His natural politeness disarmed me, but I was glad to see a small chink in the protocol.

I tried not to smile. "I have some IKEA furniture that needs putting together. I hate that crap. I don't really have the patience for it." I shrugged.

"Oh!" he said, smiling. "I'm good with tools. And I have lots of experience with IKEA furniture."

I nodded, giving him a look-over, deciding that, whatever the outcome, I should give Vincent a chance. I reached into my back pocket and pulled out my business card. "Are you free this weekend?"

He smiled. "Yes, Sir…all weekend."

He was eager, and I liked that too.

"I don't need you all weekend, but I want you at my place Saturday morning, nine o'clock sharp."

He smiled again. "Okay. Thank you for giving me a chance, Sir."

"I don't do this very often…ever, these days. If I weren't so close to Daphne, I'd have told her to find someone else for you."

He looked forlorn all of a sudden. "I like Daphne a lot."

"So do I. We have that in common." I smiled, for real this time, and he brightened. "Look… I need to go. I have some work I have to do." I stood.

He pushed his chair out and stood also. *So polite.*

"I want you to stay and finish your latté. I want you to think about what it might mean to serve me. I'll ask you to do many things and I'll expect you to perform those tasks with eagerness and competence…and without complaint."

I could see how hard he was, just from this conversation, and I couldn't help feeling aroused myself, but I pushed that down. We weren't going to jump into a sexual relationship right off the bat, if ever, necessarily. I was having fun dominating him but I enjoyed dominating anyone who would stand for it. The fact that he was an eager, attractive and very polite young man just made it more interesting. The fact that he found me and my manner a turn-on was promising.

I let my gaze drift from the bulge in his jeans to his face, where he was blushing adorably and trying not to meet my gaze as he nodded.

"Glad to meet you, Vincent." I held out my hand.

He hesitated, then took it. His touch was soft and firm at once. The backbone I wanted was there, thank goodness.

"Glad to meet you, Nic. Thank you for taking a chance on me. Daphne said you were amazing and I feel like she undersold you."

I rolled my eyes. "Flattery will get you just about anywhere. See you Saturday." I started to turn then looked back. "Don't be late."

"No, Sir. Thank you, Sir," he said and sat down like I'd told him to.

I forced myself to turn and stride away, even though I would have liked nothing better than to have spent the next hour chatting with him. That, more than anything else, was the warning I should have heeded.

* * * *

The rest of my week passed normally, as far as normal went. I had several projects to work on at the office, none of them due anytime soon, so I was able to take my time and be thorough. Basically, to enjoy the process, which was good because I needed the work to take my mind off Vincent.

The more I tried not to think about him, the more I couldn't help it. I didn't even have a vivid recollection of his looks—just impressions. Soft brown hair, sleek form, shy smile...the light of intelligence shining in blue eyes.

And deference. I was thankful he knew what he was getting into with me, because I wouldn't have been able to dampen my Dominant side if I'd met him casually. And God knows how he'd have reacted to *that*.

Instead, he'd come *looking* for what I could give him, actively seeking submission and service and an introduction to domestic discipline. Well, he was in luck because I could certainly dish it out. I'd keep it as non-sexual as I could to make sure he liked it, then go where it led. *Maybe*. I had no problem with *him* getting something sexual out of it. I couldn't really avoid it if that was how he was wired. And since he had gotten a boner from just talking to me, I expected it was.

But I was *not* going to get sexually involved with him, at least not right away—maybe not at all. That wasn't what this was about. If everything went well, it would be about guiding him to discover his kinks and fetishes, leading him through exercises to pinpoint what he liked, what he responded to, what he required to make himself feel whole and alive.

* * * *

Saturday, from the moment I got out of bed, I felt jittery and nervous and it pissed me off—mostly because I didn't understand why. I hadn't even wanted this, and now I was worried he wouldn't show up?

Maybe because I knew it would be better for me if he didn't. I wasn't sure I was ready to do this and that was basically what I'd told Daphne. Only now that I'd met him, I was tempted and the ball was already rolling.

I showered and washed my hair, tousling the short strands with gel and letting them air dry, then dressed in soft, faded jeans that hung low on my hips and a Twenty One Pilots tee I'd had for years. I needed to feel like myself and that I wasn't trying to impress anyone. He could take me or leave me.

I wanted to stand by the living room window and watch for him, but I didn't, even though I was curious to see if he came by car or bus or Uber. Forms of transportation could say a lot about a person.

Instead, I busied myself in the kitchen, preparing a pot of coffee—I knew he liked lattés—and setting out two nondescript mugs. I'd use the fancy ones next time if he was a good boy today. Why was I already thinking about the next time? Odds were he'd decide I was too much and leave early.

When the doorbell finally rang, I felt a sense of relief and anticipation…and also dread. Because I'd protected myself from anything like this for so long, I was scared to get back in the game.

By my watch, it was nine o'clock on the *dot*.

I schooled my features and opened the door.

"Vincent, you're on time," I said with a neutral expression. Merely a statement of fact, not approval.

"Hello, Sir."

"Come in. Take off your shoes and hang up your jacket, please." I backed up, letting him into my small entryway.

"Wow, this is really nice," he said, looking around at my home while I tried to adjust to the weirdness of having this attractive young man in my living space. He didn't make me nervous at all, just pissed off. Why did he have to be *so* cute? *Seriously, Daphne, I'm legit going to kill you for this.* She knew how much I'd like him. I felt like I'd been set up.

"Thank you. Have you eaten today?" Why not get right to business? It would take my mind off the fact that I found him so hot, because that was irrelevant at the moment.

"Huh?"

"Have you had anything to eat, Vincent?"

He finished hanging his jacket and followed me through the living room to the kitchen. "No. I don't usually eat breakfast. I brushed my teeth, though," he assured me.

I felt a hint of amusement at this reassurance but didn't show it. That wouldn't do. "Sit down."

He did. "Oh, you don't have to make me breakfast or anything, Sir," he said. "I'm not really hungry in the morning."

I didn't respond, just finished putting the coffee on and reached into the cupboard for a plate. I opened the bread box and took out a cranberry muffin, peeling the wrapper and cutting it in half. I placed the half-muffin on the plate and put it on the table in front of him, then took the opposite chair.

"I want you to eat breakfast if you're coming to my place. It's important to keep your energy up and it's a healthy thing to do anyway." I sat back in my chair and observed him.

He didn't argue, just looked at the muffin. "Okay."

"Do you have any food allergies?"

"No."

"Good. After you eat that, we'll chat." I folded my arms over my chest and listened to the coffeemaker spitting and growling.

He picked up the muffin and took a bite, chewing slowly. He looked at the table and seemed a little bit pissed off, but he did what I'd asked of him, a slight blush creeping up his neck, like he was starting to wonder what he'd gotten himself into.

It was one thing to submit to sexual dominance, another to do what you were told about random things, but he might as well get used to it. He was to do what I told him, period. Right now, as a guest in my home, he was free to tell me to go fuck myself and walk out. Actually, he could always do that, but I hoped he wouldn't. Or did I hope he *would*? He looked entirely too good sitting at my table in black jeans and a gray cotton shirt.

When he'd finished eating, I took the plate away and poured fresh coffee into the two mugs. "What do you take in your coffee?"

"Cream and sugar, please."

Ah, a sweet tooth. I would make use of that later. "I have milk, not cream. Will that do?"

"Yes, Sir. Thank you."

I brought the mugs to the table and sat down again. "Did you have any trouble finding the place?"

He shook his head. "No. I looked it up on my phone."

"Did you drive or take the bus?"

"Uber. My car kind of died on me and I can't afford to get it fixed."

"I see."

"Thanks for the muffin. I kind of got in the habit of not eating until lunch."

I shrugged. "I don't care what you do when you're not coming here. That's your business. But if you're planning to see me, I want you eating properly."

"Yes, Sir."

"And most of the time, you will be serving *me* food, not the other way around."

A tiny little quirk moved the corner of his mouth, and the blush spread. "Of course. Sir."

We drank our coffees and I tried not to stare at him too much, tried not to look at the way his brown hair fell in soft waves across his eyebrows, the way his chin curved and jutted gracefully beneath those perfect pink lips, the way his arms rested gently on the table. He had attractive hands with long, guitar-player fingers. Perhaps even better for piano?

"Do you play the piano, Vincent?"

He blinked. "No, Sir. Why?"

"Your fingers are the right length for it. Not everyone can, but you'd be well suited to it. Do you have any interest in learning?"

He smiled, and it smacked me in the chest the way it lit him up. "Actually, yeah. I just haven't really had the time, you know?"

I nodded, my brain already wrapping around this idea. "If you have the time to be my submissive on weekends, you have the time to learn the piano."

"Yes, Sir. Really? You can teach me?"

I gave him the tiniest hint of a smile. "Yeah. I have an MA in music from the University of Ottawa."

He seemed surprised by this information. I guess Daphne *hadn't* told him much about me.

"Wow. I'm feeling really intimidated now." He glanced down at the table, then met my gaze. "I like it."

I swallowed hard and tried to tamp down my sudden arousal. I needed to be good and not get distracted. "Good. I plan to intimidate you fairly often."

His eyes widened and he swallowed, hard *and* shifted in his chair.

All to the good.

"Yes, Sir. Thank you, Sir."

So fucking polite. I wanted to crack that politeness wide open and find the real Vincent underneath — the rude one, the indecent one, the raw and needy one.

"But shouldn't I be paying you, if you're going to teach me piano?"

I shook my head. "Not if it's part of what we're doing here. Part of the way you'll serve me is by learning to play the piano. It's not easy. It takes practice and dedication. But if you put in the time, it can be very rewarding."

He thought about that. "Okay."

"That work for you?"

"Yes. I think so. Only…"

"Yes?"

"I mean, I just…"

I stared hard at him. "Vincent, you need to be honest with me if this is going to work. What do you want to know?"

"I mean, will I have rules when I'm here?" The innocence of this query disarmed me. "I want to have rules."

This time I truly did smile. I lifted my coffee to my lips and sipped. Then I placed my mug down. "Yes, you will have rules."

I heard him sigh, as if with relief. "What are they?"

I gazed at him a little longer, realizing that this was where it would begin. If I didn't want any part of this,

I needed to say so. Instead, I stood up and walked over to the counter, picked up a notepad and pen and returned to the table.

"That's what we need to figure out today. What rules will work for you and what rules won't. I don't want to set you up for failure." It had been a long time since I'd done this, but the feeling of order and control was familiar and reassuring. I'd missed it, if I were being honest.

"Okay. Thank you." He looked down at his feet, then back up at me. The honesty in his gaze was terrifying. "I like to follow rules."

"I can tell. I mean, that's why you're here, right?"

"Right."

I nodded, trying to be open and as friendly as possible in this circumstance. "You're in luck, because I like to impose them."

He laughed then blushed even more. "What you asked me, before, at Starbucks? About whether I wanted to be dominated sexually?" His eyes were burning orbs and I struggled to protect myself from that energy. "The answer is yes. It's actually *hell, yes*."

Chapter Three

I, too, felt a sexual pull between us but I couldn't possibly acknowledge it yet. It was too soon and I didn't want to.

"That's good to know. But neither of us are ready for that yet."

He looked disappointed. "Okay. Sure."

I needed to clarify. "Look... If you're a natural submissive, which I suspect you are, you might get any amount of sexual enjoyment from the things we're going to start with, even though what I get you to do won't be immediately connected to your sexual responses. Please feel free to become aroused at anything we do. I won't penalize you for that."

The wrinkles in his forehead smoothed. "Thank God."

I raised my eyebrows. "I don't care if you get hard, but you'd better not come from doing my dishes dressed in a miniskirt and tank top or the punishment will be severe."

He visibly shuddered at those words. *Oh hell, this boy is perfect.* He would struggle to keep this platonic while I enjoyed every moment of watching him. I could tell he was imagining just what punishment I might dole out for a little premature ejaculation at the kitchen sink.

Fuck me. I am so doomed.

He swallowed thickly, and I knew he was sporting wood at my kitchen table. "Yes, Sir."

We needed to get this formalized and soon. I lifted my pen.

"Okay, so my rules... Please let me know if you have any problem with what I am telling you."

He nodded.

"The most important rule is honesty. We need to be honest with each other to make any of this work. And, by honesty, I mean *total* honesty. If I ask you how my hair looks and it looks like shit because I forgot to rinse out the conditioner, I expect you to tell me that. Respectfully, of course."

"Is that... Is that likely?" he asked, which almost made me laugh, but I caught myself before it happened.

"That I'll forget to rinse out my conditioner or that I'll ever ask you how my hair looks?"

"Um, either?"

"No. It's just an example, Vincent. Total honesty, all right? Don't worry about hurting my feelings, just be respectfully honest about yours. Got it?"

"Got it."

"I don't even use conditioner. I don't have time for that shit."

He laughed softly, and I couldn't help smiling. God help me, he was adorable.

"I want you to eat properly on the days you come here. But we've already discussed that."

He nodded.

"I want you to shower before coming over. Although we won't be doing anything overtly sexual, you may not be wearing many clothes, so I'd like you to be clean and groomed. By groomed I mean freshly shaved on the face, pubes trimmed or shaved. I don't care which. You can leave your armpits alone but make sure you use antiperspirant. You should bring some with you because you will be doing physical labor and I might ask you to reapply."

He licked his lips.

"No underwear, please."

He blinked. "I thought this wasn't going to be sexual."

"It's not a *sexual* request. I'm asking you to disobey social norms in a way that will make you feel vulnerable. Got a problem with it?"

He shook his head. "Nope."

"Good. Next...you do what I tell you to do, without argument, unless you have a real problem with it, in which case you may safeword. Would you like to pick your own safeword or would you like me to pick one for you?"

He thought about that for a moment. "I'd like you to pick one, Sir."

I'd already picked one for him and was hoping he'd want me to. "Fine. Your safeword is 'latté'."

He looked embarrassed.

"Can you remember that?"

He gazed at me. "Yes, I think I can remember that, Sir."

Sarcasm. I raised my eyebrow and tilted my head.

"I'm sorry, Sir. 'Latté' is fine. I can remember that."

"Good. You can always default to 'Starbucks'. Either is fine."

His lip quirked. So did mine. *Oh, we are two peas in a pod.*

"Yes, Sir."

"We need to discuss what you're willing to do for me, Vincent. I don't want to make you too uncomfortable — at least, not at the beginning."

I wanted to make him just uncomfortable enough. Later, after I'd gotten to know him well, I could try to push him past his soft limits...never past his hard ones. But I needed to know what those were.

"Let's start with soft limits. We're not talking about anything sexual right now. We'll revisit this when I'm comfortable, *if* I'm comfortable, taking that next step with you. So, basic stuff. I should start by asking if you have any medical issues that might interfere with your performance or that might require some adjustments on my part. Any chronic illness that I need to be concerned with?"

"No, Sir. Nothing. I'm healthy."

"Do you get regular exercise?"

"Yes, I go to the gym three times a week and I like to run."

"Excellent. I'm going to proffer some scenarios and I want you to tell me if they appeal to you, don't appeal to you or are completely not your thing. Please be honest. Your answers will guide me over our first few weekends together."

He nodded.

"Just say 'good' if you like the idea, 'okay' if it's something acceptable and 'nope' If it's something you don't want to take part in."

"Yes, Sir."

I marked something down on my notepad. "Okay." I gave him an encouraging smile. "No wrong answers."

He smiled.

"We'll start off with standard stuff. I tell you to take all your clothes off and scrub my bathtub while I watch."

He blushed. "Okay."

I nodded, wrote that down. "I tell you to sort all the clothes in my dresser by color. You can keep your clothes on."

"Okay."

"I tell you to dress in lingerie and cook me dinner."

He inhaled with an unintended whistle. "Good."

Uh-huh. "I pick out some lingerie that you are to wear under your clothes and make you go grocery shopping with me."

He put his hand to his forehead. "G-good."

More writing. The next thing I said without looking up, because I was pretty sure what his answer would be. "I dress you in something pretty and make you sit for a piano lesson."

I heard what sounded like a breathy whimper. "Good," he said in a high-pitched voice.

"Excellent. Well, at least we know where to start."

He shifted in his chair and gripped the edge of the table. "I'm really hard right now, just imagining all those things."

I looked up and met his eyes. "How interesting. Thank you for telling me. I want you to tell me these things during our sessions. It's important that I know, even though neither of us is going to do anything about it."

He swallowed. "Yes, Sir."

I sat back, putting my pen down. "How about you strip for me right now. I'd like to see what I'm working with, in terms of visual enjoyment."

He stared at me for a long moment.

"Feel free to safeword. If you like, we can wait until next weekend to begin."

He shook his head slowly. "No, I..." Then he pushed his chair back and stood, his fingers going to the buttons on his shirt. "I still don't see how this isn't sexual, Sir."

I grinned. "It isn't sexual, because I'm able to appreciate the beauty of a naked man without it necessarily being sexual. In fact, I'm generally only sexual with women."

"It feels sexual to me," he said, blushing as he unbuttoned and peeled back his shirt.

"I don't really have power over your perceptions of what we do here. In any case, that doesn't bother me. It can be sexual to you but not to me. Don't worry about it. Unless you don't want to do what I'm asking, in which case, use your safeword."

"Okay. Thank you, Sir."

My eyes raked his torso as he snaked the shirt off his arms and balled it up in his hands.

"Fold it and put it on the chair."

He shook it out and folded it properly, placing it on the chair.

"That's better. Now, pants," I said, straightforward and pragmatic. I really wasn't doing this for my own enjoyment, but for his. At least, that's what I told myself as I watched his fingers go to the button on his jeans. He hesitated.

"Is there a problem?"

"I'm wearing boxer briefs. I didn't know..."

He was so sweet. "How could you know? It's okay this time."

He nodded then undid his jeans and pushed them down, stepping out of them. He folded them and placed them on the chair with his shirt.

I could tell he felt uncomfortable but I was sure he'd stripped for Daphne. Was it me or just the fact that we were virtual strangers?

He started to push his boxer briefs down. I could see the outline of his erection underneath the fabric.

"Wait a second."

He looked down at himself but raised his eyes curiously to me. "Sir?"

In that moment I felt it—my arousal at the innocence in his expression as he waited for my next instruction and at the way he looked in his boxer briefs, which was pretty fucking amazing. But I tamped it down immediately and got back to business.

"How are you feeling right now?"

He blushed. "I'm...nervous."

"Why? Surely Daphne had you naked most of the time if I know anything about her."

He seemed confused, and those little wrinkles formed on his forehead again. "Yeah, but she was, I don't know... She was a stereotypical Dominatrix and I kind of knew what to expect. I don't really know what to expect with you."

That made sense. "What are you nervous about, exactly? What I'm going to do once you're naked? I already told you we're not stepping anywhere near the sexual arena today."

"No, it's not that." He played with the waistband of his boxer briefs. His erection didn't flag one bit from this line of questioning, I was pleased to see. He was still into this...big time.

I softened my voice and stood up. I needed to be closer. "What is it then?"

His eyes widened and he dropped his hands. "I'm nervous...about what you think of me. Of my...body. What if you don't like it?"

I raised my eyebrows, knowing he didn't have to worry about that at all. "Is that important to you? That I like the way you look naked?"

"Well, yeah. Of course."

I walked around him, looking him over as he tracked me with his eyes. I reached out and put a hand on his cotton-covered buttock, making him start. I was just touching him to see how firm his ass felt and how jumpy he was. I needed to get a read on whether he was okay with me touching him in general.

When our eyes met, I gave him my full smile finally. "I don't think you have to worry about that."

"Really?"

"I think you have an amazing body."

"Oh, thank God. Really?"

I laughed. He seemed so desperate for approval. "Yeah, really."

"But you said you're mostly attracted to women."

I raised my eyebrows. "I've mostly *dated* women, *had sex* with women, but that doesn't mean I'm not attracted to men. I'm *very* attracted to some men. It just depends. I usually don't pursue men and they generally don't pursue me, for whatever reason. Probably because of the way I look."

"You look amazing to me. I think you're incredibly hot." He glanced down at himself. "Obviously."

"That"—I gestured to his hard-on—"could just be from the situation."

"It's not."

"I see."

He looked worried again. "Is it a problem that I find you so hot?"

I circled him again. He followed my gaze as I looked him over then sat down.

"Hmm-m, I don't think I have a problem with it." I took a sip from my mug, still examining him — the spread of his shoulders, the flat planes of his stomach, the trail of dark hair leading into his boxer briefs. "You can take the briefs off now."

The blush rose in his cheeks. He hooked his thumbs under the waistband and lifted it over his arching cock, pushing the cotton briefs down his legs and stepping out of them. Pretending not to notice me, he folded them and placed them carefully on the chair.

"Did you find Daphne hot?" It was a crazy, stupid question and I didn't know why I'd asked it. Everyone found Daphne hot. She was sex personified. But I was curious. Maybe that had been the problem.

He turned to face me and didn't seem to know what to do with his hands. They hung awkwardly at his sides while his beautiful cock jutted slightly left toward his belly, the tip protruding sleekly from his foreskin.

"Hands behind your head. Feet spread apart." I nodded when he moved into the correct stance. "This is the display position. When I ask you to display, this is how you'll stand. Got it?"

"Yes, Sir."

"When you are here, you are here for my enjoyment. You will be naked if I require it or you will be dressed in what I want you to wear."

He breathed in and out quickly and I saw his cock twitch.

"Now answer my question."

"About Daphne?"

"Yes."

"I mean, I did at first. How could I not?"

"Exactly."

"But the more we got into the sex play, I realized she didn't really do it for me. But it didn't matter because"

— he looked down at his cock and shrugged, gazing up at me bashfully — "I don't really have a problem getting hard at the drop of a hat. Submission is a huge turn-on for me, even without the direct sexual component."

"I'm starting to realize that."

"So, I mean, she could get me off just by telling me to do stuff, stuff that made me uncomfortable, stuff that made me feel objectified. I like that a lot."

"Objectification. Humiliation?"

"Sure. Sometimes. I'm more into straight-out objectification, really. I don't need to be name-called or shamed or anything, just treated like an object." He glanced at me shyly. "A pretty object that she used for her pleasure without any regard to how it was responding. Kind of takes the pressure off, you know?"

I did know. "Sure. Lots of people enjoy objectif-ication."

He stared at the ceiling for a moment, looked back at me. "I'm kind of into medical kink."

"Really."

"It's the objectification thing. Having to submit to personal examinations. Feeling like I'm not supposed to be aroused, but I am."

Our eyes locked and I felt time stop while I considered this. Maybe Daphne was right and he *was* just what I needed. Maybe I was what *he* needed.

I stood up suddenly. "I want to take you shopping," I said, backing out of the room. "Get dressed. We're going to the mall."

Chapter Four

When I got back to the kitchen he was waiting for me, dressed again and sitting in the chair. When I entered the room, he stood.

"Ready?" I asked.

"Sure."

We put on boots and jackets and I locked the door behind us. Then I handed him my keys. "We'll take my car. You drive."

He seemed surprised but all he said was, "Yes, Sir," and walked to the driver's side of my Honda CRV. He stood there looking at the key fob and the car door, perplexed.

"Touch the circle on the door handle."

He did and the car made a beep as it unlocked. "Holy shit, that's so cool," he said, sounding like a ten-year-old. I loved him for it.

"Modern technology."

"So cool," he repeated as he got in and I joined him on the passenger side. I laughed as he looked for the ignition and held the fob up with a questioning look.

"Press the button." I pointed to the ignition button. "The car knows you have the key and it will start."

"Holy fucking shit," he said, and pushed the button. He laughed when the car roared to life. "That is the coolest fucking thing I've ever…"

"You can adjust the seat. There are buttons at the side there."

We spent some time getting him fitted, and I even had him save his settings as Driver 2. He was having so much fun that I'd definitely let him drive this car again.

"Where are we going, Sir?" he asked, a broad smile on his handsome face and something inside me melted, despite all of my walls.

"Hmm. Is there a La Senza at the Rideau Centre?"

He froze in the act of shifting into reverse. The smile faded as his face flushed a deep pink.

"I don't wear lingerie," I explained, "so we need to buy some. Because I'm putting you in lingerie as soon as possible, Vincent."

His mouth dropped open and his breaths came out in frantic little huffs. He nodded but looked straight ahead. I stared at him until he slid his eyes to me and whispered, "Yes."

"Yes, what?"

"Yes, there's a La Senza at the Rideau Centre."

"Good. Then that's where we're going."

He sighed as a shudder passed through his whole body. "Yes, Sir."

* * * *

He was a good driver. Excellent, in fact. I was only nervous for the first few minutes because one never knew. But it was always good to find out.

We parked in the underground parking garage and walked up the steps to the main floor. "Check the directory," I said, pointing to it.

He did so and found the popular lingerie store on Level Two. We took the escalator up to that level and made our way there. He slowed as we got nearer.

"Have you ever shopped for lingerie in person? And you don't have to do the 'Sir' thing in public, unless I specifically request it," I said, knowing what his answer would be.

"No."

"Online?"

"Yes."

"How convenient and unadventurous."

He stared at me and I got that he thought ordering lingerie online to wear for kicks was pretty adventurous. I grinned, because it wasn't *nearly* as adventurous as I'd like him to be. Clearly, since I'd brought him here.

He challenged me. "Have *you*?"

My grin got bigger. "As a matter of fact, I have. I like to buy pretty things for *other* people to wear."

He blushed. "Okay, fine."

"Come with me," I said, taking his hand and leading him into the store. He was surprised and, honestly, so was I, but I liked the feel of his hand in mine and he didn't pull away. He seemed reassured and that was good. I was here to take care of him as well as to push his boundaries.

We walked in together and I was pretty sure the store clerk did a double take, because we looked like two guys holding hands. I generally passed for male. Sometimes I forgot that I didn't *actually* have a dick and balls, but the world had a way of reminding me. Not that I wanted a dick and balls... They were cumbersome at the very least, and so vulnerable.

"Hi there," she said, glancing at our joined hands and giving us a genuine smile. "Can I help you with anything?"

Vincent looked panicked but I squeezed his hand before letting it go and answering the sales associate. "Not at the moment. We're just going to look around."

"Okay. Let me know if you have any questions." She left us to ourselves and I led Vincent past the sale bins and to the back of the store where the nicer lingerie was kept. I stopped in front of several display racks and said, "Show me what you like, Vincent."

He looked rather pale and I knew this was difficult for him, but I wanted to see how far he'd go with me, how far he'd trust me, when we were only talking about a little kinky shopping. There were much more interesting things I wanted to do to push his boundaries but we needed to start small.

He looked at the rack nearest him. It contained a display of black teddies, with a bunch of lacy camisoles on the next rack. His eyes passed over those and went to the next rack with red slips and nightdresses. Nothing so far.

But when he looked at the rack beside it, his eyes lit up and he fixed on the lacy boy shorts in soft pink and baby blue. Then he looked at me.

"*Those.*" It was the softest whisper.

I reached out and took a pair of the pink ones down. "These?"

He nodded, flitting his gaze around to see if anyone was watching.

"Very nice. The color will look lovely on you."

He blushed and seemed to be visibly trembling. Now that I knew the colors he liked and that lace was a go, I looked around a bit myself. I found a lace camisole with spaghetti straps in a matching pink and took it down. I held it in front of him with the panties and raised my eyebrows in question.

He nodded. I smiled. On impulse, I grabbed the same items in baby blue because I thought he'd look great in either color and I'd want to change things up now and then.

"You're going to be my very pretty boy, aren't you?" I whispered to him, leaning so close that my breath surely tickled his ear.

"Oh God," he said, and I almost felt the energy pulsing inside him. His jeans were tight and his face was flushed.

"Come on. Let's pay for these," I said.

He followed me silently to the counter. I knew he was embarrassed, wondering what the other customers were thinking and what the sales associate would say when she rang them up.

He grabbed my elbow before we got to the desk. "I can't do this."

"Yes, you can. It's nobody's business who these are for. They could be for your girlfriend and I'm helping pick them out."

He seemed to calm down. I didn't tell him that his obvious embarrassment was giving him away more than anything else.

"We'll take these," I said, laying them gently on the counter.

"Great!" the sales associate said cheerily. "Oh, those are so pretty! That's from my favorite collection." She smiled warmly at Vincent and I felt a surge of jealousy rise up unexpectedly inside me. "Your girlfriend will love them!"

I could see she was fishing for information and I was kind of appalled at her blatant assumption, so the next thing to come out of my mouth was, "They're for me."

Both Vincent and the sales associate stared at me. But the smile that emerged on Vincent's face and the confused look on the sales associate's were worth it. The sales associate laughed as if I were joking, and scanned the items. Then Vincent surprised me.

"He's going to look so sexy in those," he said, with only a slight stutter and a cheeky glance my way. I couldn't help smiling at him as my heart did a little flutter. I stamped it out like it was a pesky mosquito and asked for a bag.

"Of course," the sales associate said, blushing furiously and acting uncomfortable. I loved what Vincent had just done more than I loved the fact that he was going to be wearing those lacy undergarments all afternoon if I had my way — maybe every time he came over. Maybe I'd buy more so he would never have an excuse not to wear something lacy and soft. I decided to change my *No underwear* rule to *Only lacy underwear*. Just for him.

And this little exchange told me a couple of things. He wasn't embarrassed to be mistaken for a gay guy, and he wasn't embarrassed to be with me, even though I looked like a gay guy. Not that there was specifically a gay-guy look, but I was feminine enough to not be mistaken for a straight guy.

He was only embarrassed about the fact that the lingerie was for *him*. There was a deep-seated shame there that I planned to explore. And exploit? Well, sure, and teach him there was absolutely nothing to be ashamed of.

"You hungry?" I asked, seeing that it was close to lunchtime.

"Yeah. The food court's pretty good here."

"What do you like to get usually?"

"New York Fries. Or A&W."

"Let's go. It's on me."

"No, Nic, I can't let you pay for—"

I stopped dead and turned, pinning him with my most Dominant gaze.

"Oh shit," he said breathlessly and I almost *saw* the jolt go from his eyes to his cock.

My voice was like steel. "You can't *let* me? You can't *let* me do *what*?"

He shook his head and licked his lips. "Never mind. Thank you, Sir. I'm starving."

I nodded. "That's better. Come on."

He followed me to the food court where I pointed to an empty table. "Sit down and wait for me."

He slid into a chair, holding his La Senza bag tightly on his lap, as if he would fight anyone who tried to take it from him.

As I walked to the New York Fries booth, I felt something inside me that resembled the closest thing to happiness I'd experienced in months. Maybe years?

Zane and I had parted ways months before, but maybe I'd never been happy with him. I had thought I was. But this was…different. This was *pure*.

There was plenty of time for it to crash and burn, so I tried not to put too much importance on how I was feeling right this minute. But I liked it.

I went back to the table with two orders of fries and drinks. I knew it wasn't very healthy but, hey, we had to live a little. This was kind of a special occasion. At least, it felt like one.

There was a woman sitting in my seat across from Vincent when I got back to the table and I felt my skin prickle and my insides twist. God, was I jealous already? I tamped that down and plastered a fake smile on my face.

"Hello," I said, my voice cool.

Vincent stood up, still clutching his bag of pretty things. "Nic, this is Lilly. She was in my accounting class in University." He seemed uncomfortable but it could have been because he was holding a bag of lacy unmentionables that his new gender-fluid Dom had bought him.

But Lilly gave me a look I didn't like—condescending and proprietary at once. She was pretty, annoyingly pretty, with long red hair and expensive clothes. "Hi."

I smiled and aimed mental daggers at her. "That's my chair."

She seemed taken aback. "Oh, sure. I just sat down for a second to catch up with Vincent." She stood and moved out of my way.

That's right, bitch. Get away from my pretty boy.

I placed Vincent's fries and drink in front of him without telling him to sit down, which would have sounded strange to Lilly and probably would have embarrassed Vincent. Luckily, he sat and picked up his fork, giving Lilly a perfunctory smile.

I took my seat, ignoring her, and began to eat.

"So, Vincent, It's great to see you again," Lilly said, standing beside us.

"Yeah. Nice to see you, too." I could tell he didn't especially like her either, but, like most people, he was a prisoner of a social convention that dictated he needed to be polite in this awkward situation. I, on the other hand, was not.

I ignored her and asked Vincent how the fries tasted.

"Really good. Thanks."

Lilly tried engaging *me* this time. "Vincent and I know each other from *way* back. He helped me a lot with the accounting assignments in school."

"That seems like something Vincent would do. He's very accommodating." I grinned at Vincent and he squirmed a little.

Lilly laughed. "Yeah, he's a super-nice guy."

"Super nice," I echoed, chewing on a French fry and trying not to laugh at the way he was looking at me.

"I wonder if I can find another chair somewhere," she said, looking around at nearby tables.

"Actually," I said, as Vincent's eyes widened, "if you don't mind, we'd like to eat our lunch together without an audience."

He blinked, like he couldn't believe I'd just said that. But it was true and I believed in honesty above all.

Lilly seemed shocked also. I smiled at her as I waited for her to leave us alone.

"Oh, okay, whatever," she said, throwing a deprecating look my way and turning to address Vincent.

"Give me a call sometime, okay? I'd love to reconnect with you," she said, glancing my way disdainfully. "When you're not *busy*."

Oh, if eyes could have shoveled shit, she'd have been burying me in it.

Vincent smiled. "Sure," he said. Then, "Bye."

And I loved him for it.

She nodded, "Okay, bye," and finally took off.

I kept eating my fries, not saying anything.

"I'm sorry," Vincent said.

"Not your fault."

"She's not shy."

"Or polite. But then, neither am I." I chewed another fry and took a sip of my Coke. "Is she a friend of yours or just an acquaintance?"

He shook his head. "We knew each other in class. She wouldn't leave me alone. I think she wanted to date me."

"Probably," I said. "Who wouldn't?"

He blinked. "Pardon?"

I stared at him. "Who wouldn't want to date you, Vincent? You're sweet and pretty fucking attractive."

He blushed but looked at his fries. "I'm really not..." he said, then shook his head.

"What? Tell me. You're really not...?"

He shook his head again. "I'm not... I'm not confident enough to be in a relationship that's not" — he glanced at me — "like this one."

"You mean with you in a submissive role?"

"Yeah. I mean I've tried to be normal. You know." He put his fingers into air quotes. "I've tried to *act* like a man."

I chewed my fry and raised my brows. "And how is *that*?"

"You know, confident, dominant, assertive." He blushed. "But I'm not like that. I mean, it doesn't come naturally. Why am I supposed to be that way just because I'm a guy?"

This genuine question disarmed me completely. I gazed at him like he was my long-lost best friend.

"Why indeed? I don't understand it," I admitted. "And if you think I haven't been fighting those same expectations since I was a bossy little tomboy, you'd be mistaken." I grinned at him and he smiled—that full, beautiful smile he hadn't given Lilly even a hint of.

I continued. "Look… I learned to dismiss other people's expectations of me ages ago. They only limit you and stop you from being purely who you are."

He looked relieved. "Yeah. Exactly."

I sat back and sipped my Coke, enjoying the cold, sugar-filled hit after the warmth and richness of the fries. "Are you having fun?"

"Pardon?"

"Are you having fun being here with me?"

I was good at reading people, and I was pretty sure he was. On the surface, it wasn't the most fascinating 'field trip', but I sensed that he got excitement out of not knowing what to expect and knowing that our relationship would be unconventional and mostly hidden from the public eye. I knew that excited *me*.

"God, yes. I *love* this. I love that you bought me these and I can't wait to try them on."

I smiled because that was the reaction I'd hoped for.

"Well, then, eat up and we'll head back to my place where you can do just that."

He nodded, blushing, and finished his fries with a blissful expression on his face.

As we were leaving, we had to pass a wall of mirrors and I got a glimpse of the two of us walking together. Vincent looked as hot as I knew he was and I looked…not so bad either, really. I was shorter, and my clothes were a bit more edgy since I'd worn my leather jacket and my bad-ass biker boots. We definitely looked like a gay couple—or at least I thought we did. My blond hair was spiked up and the shaved sides made my face look thinner and more masculine. My gray eyes looked alive for once and my mouth was relaxed. I looked content.

And how could I not be with this lovely boy by my side and an afternoon fashion show to look forward to? Even if it didn't work out in the long run, I would always have this day to remember. I mentally chastised myself for even thinking about the long-term.

Chapter Five

When Vincent pulled smoothly into my drive and put my car in Park I told him, "You are an excellent driver, Vincent. I plan to exploit this skill."

He blushed. "Thank you, Sir."

"Which means I will be getting you to drive me around pretty often."

"Okay."

"I'll try to make it worth your while," I said, holding up the La Senza bag.

He laughed. "Thank you, Sir."

So fucking polite.

I wasn't sure I could wait as long as I should to start digging beneath that very well-behaved exterior.

We exited the vehicle and walked to the front door. He passed me my keys and I unlocked it so we could go inside. We hung our jackets and took off our boots.

"I love those boots," he said softly. "They suit you."

"Thank you. They're my favorites." I catalogued his appreciation for my boots in the back of my mind along with *Likes wearing lacy lingerie in pastels* and *Gets hard from almost any direct order*.

"Come with me."

He followed obediently to the master bedroom, where I placed our bag of purchases on the end of my bed.

The furnishings were fairly standard — queen platform bed, navy comforter, a few pillows, dresser and side table and a full-length mirror leaning against the wall by the window.

He looked around quickly, flitting his gaze to the ceiling and the walls. He was probably checking for eye rings and suspension equipment. Daphne had lots. He didn't ask about it, just licked his lips and glanced at me, waiting.

I assessed him, anticipating how good he was going to look in the lingerie. "We can do this either of two ways," I said.

He shivered and wrapped his arms around himself, but his eyes were wide, the pupils dark. He nodded.

"You can get undressed in here with the door closed and put them on then come out when you're ready, or…"

He was waiting for me to give him another option, so I did.

"Or we can do it together. I can watch you get undressed and I can help you put them on. It's completely up to you."

His mouth twitched and I was surprised to see amusement there.

"What?" I narrowed my eyes.

He looked at the floor. "In a completely non-sexual way?"

The statement hung there and I realized how ridiculous it seemed. But I played along.

"Of course. Nothing sexual about it. I'd like to see how the lingerie I purchased looks on the person I purchased it for. Nothing sexual about that. Plus, we need to make sure it fits."

We both knew I was fucking lying. So much for that whole honesty thing. And he called me on it, the devil.

"I thought we were supposed to be honest with each other." He whispered it, as if he were afraid he was being too bold or that he was wrong and I didn't feel anything sexual about seeing him in pink lingerie.

Right.

"Snap," I said. *You got me.* I sat on the bed, looking at the wall. "Okay, here's the situation right now, Vincent. The truth is I'm incredibly turned on but I don't want to be, and even so, I'm not going to do anything directly sexual *with you* or *to you* until we know each other a little better and this" —I gestured between us—"thing, whatever it is, becomes a little more defined."

"Okay," he said, sounding relieved. "Really? You're really turned on?"

"Against my better judgment, yes."

"Why don't you want to be?"

I cleared my throat. *Goddammit.* I mean, I could have refused to answer, but I wouldn't. "Because I don't want to jump into something with you that will make me feel vulnerable. I need to be in control and with my wits about me, at least to start with."

"Okay. But *I'm* feeling pretty vulnerable here," he said.

I turned to look at him. "But that's what you want." It was a statement.

"Yeah, okay. That's true. I like it," he admitted. As if I didn't know that.

"Yeah, well, I *don't*. I like to be the top, so *let* me be the top, okay?" It was a plea from the heart, and he recognized it as such.

He nodded quickly. "I will. I'll let you do whatever you want, the way you want. But, for the record?"

I raised my eyebrows.

He continued. "I have no problem getting sexual with you, whenever the time is right."

Now *I* was the one who blushed and that was exactly my point. With one statement he'd made me feel so good that I wanted to walk over there and fold him into my arms.

WTF? I shook my head, as if to rid it of these feelings.

"Okay, sweet talker. Which is it? You want some help or not?" I opened the bag and took out a package wrapped in crinkly white paper, unfolding it to expose the pretty pink camisole. I hooked my thumbs through the spaghetti straps and held it up.

He sighed and a shudder passed through him.

"Help," he said, and it was like he was asking me to rescue him from the idea that he had to do this alone.

I nodded curtly. "Strip…slowly." I sat down on the edge of the bed, putting the camisole to the side and unwrapping the boy shorts, watching unabashedly as he removed his clothes. He'd done this before and he would do it again, many times, so I settled in to watch and enjoy.

When he'd gotten down to his boxer briefs, he glanced at me then pushed them off and straightened, keeping his head bowed. His cock, as before, was rock-hard. I wondered what it was like to possess something so revealing, so vulnerable — what it was like to show one's arousal so obviously. I was beginning to realize that I was just as turned on as he was, but I could pretend that wasn't the case. I had the privilege of hiding my feelings…and I did.

I kept my expression neutral and stood up, holding the delicate camisole. "Turn around."

He did. I'd placed him deliberately in front of the mirror so he would be confronted with his naked image when he glanced up. He reddened and quickly cast his eyes down.

"Look at yourself, Vincent. Tell me what you see." Yes, I was going to make this excruciatingly intimate. He would love *and* hate every minute of it.

He forced himself to look. He quickly scanned himself, creases appearing on his forehead as he considered his nakedness.

He cleared his throat. "A naked man."

"How naked?"

"Completely, utterly," he whispered.

"Young or old?"

"Young."

"Handsome?"

He tilted his head. "I mean…yeah?"

"Oh yeah," I affirmed.

A slight smile appeared, then vanished.

"Is this naked man embarrassed? Ashamed?" I asked.

He considered the question. "Not ashamed. Just" — he shrugged — "shy?"

I let myself smile. He could see me in the mirror. "I love your bashfulness, Vincent. It's endearing, sweet and so lovely, even as it deviates from typical masculinity. Especially *because* of that."

He met my eyes in the reflection. "Thank you."

"You're welcome." I slid my hand between his legs and stroked the inside of his left thigh, before gliding it all the way down to his ankle. I crouched down and held the boy shorts for him to step into. Then I stood, slowly pulling the gossamer material up his legs. As the pink lace glided over his skin, his lips parted and he sighed. I slid it over his ass and erection and fiddled until it sat perfectly on his slim frame. The fabric was stretched tight over his full cock and his firm ass and he looked fucking sexy. His breathing ramped up as he looked at himself in the mirror.

"Holy fuck," he said with a tremor in his voice.

"Holy fuck, indeed. You look stunning, Vincent."

"I feel...pretty," he whispered, turning to see how they looked from the side.

I ran my hands over his hips and cupped his bottom, tilting my head to see him from every angle. "You *are* pretty. Here... Turn around."

He turned to face me, and all I wanted to do was pull the lace away from his cock and take him in my mouth or in my hand, make him come standing here in my bedroom, eyes and mouth wide with surprise, moans echoing off the walls.

The urge was strong but I resisted it. It was too soon for something so intimate. But the fact that I *wanted* to do it was telling.

I swallowed and turned away, grabbing the camisole from the bed and holding it in front of him. "Put your arms through the straps."

I had him lift his arms so I could pull the camisole down past his head until it hugged his torso in a most beguiling way. I smoothed the hem where it rested an inch or two above the boy shorts, then straightened the straps and stepped back.

Oh yes. He was a vision in powder pink with his lean muscles and light body hair, his thick cock trapped and so, so hard.

His hand moved and before I could say anything, he pressed his palm against his erection and closed his eyes, giving himself some relief.

"No, you don't. Hands off, please," I said and he jerked his hand away as if he'd been very naughty — as, indeed, he had been, but not on purpose. I realized I'd forgotten to tell him *this* rule.

"Sorry, but that's another one of my rules." I snaked my finger up his neck and tilted his chin so he looked at me. "You aren't allowed to touch yourself intimately while you are here."

He considered this. "Okay."

"Or when you're at home."

He blinked. "What?"

"I don't want you pleasuring yourself at all while we are doing this."

He struggled with this idea. "But…that's not really fair."

I sat down on the edge of the bed again, running my eyes over him from head to foot, drinking him in, memorizing how he looked for later when I was alone. Because the same rule did not apply to me.

"How so?"

I could see him trying to figure out how to disagree with me without offending me. "Well, because you say this isn't sexual, but you tell me I can't get myself off, even when I'm at home?"

"Vincent, it's about control."

"Okay, but—"

"I want to control you." I pinned his adorable blue eyes as I said this with all the Dom I had in me, holding his gaze and being as direct as possible. "There's no other reason than that."

"Whoa." He swallowed, and I swear I saw his dick pulse behind the pink lace. A small dark spot appeared at the waistband, which sat at the tip of his cock. "Okay."

"I want to control you in every way that you'll let me," I said, still holding his gaze. I licked my lips. "Simply because it pleases me to do it."

His mouth dropped open. I saw him start to reach for his cock then drop his hand to his side.

Good boy.

"But let me reiterate you are free to say no, that it's not what you want. I can adjust my rules to a certain extent. But the 'hands off your junk' policy here in my home will stand." I got up and walked to him, dropping my voice. "Do you want me to control you while you *aren't* here?"

He inhaled a shaky breath as his hands became fists at his sides. "Yes."

"Perfect," I said, turning him so he could get the full effect of the outfit in the mirror. "Then we are going to have so much fun."

* * * *

An hour later, I was sprawled on my living room sofa with *House Hunters* on, watching as Vincent wiped the baseboards with a wet cloth—on hands and knees of course. His ass in the pink lace was a vision. His muscles rippled in a delightful way as he completed this most menial of tasks. It was quite literally something I'd never do. But I was pleased to have *him* do it. I'd already had him dust the flat surfaces and sweep the floor.

He walked over to me, kneeling before me holding the cloth. "All done, Sir."

I reached out and ruffled his hair, glancing to see that his erection was still there and still solid. I had to love a man who got off on cleaning baseboards, because I certainly didn't, although I was sure it wasn't the baseboards. It was me *telling* him to do it, *watching* him do it.

"Very good." I sat up quickly, surprising him with the sudden movement. I'd been eagerly awaiting this moment. "Time for a piano lesson."

He blinked. "Okay."

I raised my eyebrows.

"I mean, yes, Sir."

"Better. Go sit on the piano bench and place your hands on your thighs."

"Yes, Sir." He grinned. He was into it. I was glad because I really wanted him to learn to play.

I slid in beside him on the piano bench and my nose got an extra strong whiff of the moisture leaking from Vincent's dick. I closed my eyes for a moment, savoring it. It was something I'd not enjoyed for some time. It was the scent of potency, testosterone and male excitement, and I'd forgotten how much I loved it. Again, I felt the very strong urge to taste him, but I wouldn't. *I wouldn't.* I was not doing this for my own enjoyment. Not yet, anyway. I was doing this for him.

At least, that's what I told myself.

"Have you ever played before?"

"No. But I've always been curious. I don't know if I have the talent."

"Despite what most people believe, talent isn't the most important thing a beginner piano student needs."

He regarded me quizzically. "What is the most important thing? A good teacher?"

What a sweetheart. Was he deliberately flattering me?

"Well, yes. But what I was going to say is that a beginning student needs to understand that practice and repetition are more important than talent, at least at first."

He blinked. "I don't have a piano at home."

"I didn't think you did. But if you are going to spend Saturdays with me, you'll have time to practice."

He looked down at the keys, the blush getting stronger and a small smile appearing. "Am I going to spend Saturdays here?"

"If you want to. It doesn't have to be every weekend."

"*Can* it be every weekend?" he asked shyly, looking at his fingers splayed on his thighs. "I mean, I'd learn the piano faster."

I couldn't help smiling too. "That's certainly true." I placed my fingers on the keys and started playing the chorus from *Let It Be,* which was the first thing I was going to teach him. "Don't you have family and friends that will want to spend time with you?"

His smile disappeared and he rubbed his thighs. "Not in town. Not really."

"Oh," I said, curious. "You're on your own here?"

"Except for my co-workers, and one or two acquaintances…yeah." He pursed his lips, then pushed out a puff of air. "I sort of followed my girlfriend here. Then we split."

There was pain in his expression.

"How long ago did you break up with her?"

"It's been a while."

"How long?"

He thought for a moment. "Five months."

"Do you mind if I ask what happened?"

"I don't mind. It was because I wanted *this*." He gestured to himself and to me, and I understood what he was telling me. He lifted his eyes from his hands and met mine. "And she didn't."

"Okay."

"Anyway, I'm fine with it. It just means I don't have a huge friend network here and most of my family are out East. I mean, my aunt and uncle are here, but they're kind of religious fanatics, so I don't keep in touch."

"I see."

"So, um, I'm all yours on the weekends…if you want me." He stared at his hands again.

I stared at his hands too. They were nice hands. His fingers were perfect for playing the piano…and for other things. I licked my lips. "I want you. Just Saturdays for now."

The smile returned and he nodded. "Good."

I went over the basic rules of piano playing—note placement, finger numbering, chords, all-while-trying not to imagine those fingers doing other, much more intimate things. It was difficult and it took all my professionalism to push those thoughts from my mind.

He was a good student and seemed interested in learning from me, above and beyond that he enjoyed me telling him what to do. But there was that too.

By the time we were done with his first lesson, he could do his scales and play the chorus to *Let It Be* with a bit of skill. I was pleased.

I saw him surreptitiously move his hand to his dick for a second and something inside me went off.

"Vincent."

He froze, moved his hand back to the piano keys without looking up and started to do the scales as if nothing had happened.

"Stand up."

He hesitated. "I'm sorry," he mumbled. "I forgot." He was whispering and staring at the keys and that blush got darker, his cock got harder and that made me so, so happy.

I shoved the bench back and stood as he was forced to stand also.

"Lean forward with your arms on the top of the piano."

He did as a tremor went through his whole body. "Fuck," he said, as he assumed the position.

"Head down on your arms."

He lowered his head and closed his eyes. I drank in the sight of him — slightly tanned skin, pink lace, firm muscles and lean limbs displayed for his punishment.

"I'm going to spank you, Vincent. You're a naughty boy."

He shuddered. He rubbed his forehead against his bicep. "Yes, Sir," he squeaked.

Oh, God, he's perfect. So beautiful in his submission… So delicious in his state of arousal at what was a pretty basic and simple punishment… Beginner BDSM as well as Beginner Piano. *My sweet ingenue.*

I had no doubt that Daphne had done more extreme things to him, but he was a beginner with *me*. I planned to go so slowly with him until he'd be begging for more at each visit. I *wanted* him begging. I wanted to drive him mad with desire, crazy with anticipation.

He knew as well as I did what there was to look forward to. The fact that this simple thing affected him so strongly gave me an idea what we were in for, and it was starting not to scare me so much. It was starting to make me just as excited as he was.

I placed my right hand on his elbow to hold him in place, while my left hand stroked over the lace on his ass. I did this for a few moments while his breath hitched and quickened. Then I pulled back and gave him a hard swat.

He grunted.

I did it again.

He moaned.

I began to spank him in earnest as he struggled to stay still. I didn't go for too long. This was just a warm-up. When I stopped he was panting but not winded.

"Lower the panties, Vincent."

His eyes flew open, then quickly closed. "Oh God."

"Don't move, except to expose your ass to me. Got it?"

"Yes, Sir." It was a whisper as he moved his arms back, keeping his forehead pressed to the piano and fumbled with the panties until he got them down.

"Good boy," I said and the breath he let out shuddered through him.

"Arms back up on the piano."

He resumed the position and I had a chance to fondle his bare ass, which I proceeded to do. His skin felt softer than I would have expected. *He must moisturize.*

"Your skin is very soft," I commented, smoothing the flat of my hand over his warm skin that was already a nice pink color from the spanking.

"Well...I moisturize," he murmured and smiled as if he realized the banality of his comment.

"I can tell."

"Is that too girly?" he asked shyly and I could hear a million apprehensions in that question.

I squeezed his buttock gently as I replied. "It's perfect, Vincent. *You're* perfect."

I heard a strange sound and looked at his face, which he'd pressed against his arm. I realized he was crying just as I realized I had said that last thing out loud.

"Hey, hey," I murmured, leaning in and kissing him on his cheek because it seemed like the thing to do. "It's okay. It's okay."

He let the tears come. "Sorry… God, I'm sorry," he said. "I don't know why I'm crying."

I took a shot. "Relief?"

He sighed. "Yeah. Probably." He laughed and rubbed the tears away on his arm. "You don't think I'm a pussy just because I like girly things."

I smiled a bit sadly at his words. "I think you're amazing, Vincent. I think you're sexy and cute and pretty and manly and so, so very *brave.*"

He opened his eyes and stared at me from the top of the piano. "Thank you."

"You want the rest of your punishment? Or do you want to go home now?" I rubbed the skin of his ass. "There's no wrong answer."

"I want my punishment," he said without hesitation.

So, I spanked him. I spanked his bare ass with no mercy. He shed more tears but he also moaned with bliss and pushed his ass out to receive my hand, which began to ache after a while.

"Okay, we're done," I said finally, stepping back and trying to control my own breathing. "Go to the bedroom and get dressed. Then come and sit with me."

Fifteen minutes later we sat together on my sofa and talked about what had happened. I didn't want him leaving without some aftercare.

"How is your ass feeling?"

"Good. Sore, but good."

"Do you have arnica cream at home? I figure if you've been seeing Daphne for as long as you have that you do?"

"Yeah. I have some."

"Put some on if you need it. That wasn't much of a spanking, really."

"I know," he whispered. "Thanks for going easy on me."

"You're welcome. Do you want to come back next Saturday?"

"Yes, please. Definitely."

"Good. I want you to wear the blue panties and camisole under your clothes next Saturday, Vincent."

"Shit. Okay. Yes."

"Yes, what?"

He grinned. "Yes, *Sir*."

Chapter Six

I asked Vincent to let me know he got home safely. I'd input his contact as 'Trouble' for reasons that should've been obvious.

Trouble: I'm home. I had a great time.
Nic: I'm glad. So did I.
Trouble: See you next week.
Nic: Nine o'clock. Don't be late.
Trouble: No, Sir. Good night, Sir.
Nic: Good night. Are you still hard, Vincent?
Trouble: Surprisingly, no. Thank God.
Nic: Yes. No wanking, remember?
Trouble: I remember.
Nic: I will know if you do, Vincent.
Trouble: How is that possible?
Nic: Because I'm good at what I do. *Smiley face*
Trouble: Very good. *Super smiley face*

Now I had a super smiley face as well. But I put my phone away.

As I puttered around and my brain spun with memories of my day with Vincent, my heartbeat increased and I realized I was sweating like a mofo. I felt overwhelmed and trapped. He was beautiful and amazing and I was really into him, but that scared the fuck out of me at a very basic level. I'd always had a commitment phobia, and right when I found someone who pushed all my buttons was its cue to go off.

I called Daphne because she knew that.

"Hi, Nic. I've been waiting for you to call."

"Daphne, I'm having a panic attack."

"Oh goodie! That means it went well?"

I snorted out a laugh because she was right on the ball, but I still felt like running away and changing my address so Vincent would never find me. "Yeah, he's fucking perfect. It's *terrible*, Daphne. What have you *done*?"

I heard the sounds of a chair scraping across the floor as Daphne sat down. "Sweetie, I want you to take a seat and talk to me. What are you so afraid of?"

I sat on the sofa and rocked back and forth while I forced myself to take a deep, calming breath and think about my answer.

"That he really likes me."

"Why does that scare you?"

"What if I disappoint him? How can I live up to the image he has of me?"

"What image does he have?" Daphne's voice was firm and calming.

"I don't know. Of 'the perfect Dom'?"

She laughed. "Whoa, Nic. I mean, that's a bit narcissistic."

"True."

"You don't know what he's thinking. But the fact you think it might be that means that the day went well, which makes me happy."

I took a deep shuddering breath. "Oh God, Daphne. I don't know if I can do this. I want to run."

"You are *not* running, Nic. My reputation is at stake. I told Vincent you were wonderful."

I groaned. "Why the hell did you do that, Daphne?" I felt the panic rise. *What am I going to do?*

"I'll tell you what you're going to do, Nic."

Thank God for Daphne. "Okay. Okay."

"You're going to run yourself a hot bath."

"Okay."

"You're going to pour yourself a glass of wine."

"Okay."

"Then, you're going to get yourself off."

"What?"

"Mast-ur-bate," she said, enunciating clearly.

"Okay. Fine."

"Twice."

"Twice?"

She laughed again. "Or even three times. If Vincent was that good, it shouldn't be too difficult."

"Fine."

"Because you know as well as I do that unreleased sexual tension feels a lot like anxiety."

That was absolutely bang on. "Right. True." It was a good plan. And it might just work.

"You are not allowed to text Vincent anything. If you decide you don't want to see him anymore, you will have to tell him in person."

"Ah, hell. You are a cruel, cruel mistress, Daphne. And I love you so much."

"Awe, baby, me too. Me too."

I took some deep breaths and went about following Daphne's orders to the letter. The nice thing about having friends who worked as Dominants? They could make you behave when you needed them to.

The bath was lovely, the wine delicious. By the time I crawled naked under my sheets with my favorite glass dildo, I felt much, much better.

The thing about a nice tempered glass dildo? They were hard as rock. And you didn't need any lube. If you were the least bit wet, they just slid right in. No fuss, no muss. Instant pleasure.

It took me about two minutes to come the first time, which showed just how aroused I was and probably what had triggered the panic attack.

My second orgasm came after another ten minutes of visualizing Vincent sitting at my piano in his pretty pink lingerie, then bending over it for his spanking. Fuck, that image would stay with me for a long time.

I already felt a ton better.

The other great thing about glass dildos? They pressed solidly against my G-spot so I came like a banshee if I rubbed my clit at the same time. I'm talking whole body orgasms that left my limbs like Jell-O and my brain like mush.

Still, I went for number three. This time I imagined Vincent's long fingers inside me, front *and* back, his tongue on my clit and his bottom red from the spanking I'd given him. I was getting closer and closer, then imagined tying him down and riding his cock until he begged me to let him come and *that* was it. *Over the edge and to the moon.*

Afterward I lay splayed out in my big bed, panting and exhausted and feeling much better about everything.

Before I went to sleep, I texted Daphne:

Thank you for the advice. You were right, as usual. Love you.

She texted back almost right away:

When do you see him next?

A week from today.

Wow. You might have to repeat this entire ritual next week. Or every night until then?

I feel a bit bad for Vincent now.

Why?

Because I told him he wasn't allowed to get himself off and here I am enjoying three epic orgasms, all because of him.

Oh God, Nic, you have to tell him about them! He'll feel so hard done by, so used and abused. He'll **love** *it!*

Yeah, probably. Am I a sick pervert, Daphne?

Yes. *The best kind. Lol.*

* * * *

Sunday morning, about nine-thirty my phone rang. It was Vincent, aka Trouble.

"Hello?"

"Hi, Sir? I'm so sorry to bother you. Am I bothering you? I didn't wake you up, did I?"

He sounded good on the phone. I hadn't really noticed the soft, deep timbre of his voice until this moment.

"No, you're not bothering me. And yes, I'm up."

"Oh. I…uh, I just remembered you saying something about IKEA furniture and I remember seeing a box in your living room yesterday. Like I said, I'm really good at putting IKEA furniture together, and if you wanted… I mean, I could come over and help you with it. Or I could do it *all* for you. Sir?" He sounded eager and apologetic, and it was so nice to hear his voice. My panic from the night before seemed irrelevant.

"You mean today? It's Sunday. Don't you want to relax?"

"I mean, if it's not convenient… I just… I'm not doing anything and I'd love to put some furniture together for you."

I tried not to laugh because he was desperate and it was so sweet. And I did want him here.

"It's perfectly convenient. Would you like to make me lunch, as well?"

I heard his indrawn breath. "Oh! Yeah, of course. I'll make you lunch then I'll put your stuff together."

"Can you be here at eleven?"

"Yes, Sir. Of course."

"See you soon, Vincent."

While I waited, I finished my coffee and took a leisurely shower, looking forward to seeing Vincent again. He arrived on time, looking apologetic but cheerful. He was wearing faded jeans and a navy T-shirt under his jacket, as well as a wide smile on his face.

"Hi, Sir. Thanks for letting me come over."

I grinned, finding it easy to do. "Well, you gave me an offer I couldn't refuse. I'd like tomato soup and grilled cheese for lunch. Soup is on the counter and you'll easily find the fixings for the sandwiches. You can make some for yourself, too."

"Of course. Thank you, Sir."

"Are you a good cook, Vincent?"

He shrugged as he removed his shoes. "I'm okay. I can definitely do soup and sandwiches."

"Excellent. I'm going to have you strip to your cute little panties. But you can leave your T-shirt on so you don't burn yourself or get any splinters later."

Vincent froze, staring at his feet. "Um."

"You *did* wear some cute panties, didn't you, Vincent?"

"I kind of forgot. I'm *so* sorry, Sir." He looked up at me, mortified.

I tried to look severely disappointed. "Well, I should have reminded you. But please be aware that I expect you to wear pretty lingerie under your clothes whenever you come to my home. I should make you strip to nothing, but in the interests of keeping my hands to myself today, the boxer briefs will be fine."

He nodded sadly but glanced up hopefully. "I can work naked if you want."

I smiled. "It's okay, Vincent. Just keep your T-shirt and boxer briefs on. But I will expect you to wear the baby blue panties on Saturday."

"Yes, Sir. Of course, Sir."

He looked so good in his white boxer briefs and navy T-shirt that I felt kind of relieved that he'd forgotten the panties, because it was a struggle to keep my hands off him as it was. But I was determined not to touch him today. He was only here to perform some entirely non-sexual service for me and I thought that would be good for both of us.

Things had gotten down and dirty fast the day before and I felt like we needed to slow down. I wanted to get to know Vincent as a person, not just a young man who seemed willing to let me do whatever I wanted with his body.

I busied myself with a few things in the living room while he made lunch. When he was done, he served it on the kitchen table and we sat and ate together. Next time he made us lunch, I was going to feed him, but for now, I left it like this.

"When did you realize you liked wearing women's panties, Vincent?" I asked because it was an aspect of him I was *very* interested in.

He sipped some soup off his spoon. "Uh, a few years ago I guess?"

I let my lips slide into a pleased smile. "And, uh, *how* did you find out, if I might ask?" I was picturing him trying on a pair of his girlfriend's underpants as a joke or something and figuring out how great they felt and looked on him.

He rubbed his thumb against his eyebrow. "Well, I uh, saw a guy in a magazine wearing them and I couldn't stop thinking about it. So, I ordered a pair of panties online. I only wore them once in a while."

"Did you masturbate in them?"

"Uh. Yeah. Of course" —he looked at me shyly— "Sir."

I spoke slowly and deliberately, like I was actually using my words on his body. "And how did you feel, when you stroked yourself off in those pretty panties?" I said, taking a bite of my grilled cheese.

His forehead creased and his blush spread. "Good, Sir. Pretty. Hot. Sexy. Sweet."

"You, Vincent, are all of those things. This is delicious, by the way."

He blinked. "Thank you, Sir."

After lunch I helped him unpack the bookcase I'd ordered from IKEA. But once we got the pieces out of the box, I left him to it. I had no patience for that. I mean, I could spend three hours edging a submissive but I hated, hated, *hated* putting furniture together — especially IKEA furniture.

Vincent, however, seemed to enjoy it. He organized all the pieces in sections on the floor and checked everything off in the instructions as he sat cross-legged in his cute little boxer briefs and T-shirt. He took his time, concentrating on following the instructions and getting things just right. I was impressed and, for some reason, proud.

I sat on the sofa pretending to work on my laptop but subtly observing Vincent. I liked the way he thought, the way he moved, the way he focused intently on the task. He was so graceful, both when he submitted to me and when he put IKEA furniture together.

At one point he needed my help to hold the pieces steady while he placed the finishing screws. We were both breathing heavy, trying to ignore our mutual attraction, and it felt kind of like a *real* second date, when the attraction was growing but nobody wanted to make the first move.

But it was torture for me, since I knew that all I had to say was, "Take off your clothes, Vincent," and he would strip for me. Then I'd be lost. We both would.

When he was done and we placed the bookshelf against the wall where I wanted it, I told him it had been lovely having him here but he needed to leave.

"Put your clothes on. Are you taking an Uber?" I should have offered to drive him, but I was too afraid of my own desires. Having Vincent beside me in the close confines of my car would have been too much.

"Yeah. I'll order it now."

While we waited for his Uber to arrive I thanked him for the work he'd done for me today. "I'm glad you came over."

He beamed. "Me too." Then his face fell. "Saturday seems like a long time from now."

I winked. "You'll be okay. I'll be thinking of you. Does that make it better?"

"Yes, Sir. Much."

"Don't forget, no jerking off."

"Yes, Sir. I remember."

* * * *

I got through the week fine but couldn't stop thinking about Vincent. I masturbated every fucking night and only felt slightly guilty that I'd prohibited Vincent from doing the same.

By the time Friday came around I was so eager to see him that it was ridiculous. I stayed up late chatting with Daphne on the phone about some of her latest clients and the interesting things they wanted her to do to them. There was this guy named Brian who lived for cock-and-ball torture apparently, although he also liked extreme humiliation and role play.

"I'm glad your work is rewarding, Daf," I told her, finishing my wine. "I've got to go to bed. It's past one o'clock and Vincent's coming tomorrow."

"Did he text you at all?"

"A couple of times. He texted today to make sure we're still on for tomorrow and to tell me he's been a good boy."

"Oh, Nic, he will be such a good boy for you. I know it. I mean, he was a *very good* boy for me."

For some reason I didn't want the details of Daphne's interactions with Vincent. I told her good night and hung up. It took me some time to fall asleep. I felt more excited about the next day than I should have been.

Dreams came, vivid and arousing and I woke to the sound of my doorbell ringing. It dragged me out of a deep, fitful sleep.

Who the fuck is here so early?

I glanced at the clock.

"Shit. Oh fuck!" I mumbled, sitting up fast and blinking like a deer in the headlights.

Nine o'clock on the dot. Vincent was on time and I'd slept through my alarm. I scrambled out of bed.

Grabbing a pair of black cotton boy shorts and an oversized T-shirt, I pulled them on as I made haste to the front door. I opened it with one hand and tried to tame my bedhead with the other.

"Hey, hi. Sorry… I slept in by mistake."

Vincent stood there in a pair of black jeans and a black knit sweater, blinking at me with a strange look on his face. He didn't say anything.

"What?" I said, my tone angry. I *hated* rushing and I *hated* being caught unprepared.

"You... You look even hotter than you did last week. I just got, like, an immediate hard-on."

I closed my eyes, shaking my head out of desperation. Why did he have to be so sweet? "Vincent."

"I'm sorry. I shouldn't have said that."

"It's fine. Just...come in. You want some coffee?" I was so flustered and I also *hated* that.

Vincent seemed amused and turned on by my confusion. He tried to hide a smile. "Why don't *I* make the coffee?"

"That's a *great* idea. Make us coffee, Vincent," I said, trying to get my Dom-self back.

"Okay, Sir," he said, toeing off his shoes and moving past me like he was on a mission.

I stared after him as he moved into the kitchen and located the coffeemaker. I wondered if he'd followed the instructions I'd given him.

"Are you wearing the lingerie like I told you to?"

He blushed and nodded, filling the carafe and pouring the water into the device.

For the first time that morning, a glimmer of hope for the day surfaced. I was sure once I had my coffee I'd be fine, but I didn't like waking up like this.

I sat at the kitchen table and watched him open the wrong cupboard. "How does it feel? Wearing lacy things under your regular clothes?"

He glanced at me and smiled. "Good. Where's the coffee?"

"Cupboard on the right. By the window."

He found the container and brought it down to the counter.

"I'm going to need it smooth and strong, Vincent. Just like you, my brave submissive."

He looked over. "Is that what I am?"

"Is that what you want to be? Mine?"

"Yours. Yes." He scooped measure after measure of coffee into the basket.

I stared at the table. "After last week, I already consider you mine. Do you want to know what I did Saturday night? Besides having an anxiety attack?"

He looked over. "You had an anxiety attack? Why?"

I shrugged. It was already old news that I wasn't concerned about. "I get them sometimes when I'm overwhelmed."

"Why were you overwhelmed?" he asked, pausing in his task. "Because of me?"

I didn't answer his question. Instead I stood and walked over there. "Did you obey my instructions, Vincent?"

"I'm wearing the lingerie. Yeah."

"No, I mean, about not getting yourself off."

He blushed harder. "Yeah. It was hard." He realized what he'd said and laughed.

"You know what *I* did last Saturday evening?"

He shook his head, staring at me with those curious blue eyes.

I leaned against the counter and reached out, pushing the lock of brown hair off his forehead. "I pictured the way you looked on my piano bench in your pretty pink panties and gave myself three fucking epic orgasms."

His eyes widened as he tried to picture it. "*Three*?"

"Three," I affirmed, holding up three fingers.

His eyes zeroed in on them. "With your fingers?" he whispered, as his breathing quickened.

I grinned slowly. "With my big glass dildo."

"Oh, fuck," he sighed. "Why didn't you tell me on Sunday when I came over?"

"Well, Vincent, because I knew that information would make you hard and I was really trying to be good on Sunday."

"You really are evil, you know?"

"Oh, I know." I looked him over, seeing the bulge in his jeans. "How does it make you feel, knowing that while you were holding yourself back, I was getting myself off to images of your fine ass, Vincent? Because I think I've masturbated every night this week."

My eyes flew to his hand as it moved toward his groin, but he stopped this instinctive movement and dropped it to his side.

"Good boy," I said, licking my lips. "Now answer my question."

"It feels good, like you used me." He stared at the floor. "I like to be used."

"Yes, you told me."

He nodded, still looking at the floor. "So…" he said.

"Mmm-m?"

"Do you still think there's nothing sexual between us?" It was a fair question and a bold one. But he already knew the answer and so did I.

"No."

"So, there is?"

"Yes, I think it's pretty obvious."

"Yes."

"And against my better judgment."

He grinned and met my eyes as the coffeemaker grumbled and spat. "Judgment, smudgment."

I couldn't help laughing at that ridiculous assertion. "Ah, Vincent, what am I going to do with you?"

He stared at me, humming with anticipation. "I don't know. But I can't wait to find out."

The first thing I did was tell him to be quiet while I drank my coffee. I took down two mugs and gave him the one with 'Slave' on it. I took the one that said 'Master'. I mean, *obviously*.

He smiled when he saw but remained quiet. We sat at the table and sipped in silence.

"This is very good coffee, Vincent."

He opened his mouth then closed it. Bobbed his head.

I grinned. "You will make this every time you come here in the morning without instruction, enough for us both."

He smiled.

"Is your cock still hard?"

He nodded.

"Take it out, please."

He blinked at me over his coffee.

"*Now*."

He put his mug down and reached one hand to his fly, popping the button and pulling the zipper down. I couldn't really see under the table but I watched the expression on his face as he freed his erection from its lacy confines.

"Just hold it in your hand."

He stared at me, doing as I asked, blinking silently. His chest moved out and in. His lips parted.

"You can talk now. I want you to describe it to me."

"Pardon?" he said.

"Tell me about your cock."

"Um, okay. It's pretty hard right now."

"How big is it when it's erect?"

"Um. Big?"

"You've never measured it?"

"Uh, nope." He seemed embarrassed, like that was a pretty big oversight on his part.

I was just surprised. I thought all men measured themselves.

"Stand up and get the tape measure from the drawer." I pointed to the top drawer by the sink. "That one."

He pushed his chair back and walked to the drawer, still holding himself, which was good because I'd never told him to stop. He used his free hand to pull the drawer open, found the tape measure and brought it to me.

"Thank you," I said, taking another sip of my coffee. It tasted really good. He made excellent coffee on top of everything else.

I took the tape measure from him and sat back in my chair, looking at his long fingers wrapped around his dick.

"Stroke yourself. Get it nice and full for me."

He gasped as he started moving his hand back and forth. His eyelids drooped as the pleasure hit. I watched his cock grow and the head emerge from the foreskin.

It was a really nice penis. Because...of course. And I'd already seen it, but not this close.

"You have a really nice penis, Vincent."

"Thank you," he gasped. "I mean, *I* like it."

I grinned. "I like it too. Okay, you can let go."

He let go and instead of immediately measuring him, I wrapped my fingers around him. I mean, I wanted to make sure he was at his thickest and longest, right? I was doing this for science.

"Oh. Fuck!" he moaned as I started to stroke him, making his cock even harder and longer.

I grinned up at the look on his face — surprise, arousal and bliss. I couldn't resist any longer. As he tilted his head back, I leaned forward on the downstroke and plunged my mouth over his glans.

The sound he made echoed off the walls. It was a wordless plea to continue and I did, until he couldn't get any harder without exploding all over the kitchen table.

I popped my mouth off him and pulled the tape out from its holder with a whoosh. Vincent gasped and struggled not to grab himself as I took the measure of his cock while it swayed against his sweater.

"Fuck, fuck," he panted as I did my work and glanced up at him. He looked down with adoration and expectation.

"Six-and-a-half inches, Vincent. Quite respectable." I turned the tape sideways to take his girth. "And four inches at the widest spot."

"Oh, God," he whispered as his hips unconsciously pushed toward me. A bead of moisture oozed from his glans.

"Okay," I said, pressing the button on the tape measure. The tape zinged back into its holder with a snap. "Time for some piano practice."

Vincent stared at me wide-eyed. Had he expected me to suck him to orgasm?

Silly boy.

"Wh-what?" he said.

"Pull your panties up, stuff yourself back into your jeans and go sit on the piano bench. I'll be there in a minute." I drank the last bit of my coffee and put the empty mug on the counter as he struggled to obey. I left him trying to put his large and erect cock back in his pants as I went to find some items I'd need for his lesson.

When I came back to the living room, Vincent was sitting obediently at the piano, his hands on his thighs, his head bowed. He looked uncomfortable, which I'm sure he was if his dick was wedged inside his tight jeans. He might have to consider altering his style a bit if he continued to come see me. *Y'know, wear looser pants*. Then again, I would probably have him naked or almost naked much of the time. But right then, I wanted him in his clothes.

"I like your outfit, so I'm going to keep you in it for now."

He dipped his head but didn't say anything.

"Practice your scales, please."

He hesitated.

"Is there a problem?"

He cleared his throat. "I need to tell you something."

My stomach lurched. *He's changed his mind. He's not into this. He's not into me.* A thousand awful things came to mind.

"Okay."

"I almost came in your mouth…in the kitchen."

That is *so* not what I expected to hear. Also, did he think I didn't know? I wanted to snort a laugh but I kept it in. Ridicule, at least at that moment, was not what I was going for.

"I know."

He glanced at me out of shy eyes. "Really?"

"Really."

He licked his lips and stared at the floor. "What would have happened if I had?"

I leaned my elbow on the piano and stared at him. "Well, I would have spat it out, for one thing. I would have left you hanging and spurting all over the place."

He shuddered.

"But I'm pleased that you held back."

"Would you have punished me?"

"Oh, hell yeah."

"How?" he asked before I'd even finished speaking. *Eager little slut.*

I didn't say anything. We gazed at each other, the tension building. "How would you *like* to be punished, Vincent?"

The question hung in the air between us. Finally, he spoke.

"I want…I want to…" He couldn't get it out.

"Tell me."

"I want to…stand in the corner while you fuck me with your glass dildo." It rushed out of him like the orgasm he'd held in.

Silence while I took this in. I felt a throb inside as I pictured it.

"Oh, Vincent, we were made for each other."

He actually moaned from the idea that I would do this to him and enjoy every minute of it. His eyes closed and he rocked his hips.

"But right now, I want you to practice your scales like a good boy."

His eyes opened and he blinked. "Okay."

"But I'm glad you told me that. I will certainly keep it in mind." No promises, just the possibility of his fantasy punishment coming true—at a time of my choosing, at my sole discretion.

His face fell and I bet he wished he'd *actually* come in my mouth. Because then I would have *had* to punish him. But since he'd just betrayed how he *wanted* to be punished, he had inadvertently told me how I *should* punish him when the time was right—which would, essentially, be to stand him in the corner and completely ignore him until the anticipation and arousal drove him mad with desire.

But I'd put that in my pocket for now.

Chapter Seven

As Vincent obediently practiced his scales, I picked up the powder blue penis gag from the coffee table and brought it over.

"Take a break for a second."

He stopped and glanced beside him, did a double-take at the gag. "What is *that*?"

I grinned. "It's a penis gag. You mean Daphne never used one on you?"

"Uh, nope."

"Okay. So, this bit, the part that looks like a small, thick penis, goes in your mouth, and it buckles behind your head."

He stared at the rubber penis part of the gag. "Um…"

I raised my eyebrows. "You have an issue with a fake penis in your mouth?"

He gave a little head shake back and forth. "But, *why?*"

Ah. He was a thinker. He wanted *reasons.* "Because it presses down on your tongue and makes you feel used."

His eyes widened. "Oh."

"Wanna try it? I can get a regular ball gag if you prefer."

"I'll try it."

"Okay." I held it out for him to look at again. "I have powder blue because the women I used to play with liked pastels. Anyway, it matches your underwear. Open."

He parted his lips and I inserted the rubber cock into his mouth, feeling a little shiver go up my spine. Because, wow, I almost wished I had a real cock to put in there. Except, he might not have wanted that. Anyway, I liked what I *did* have and he'd get plenty of that in his face eventually.

I fastened the gag behind his head and pulled back to check things out. His eyes were wide and his pupils blown. *I think he likes it.*

"Thumbs-up or thumbs-down?" I asked.

He bent his elbow and gave me a big thumbs-up.

"I thought so," I said, stroking his hair, which was soft and slightly curly. He was just so handsome. I felt sorry for his ex that she hadn't done some research and tried to give him this. She had really missed out. "You look beautiful, Vincent."

His eyes closed and he made a soft noise that sounded delicious around the gag.

"If you need to safeword, I want you to shake your head quickly from side-to-side. Got it?"

He nodded.

I picked up something else from the coffee table. "I'm going to blindfold you now."

He looked at me, then at the piano keys, then back at me, his eyebrows raised.

"I'll put your hands in the right place and you will do your scales from memory. You don't need to see the keys."

He didn't seem convinced but bobbed his head.

With the black leather blindfold on, he looked even better—subdued, put in his place, *mine*. Mine to do with as I pleased. And what I pleased was to have him learn the piano.

I placed his hands where they needed to go on the keys and had him practice scales and chords with the blindfold on.

He did very well. He had a feel as well as an ear for it.

"That's very good. You're a natural, Vincent."

He glowed under my praise. I leaned in and tickled his earlobe with the tip of my tongue. "You get a reward."

I took his hand in mine and led him to my bedroom where I removed his blindfold while he blinked like a confused puppy. God he was adorable. And, yeah, *puppy*. Maybe we could get into *that* someday.

"I'm going to undress you, okay?"

He nodded vigorously and tried to smile but he couldn't because of the penis gag, which made *me* smile.

I got him to bend so I could remove his sweater, revealing a white T-shirt that I took off, and there was the baby-blue camisole which looked lovely, but I divested him of that as well.

"I want access to those nipples," I explained.

He shuddered.

Then, his pants. My heart started thudding as he became more and more naked. He really did things to me. His submission did things to me. All of it. He was the whole package. And, speaking of packages...

When he stepped out of his jeans, he looked magnificent in the blue panties, his cock pressed against his belly, the shiny tip almost pushing past the waistband. Maybe we should have bought a size larger. No, this was perfect.

"Your cock looks amazing under that lace," I told him. "Now, turn around and lean over my desk."

I was a stickler for neatness, so the surface was relatively free of clutter. There was plenty of room for a woman or man's bare torso. I had made sure of that when I'd bought it. The wood surface had been polished to a sheen and would feel good on Vincent's skin.

He looked at the desk then moved into position, leaning his upper body on it. It was a fairly high surface. The women I'd had here had needed to be on tiptoe to do this. It was the perfect height for Vincent.

I walked over to the dresser that stored my bedroom kink supplies and opened the second drawer, taking out a length of soft red rope.

"I'm going to bind your wrists, now," I said, taking his right hand and moving it to his lower back. I brought the other hand down and looped the rope around his wrists several times. I stepped back and took a look at my handsome boy bent over in the pretty blue panties, gagged and with his wrists tied together.

Now *that* was art.

"Everything okay, Vincent?"

His cheek pressed against the surface of the desk and he nodded, glancing at me quickly.

"The rope's not too tight?" I checked.

He shook his head once.

"Good. I'm going to reward you for a productive practice session at the piano. It's going to feel really good, but I don't want you to come. Understand?"

He huffed, but dipped his head.

"Good boy. You are my very good boy, aren't you, Vincent?"

His eyes closed and he made a soft sound. I knew he would try hard to be good for me.

I placed my hands on his lace-covered butt cheeks, pressing and stroking, feeling the firmness under the delicate fabric. I pressed upward and outward in a circular motion so that his ass spread as I brought my hands around, then squeezed tight, then spread, then squeezed.

Vincent moaned.

I did this for a bit, then took hold of the waistband of his panties and slid them down to the top of his thighs, giving his ass a good slap. I couldn't wait to give him a thorough over-the-lap spanking, but not yet. I would savor the anticipation instead.

As I snaked my thumb along the crack of his ass, pushing between his cheeks, I wondered if he'd ever been rimmed? I was sure Daphne'd never rimmed him. Daphne didn't have sexual contact with her clients. She dominated men for money, but she didn't consider herself a sex worker. Sure, she made them come like gangbusters, when they were allowed, but she didn't give or receive oral and she didn't have intercourse with them.

I had the luxury of doing whatever the fuck I wanted with Vincent, as long as he consented to it, precisely because he wasn't my 'client' and he wasn't paying me. We were developing a close friendship as far as I was concerned and I thought I could get as close as I wanted. And at that moment, despite my previous reluctance, I wanted to get really, really close.

"Do you know what rimming is, Vincent?" I said, pushing my thumb against his hole. I felt him clench, his gasp muffled by the gag. Honestly, in the Internet age, was there anyone who didn't know what rimming was?

He groaned.

"I'll take that as a *yes*." I liked the fact that I could do things to him that Daphne'd never done, because I was sure she'd done things that *I'd* never do because they were beyond *my* hard limits but not Daphne's—and maybe not Vincent's. We needed to actually sit down and discuss what he and Daphne *had* done, just so I had all the information and knew his likes and dislikes.

I spread his cheeks to take a good look at him. He whimpered and shifted as if he were trying to get away from me. *Good luck.*

"Be still. I want to look."

Another whimper. I glanced at his face. His eyes had closed and his cheeks were scarlet. He looked so hot with the gag on.

"Does this embarrass you, Vincent? The fact that I want a good look at your asshole?"

He huffed out a laugh and nodded, while I traced my finger down his crack and teased his rim. There was fine dark hair along the sides, as there should be, but his hole looked clean and delicate.

"In a few weeks when I do this again, you won't even care, except to be excited. I'm going to get you very used to being examined *everywhere*."

He legit groaned. His ass clenched and released while I watched. Oh, he liked that idea, as much as this first exam had made him cringe. He *had* said he was into medical play.

"You know, if I'm going to play with you, I have to make sure you're healthy and fit, and that your skin" — I traced my finger around his anus while he struggled to stay still—"isn't broken or damaged. This is very important from a safety perspective."

Which was true, actually. But, just as I'd suspected, he was unblemished in this particular spot. No signs of hemorrhoids or infections. "And, lucky for us both, you're in excellent shape here." I ran my finger down his perineum and cupped his balls in my hand. They were heavy and warm.

He sighed.

He smelled of soap and a little of sweat, but it wasn't unpleasant. It was musky and natural and heady. I leaned closer and blew on his asshole.

He jerked and whimpered. I held his cheeks apart and did it again. He moaned. Then I stretched him apart wider and ran the flat of my tongue down his crack and over his anus.

He cried out, his curse muffled by the fake cock in his mouth.

I did it again. He made a high-pitched sound and stiffened all over. Oh yeah, baby. *That* was rimming.

"Do you like that, Vincent?"

His head went up and down like mad. His eyes fixed on the wall. He moaned, long and low.

I grinned. "I figured you would."

Then I really went at him. I pressed my face into the cleft of his ass and licked, bit and sucked at his hole like the dirty slut I was, delighting in his cries and struggles as he was overcome. He pulled at the ropes, his head turned from side to side on the desk as his breathing became desperate and erratic.

But the head movement concerned me. "Are you safewording, Vincent?"

He grunted, shaking his head once.

"Shall I keep going?"

He groaned and whimpered, then assented.

Oh, thank God. He tasted fucking delicious, better than any woman I'd done this to. I mean, assholes were pretty much the same in general, but specifically they were unique, like a fingerprint. And smells were different. And seeing as I was used to the female animal and the plethora of aromas it provided, I never thought I'd be so enamored by the male musk that filled my nose and slid down my throat.

Zane hadn't been a fan of performing this particular delicacy and had never wanted it done to *him* either.

This was my first time rimming a *guy*, and I devoured Vincent and hardly noticed his desperate grunts as he barely missed exploding beneath my assault.

But I did finally hear him and felt his barely contained energy. I pulled back, licking my lips and wiping my chin where my saliva had soaked it.

"Easy, easy, hold back. You can do it."

I rested my hand on the small of his back—a calm presence as he gathered himself and kept hold. I was secretly delighted he'd responded so strongly to my skills. I had much more to show him.

But at the moment, *I* needed some attention.

"Good boy. I'm going to untie your hands now." I undid the rope and pulled up his panties, listening to him hiss as they slid up over his sensitive erection.

When I was done, I told him to stand up and face me.

He did — and regarded me with open adoration. His damp hair stuck to his forehead. His face was red and there were marks from the desk. Fuck me, I could have come just from looking at him.

I reached up and unbuckled the gag, pulling it off him. The stump of a dildo slid out of his mouth and he licked his lips, breathing hard. He didn't speak, just watched me with those beautiful blue eyes.

"No talking. Sit on the edge of the bed." Even I could hear the lust in my voice.

He did as I asked, placing his hands on his thighs, waiting.

Those goddamn fingers. I moved close and stood right in front of him, staring at the hard cock trapped under blue lace. I lifted one foot and placed it on the bed by his hip, raising my chin and gazing at him in challenge.

"Give me your left hand, Vincent."

He swallowed thickly as his dick twitched and leaked. Oh yeah, he knew *exactly* what I wanted. Well, I wanted obedience, for one thing. *And* his fingers.

He lifted his left hand from his thigh and held it out to me, as if we were going to shake. I took his wrist in my fingers and guided his hand to my inner thigh. He gasped as his palm touched my skin, then inhaled shakily as I guided his fingers underneath my loose boy shorts. I mean, I basically pushed his hand to my crotch and shoved his fingers up my *soaking wet* cunt.

"Oh Jesus *Christ*," Vincent muttered, letting me use his hand like it was a weirdly shaped sex toy.

"Finger me. *Hard*," I commanded, my voice rough with need.

He shoved his fingers into me and I squeaked out an un-Dom-like cry as he started — expertly — to do what

I'd asked of him. And he did it hard, as I'd requested. I was forced to put my hands on his shoulders and focus on balancing while he fucked me with his hand.

"Oh fuck, that's good. That's good," I moaned, grinding against him as he found and pumped my G-spot like a goddamn expert, and I came, shaking and panting and squeezing his shoulders.

"Fuck!" I cursed, gasping for air. "Fuck! Oh my God. *Fuck.*"

He looked so triumphant and turned on as I came all over his hand that it made me giddy. Had I *ever* been giddy?

"Oh, Vincent, you fucking genius. I knew those fingers were magic!"

He grinned and, yeah, looked pretty fucking smug. "Not just for piano?"

I actually *laughed*. What the fuck was wrong with me? "No, definitely not just for piano. Oh, fucking Christ, *that* felt good."

He pulled his hand out of my shorts and it was — *no shit* — glistening with my juices. Without any word from me, he put his fingers in his mouth and sucked like they were something from Dairy Queen, closing his eyes as he tasted me.

"Vincent," I said sternly.

He opened his eyes and froze, realizing I'd never told him to do that. *Had he been a naughty boy? Or would I be amused?* I could see those thoughts as they flitted through his mind.

"Take your fingers out of your mouth."

He did, following them with his tongue as if he couldn't quite relinquish them.

I put my foot on the floor and straightened my boy shorts. "Lie on your back. Stretch your arms over your head."

I saw the hint of a smile as he obeyed, stretching out as if he were doing a yoga pose, only his breathing was way too fast for yoga.

In one quick move I leaned forward and pulled the panties down to his thighs. His cock bounced free and I crawled onto the bed, grabbing it and stuffing it between my lips.

"Oh! *Shit!*" he cursed, gasping a breath and fisting the coverlet, throwing his head back as I sucked and ravaged him.

I was hungry, so hungry. I wanted him to come in my mouth. I wanted him undone. I wanted him just as surprised as I had been a moment ago.

He garbled words I didn't understand as his body jerked beneath me. When he came, I felt the rush of warm fluid before I had to hold him down. It was *that* violent. His body convulsed and he came and kept coming. I tried to swallow because I knew from Daphne that he didn't have any STIs or STDs, but I couldn't get it all and it dripped from my lips as I tried to gentle him.

Finally, he sagged and collapsed on the bed, breathing raggedly like he'd just finished a twenty-K race. I sat up and wiped my chin dry of Vincent's copious spunk. His groin glistened with it.

"I think you've killed me," he said finally, when I was just about to check in.

"Well, that would be a tragedy," I said, sliding down on the bed beside him, taking his hand and playing with those beautiful fingers, "since we've only just begun."

Once we'd recovered and cleaned up, I peeled Vincent out of the panties and let him put his clothes back on. Then I had him prepare a couple of sandwiches and we sat on the couch to discuss his experience so far.

"How are you enjoying this?" I asked, pen and paper in hand.

I'd put on some fancy sweatpants, a red tee and my reading glasses. I think Vincent liked my intellectual look. He kept licking his lips and shifting his ass on the sofa. I'd forgotten how little time young men needed to recoup after an orgasm. Scratch that, I'd never learned. *Mostly women, remember?* But women, if they were in the right environment, didn't take long at all, so I was kind of familiar with it. He was keeping up, at any rate.

He lifted his eyebrows at the question. "Do you really need to ask, Sir?"

I stared at him, my pen poised over the paper. "Yes, Vincent, I really do. I need to make sure you're on board with everything that has happened so I can plan out the next couple of visits." I put the end of the pen in my mouth and tried to look like I was devising a multitude of scenarios. — which, of course, I was.

He widened his eyes farther and parted his lips. "Oh," he whispered.

I grinned around the pen then removed it and wrote down what I'd learned.

Bondage, yes, rimming, yes, oral, yes. Lingerie, hell yes. Piano practice a resounding success. Excellent fingering skills.

I underlined that one.

Because, yeah, he'd known exactly where to put those long fingers and what to do with them. Granted, fingering wasn't exactly rocket science, but it was plain to see he'd been with women before and he'd been paying attention.

"So, let's talk about Daphne."

"Okay."

"What do you like about Daphne?"

He blinked. "She's fucking terrifying."

I snorted a laugh. "True. You like that?"

"I love that."

"Okay. Fair enough." I took a drink of my water. "Am I as scary as Daphne?"

He thought for a moment. "I mean, in some ways, no. In some ways, you're even scarier."

"How so?"

"Well, I'm not really sure what to expect from you. This is our second weekend, and it's been pretty awesome. But I know you've gone easy on me. Daphne's used…um…multiple items on my ass. You've only used your hand…and not that hard."

I nodded. Yeah, I had gone easy on him. I made a note to not be so gentle.

Harder spankings. Use tools.

"Has Daphne ever used her tongue on your ass?" I already knew the answer to that.

He blushed and gaped at me, remembering. "No. Nope. *That* was different. Definitely."

"And you liked that?"

His expression became suspicious, as if he thought I was toying with him, which I was.

"Yeah. I liked that."

"Was it scary?"

"A little."

"How?"

"Because…because no one's ever done that before. And I didn't know if I could keep from…you know…"

"Shooting? Jizzing? Spraying?" I was deliberately goading him. It was so much fun.

"Oh fuck. Yes."

"Say it, Vincent. Say *'I didn't know if I could keep from jizzing all over your desk, Sir.'*"

He stared at me, his jeans looking awfully tight. He cleared his throat. "I didn't know if I could keep from jizzing all over your desk, Sir."

It was so quiet that I could barely hear him.

"I beg your pardon?"

His face flushed and he looked down. "I didn't know if I could keep from jizzing all over your desk, Sir." This time he spoke loudly and enunciated each word.

"Yes, I know you struggled with that, but you did just fine. I've never done that to a man before. Just you."

"Really?"

"Lots of women. But you're the first guy I've rimmed."

We were silent for a few moments. Then he asked hesitantly, "Did *you* like it, Sir?"

And I was assaulted with the memories of his ass and my tongue and his desperate cries and squirming.

"Yep," I said, popping the 'p'.

He smiled shyly. "Yep? All I get is a yep?"

Oh, fuck me, he's so cute when he's coy.

"Fine. I fucking loved eating your ass, Vincent. Next time I'm gonna stick some fingers up there while I'm at

104

it," I said, pretending to be angry but giving him a cheeky grin.

"Oh, Jesus Christ," he said, spreading his legs and squirming on my couch cushions. "Oh, fuck."

"Did Daphne do a lot of ass play with you? I don't mean spanking. I mean shoving things up there."

He blanched. "I mean, some. She did some. Objects."

"What kind of objects, Vincent?" I loved that it was killing him to talk about this. He was so damned embarrassed and it was awesome.

"Uh, dildos. Beads." He looked down at the ground. Whispered, "*Balls.*"

"Balls?"

He glanced up shyly. "*Big* balls."

I blinked. *That minx.* "Daphne shoved big balls up your ass?"

"Yep."

I stared at him, seeing the amusement as well as embarrassment there.

"On a string," he mumbled, miming with his hands.

"I should hope so. We want to be able to get them out." I wrote it down.

Likes anal play — big balls on a string.

"And how did those big balls feel in your ass, Vincent?"

His eyes flew open and he coughed. "Good. Pretty good."

"*Pretty* good?"

"Okay, great. *Really* good."

I jotted that down.

"Excellent. We're getting somewhere now. I'm getting lots of ideas for next weekend."

He opened his mouth and a moan came out. It was adorable and sweet and so *Vincent*.

I spent a few moments jotting down several ideas for the future.

"Can I say something, Sir?"

"Of course." I looked up over the rims of my readers, and his eyes half closed. I wrote —

Wear glasses.

"Um, I don't need you to be scary the way Daphne is scary because you're not. And that's fine."

"I can be scarier, Vincent. I can be *so much* scarier."

"Oh my God. Okay. Sure."

"I'm kidding. I mean, I'm *not*. But I want to know what you mean."

He leaned forward. "I mean, there's *more* here, with you."

"Okay."

"I'm not exactly attracted to Daphne. I should be, but I'm not. So, she kind of has to scare me or we wouldn't have any fun." He paused, licked his lips then met my gaze. "I'm having so much fun with you, Nic. And fear isn't much of a part of it."

I didn't know if anyone had ever said anything so honest to me. "Thank you for sharing that, Vincent." I wrote something else down then looked up. "Why do you think you should be attracted to Daphne?" I asked, but I knew what he meant. I mean, most people were attracted to Daphne, including me.

He shook his head. "I mean, she's so beautiful. She could be in a magazine."

"She *has* been in a magazine. It's a fetish mag, but you're right. She wouldn't look out of place on the cover of *Vogue*."

"Well, maybe not in her slutty Victorian maid costume," he said.

I laughed. "Yeah, maybe not. Wait! She has a slutty Victorian maid costume?"

"Yeah. She wore it when she caned me one time."

My lips pursed in sympathy. "What did you think of the cane?"

"Hated it. It hurt way too much. But I liked the humiliation of it."

I wrote down *No canes*, which wasn't really necessary because I didn't have any. They were a little too severe for me.

"What about paddles? Do you like paddles?" I had no doubt Daphne'd paddled that beautiful ass a few times.

"I like paddles. I mean, it hurts, but I like that kind of pain?"

"Excellent. Rubber, wood, leather?"

"All the above?"

I wrote that down.

"Floggers?"

"Sure. They're okay."

"Not your favorite?"

"Kind of boring."

"Good to know. Did she ever use a crop?"

"No, actually, which is weird."

"Not weird. Daphne used to ride. She couldn't wrap her head around using crops on men. *People* are weird."

He laughed and shook his head, blushing.

"Yeah, I know it sounds strange coming from the mouth that ate your ass. But still…"

"God, you're funny."

"Am I?"

"Yeah. You make things more relaxed. When you want to, at least."

I raised an eyebrow at him.

"Sometimes you make things very formal and really nerve-racking."

"Yes. It's part of my persona. I thought you liked that."

"I do. But I like the funny part too. I like that you can be relaxed around me."

I smiled at him. I did find I could relax around him, more so than with Zane. But Zane and I had had a weird dynamic. I was starting to realize just *how* weird.

"Anyway, what do you think of the idea of a crop—on that fine ass and elsewhere?"

"I think… I think I'd like it a lot."

"I think you'd like it a lot also. And, lucky you, I own several. We'll have to find out which is your favorite."

He gulped. "Yes, please." And stared at me with wide eyes.

I blinked. "Right now?"

He nodded and repeated, "Yes, please," in a breathy voice.

I considered this. I didn't usually let my subs call the shots. Still, I was eager to see what he thought of my various implements. And now I wanted to find out how he'd react to them.

"All right, then. But I want to continue this discussion. I'm sure Daphne did many things to you and I want to know what they were."

"I mean, I can write it down for you," he offered.

Actually, that was a great idea. I was a little miffed *I* hadn't thought of it.

"That's a great idea. You can write an essay for me this week. Five pages minimum. Detailed descriptions of what she did and how it made you feel, starting with the most basic to the most extreme."

He looked at me with astonishment.

I smiled sweetly. "I'm not kidding, Vincent. Due next Saturday."

I lowered my head and looked over the tops of my glasses, quite deliberately. "You will be graded on composition, grammar and spelling." I chewed on my pen, thinking. "Anything less than an A gets a punishment of my choosing. A or higher, *you* get to pick."

"Okay. Fair."

He started to look pretty excited and I remembered we were going to look at the crops.

I left the glasses on and stood up. "Come with me."

Chapter Eight

The majority of my BDSM kit was in the basement, confined to a cabinet in one corner. You would never have guessed what I had hidden away in there because the room looked fairly ordinary. There was a gray laminate floor, a brown leather sofa and matching love seat and an old wing chair I had inherited from my granny.

Poor Granny couldn't have predicted I'd use her wing chair in my ipso facto 'dungeon', but there it was. It worked well because the wings were made of solid hardwood and I could tie a sub's arms down — or legs if I flipped them.

Of course, Vincent, with all of his experience, found the one not-so-subtle item in the room.

"Is that a spanking bench?" he asked, trying not to sound eager. He totally failed.

"Yes, my lovely boy, *that* is a spanking bench. Want to try it out?"

"Okay," he answered, his voice high-pitched.

"Bring it into the middle of the room."

He dragged it over and stood nervously beside it. I exploited his excitement and anxiety by remaining silent and opening the cabinet.

"Should I take my clothes off?" he asked.

It seemed the shy, hesitant sub from last weekend had found his legs. I smiled to myself. "Yes, Vincent. Please do. Everything."

I took out some wrist and ankle cuffs and brought them over as Vincent started to disrobe. He pulled the sweater over his head then the T-shirt. Now *I* was distracted.

I walked over and stood close in front of him. His hands were on his fly but he stopped what he was doing and stared at me, wide-eyed.

"Do you like to have your nipples pinched, Vincent?" I asked, his eyes flitting down to the light brown nubs of flesh on his lightly haired chest.

"Mistress Daphne clamped them sometimes," he said.

"Did you like that?"

"*Yes.*"

"Did she ever just pinch them, like this?" I asked, closing my fingers on his left nipple and squeezing.

He shut his eyes and moaned. "No...no."

"Hmm-m," I said, pinching his other nipple without letting go of the first.

His mouth opened and he made the most delicious sound.

"Are you hard?"

"Yes."

"Is this making you harder?" I twisted my fingers, squeezing.

He groaned. "Yes. Fuck. *Yes.*"

I let go. "Good to know," I said sweetly and stepped back, pointing to his jeans. "Finish up and sit on the bench."

He opened his eyes and unfastened his jeans, pushing them and the panties down and stepping out of them. His cock swayed in a most tantalizing way as he moved to sit on the spanking bench. I almost wanted to suck him again.

Instead I walked over and grabbed his erection, stroking him a few times and letting go as he gasped with shock and pleasure.

"I like your cock, Vincent. It's as eager to please as the rest of you." I grinned at him and he smiled back, his eyes radiating adoration. It seemed I'd made a good impression. And I hadn't even brought out the crops. I suddenly remembered my blindfold collection was down here.

"I'm going to blindfold you but no gag this time. I want you to be able to talk." I walked back to the cabinet and found my little box of blindfolds. The one I'd used on Vincent earlier was just a basic black mask I kept upstairs. I couldn't help smiling as I fingered through them and selected a dark purple silk mask with fine black lace over top. I had a sudden flashback of Delilah, her dark brown skin under that same mask as her mouth opened in ecstasy.

I took it over and held it up for Vincent to see. "Pretty enough, do you think?"

His gaze stroked over the beautiful fabric. "Oh, yes. Thank you, Sir." He looked as though he were about to cry. It was hard to believe no one before me had indulged Vincent's penchant for pretty things.

"You are so welcome, sweetheart," I said, reaching out and cupping his chin. I rubbed my thumb gently along the curve of his jaw where light stubble had already emerged. My sweet baby had a persistent beard that he liked to remove.

"Do you shave every morning?" I asked, curious.

"Yes, Sir," he said, almost proudly.

Perhaps Daphne had demanded it?

"Hmm. I might get you to stop."

His eyes widened but he said nothing.

"I like this roughness, especially when combined with some very feminine accoutrements."

"Yes, Sir," he said hesitantly.

"You'd look good with a beard," I decided.

"Yes, Sir."

I narrowed my eyes at him. "But you don't want to grow one?"

"No, Sir. Not really."

"Hmm-m. Well, we'll see."

I'd leave it up in the air for now. But I might wish to push this particular soft limit and see if he would grow one for me. I thought he'd look fantastic with a close beard and wearing his lacy undergarments and perhaps some other things I would buy for him.

I put the blindfold on him and buckled it behind his head. Then I made him lie back on the padded bench and proceeded to cuff his wrists and ankles to its legs so he was splayed out like a delicious banquet. I had to make some adjustments to the height of the bench to do that, so it was a bit of a procedure, but eventually I had him in place, looking mighty good with the lacy blindfold on and his dick curving over his belly, his balls tight and full.

I made a clicking sound with my tongue. "Oh, Vincent, what an image you make."

He blushed and wiggled on the bench. "Thank you, Sir."

"No, Vincent, thank *you*."

He licked his lips and his cock moved. *Perfect*. He was perfect. I tried to ignore this thought because it wigged me out and I just wanted to have fun with him.

"I'm giving you a different safeword, Vincent. I think your safeword should be 'piano'. It's probably easier to remember than 'latté'. Is that all right?"

"Yes, Sir. I like it."

"Good. Please feel free to use it. I will never be angry at you or frustrated with you for using your safeword."

"Thank you, Sir."

Walking back to the cabinet, I collected the five riding crops I currently possessed and walked back to where my submissive lay, captively waiting. "Mmmm, look at all that pale white skin. I can't wait to pink you up."

I put the pile of crops down on the love seat and selected a thick, braided one. It looked hefty and packed a good *thwunk* and a bit of a sting. It was as good a place to start as any. I realized we didn't know much about each other and that we might as well try to rectify that today.

"This is the first crop I ever bought," I said as, instead of striking him with it, I laid it down gently along his middle. I placed the handle by his dick and the tip reached to just below his chin. He inhaled the leather smell as I reached down to tickle his balls. He gasped and wriggled, rocking the crop but not displacing it.

"If that rolls off you I'm going to use it on your balls instead of using my fingers," I threatened. It was an empty threat because we hadn't even addressed the idea of cock and ball torture and I'd never go there so soon anyway.

But a little tickle torture? *Sure.*

I moved my fingers with feather lightness from his balls down his perineum to his sweet hole and back, as he tried not to struggle. He made lovely sounds as I played with his sensitive spots while his cock twitched and bounced from side to side.

I took my hand away and pulled on a black nitrile glove from the box I'd placed nearby, making sure to snap the material noisily so he heard. His lips parted and he lifted his head as if to look, then remembered he couldn't see and let his head fall back.

"Keep that crop steady," I reminded him as I went back to the tickling, now with the added tease of the latex glove, which meant I had other things in mind.

He made those soft noises again as I touched him. I tickled down from his balls along his perineum to his hole and back a number of times then stopped to drip some lubricant onto my gloved fingers. When Vincent felt the cold liquid on his perineum, he gasped and pulled at the bindings. The crop almost rolled off but he recovered himself and moaned with frustration.

"What do you want, Vincent? Tell me," I said softly, rubbing his perineum and spreading lubrication over his hole with the lightest touch.

"Oh God, please, *please*…"

"Tell me what you want."

"In me…"

"Pardon?"

"P-put your finger in me."

"Hmm-m, what if I don't want to?" I said, tracing around his hole and along his perineum like I could do it for hours — which I should. I really should.

"Oh…God…*please*…"

"Keep that crop steady and I'll consider it," I told him. "But I'm quite happy playing here for now."

He groaned.

I continued to tease him as he became more and more frustrated. "I'm going to ask you some questions, Vincent, and I want you to answer them honestly. When I'm satisfied, I'll finger you properly. Okay?"

"Okay. Okay."

"When Mistress Daphne was shoving balls up your ass, how did it feel?"

"Oh, fuck. It felt good."

"I realize that, but tell me *what* about it felt so good?"

He did as he panted his frustration. "I was so fucking *full*. Stretched *open*. *Stuffed*. It felt so good to be stuffed full like that…and so humiliating to have balls up there. Big black ones."

I almost laughed except his words and sounds were making me pretty horny. I didn't have any giant anal beads in my collection or I'd have considered using them that moment. There was a shopping trip in my future. Perhaps I'd bring Vincent along. We'd had a good time at the mall the week before.

"Good boy. I can just imagine how it felt to stuff you so full. How it looked. Would you like me to do that sometime?"

He whimpered. "Right now?"

"Not now. I don't have what I need. But soon. *Very* soon."

"Okay. Okay."

"Am I making you crazy with this teasing?" I said, playing with the swirling dark hairs on his scrotum.

"*Yessss. Please*…"

"You want my finger inside you?"

"Oh *please*, please. Fuck me with your finger. *Please*."

Oh, my dirty, dirty boy. Not so polite now, except he *did* keep saying 'please'.

"Just one finger?" I swirled my index finger around the edge of his hole as it unclenched and clenched in anticipation.

He lifted up his head and yelled, "*All* of them!" Then he let it fall back. "All of them."

I stopped what I was doing for a moment.

"Did Mistress Daphne *fist* you, Vincent?"

He was quiet, just soft moans coming now. Then, "Yes."

Wow. My insides throbbed with desire as I imagined it.

"Did you like it?"

"Fuck, yes. So much. *So* much."

"Hmm-m," I said again, swirling my finger around his hole, watching his cock jerk. "I'm not going to fist you today."

He sighed with disappointment. "Okay."

"But that's definitely something I'd like to explore with you."

He groaned and I pushed my finger into him finally.

He cried out as his stomach muscles clenched and his anus accepted my finger. I shoved in deeper and was rewarded with a groan and Vincent's mouth opening and closing.

"How's that?"

"Good, oh fuck, *more*."

All politeness gone. Achievement unlocked.

"Keep that crop from falling, Vincent," I said as I pulled my finger out and pushed back in again. He moaned and shuddered. I added a second finger, then a third. Oh yeah, I could have totally fisted him. I mean, my hands weren't even that big…but not this time.

As I withdrew, Vincent jerked and the crop fell, making a clatter as it hit the floor. He froze, panting and awaited my reaction.

I peeled off the nitrile glove, again with lots of noise, and dropped it to the floor. Then I walked over and bent down to pick up the crop, not saying anything. Vincent tracked my steps, although he couldn't see me.

"You're not really going to use that on my balls, are you, Sir?" he squeaked.

"I haven't decided yet," I said.

"I'm not really into ball torture," he gasped, squirming.

"I'll keep that in mind. You remember your safeword?"

"Yes. Piano."

"Okay. I need you to try to keep still because I don't want to hit you in the wrong spot with this. I don't want to hurt you too much." I grinned, even though he couldn't see. "Just enough."

"Yes, Sir."

I touched the tip of the crop to the rosy head of his penis, which had fully emerged from his foreskin and glistened with moisture. He was ripe for the taking. I tapped it, making him gasp and squirm. *So much for staying still.*

I glided the tip of the crop along the underside of his cock to touch his balls then poked behind them. He groaned.

"I'll start small," I said.

I traced the tip of the crop to his inner thigh and gave it a sharp swat. He gasped. I did it again. A moan this time.

"Okay?"

"Yesssss…"

He liked that. Good. I had chosen the right crop to start with.

I swatted the insides of both thighs, then the outsides, then moved down to his calves. Because I was hitting him very lightly, I could go there safely. I was just teasing him. I wouldn't have bound him this way for severe impact play. That was better reserved for the buttock area.

I traced the tip of the crop up one leg and along his hip to his belly. Again, light stingy taps over his belly, near his cock to scare him. I just wanted to get him worked up and it seemed to be doing the trick. He looked beautiful moaning and licking his lips with the purple mask over his eyes and his body displayed this way.

There wasn't much of a difference between a man's body and a woman's body when it came down to it. The vulnerable spots were basically the same, the responses similar. But the feeling of exploring a man in this way was exhilarating since I'd never done it before. Zane had never let me top him. He had taught me how to dominate *women*. And he had taught me well — Well enough that I seemed able to carry over those skills to be what Vincent needed.

I used the crop like a feather, tracing Vincent's skin along his muscles and limbs, enjoying the way he tensed and relaxed, listening to his breathing, his moans and gasps. He was as delicate as a flower in some ways, but I could already see he was incredibly strong and inviolable in others. To seek out this kind of thing from strangers took guts.

"Oh, sweetheart, you're doing so well." I loved calling him that, and he seemed to like it too. While some men would have bristled at so soft an endearment, it seemed to reach deep into Vincent's soul and water an empty well. "I can see you're very aroused."

He groaned and his cock jerked, as if to prove me right.

"I'm going to turn you over so I can demonstrate the true effectiveness of each of these crops on your backside."

He shuddered.

It only took a few minutes to reposition him on his front, with his knees and wrists bound this time. I'd lowered the bench so he was kneeling on the floor, his erect cock jutting below. His cheek lay against the padded leather as he tested his wrist bindings. The purple mask was still in place because his face looked beautiful with it on and because I wanted him to concentrate on the different sensations produced by each implement.

I was confident that he liked this position. He seemed more relaxed and able to accommodate the indignity of being bound.

"Let's get down to business." I tapped the skin of his buttock with the tip of the crop, harder than before. "I'm going to ask you some questions and I want you to try to answer them honestly. If you don't like a question, you can pass. Okay?"

"Yes, Sir," he said obediently.

I mean, this entire weekend was essentially a first date, so I wanted to know things.

"Where did you grow up?" I asked, snapping the crop against his ass.

He cried out but answered. "Toronto. Sir."

"Downtown Toronto? Or the suburbs?" I said, hitting him on the other cheek.

He gasped. "Suburbs. Big house. Three sisters."

Ah, that explained some of it. I ran the tip of the crop into his cleft, sliding it against his anus. He moaned.

"Are your parents together?"

"Divorced…when I was eight. Why are we talking about my parents?" he asked.

"Sorry. Never mind. Forget them. They're irrelevant."

He laughed, then gasped as I struck him again. "I like that, Sir."

"I like that you like it." I gave him a final strike, then laid the crop down on the love seat and picked up another. This one was green and had a smaller tip, so it would sting a bit more where the last one had had more of a *thwunk*. "This is my second crop purchase. My sub wanted something a little sharper." I slapped his buttock with it and he moaned.

"What do you think? Better than the other one or not as good?"

"Better," he said, panting and squirming.

I slapped his ass with it a few more times, then reached underneath and palmed his cock, which was hard and throbbing.

"Mmm-hmm. You *do* like that one."

He thrust into my hand, groaning. He would have come if I'd let him. I took my hand away.

"Not yet, sweetheart. We still have three more to sample."

He whimpered in a most delicious way. I worked him over with the green crop for a little longer, then switched to the red one. This one was similar to the first and dealt a heavier, less-stingy impact. I already knew he liked it and his sounds indicated he was enjoying himself.

Then I picked up the quirt. "This is my fourth purchase," I said, gliding the knotted end along Vincent's back and over his pinking buttocks.

He shuddered and groaned, pulling on his bindings. "Oh fuck," he muttered.

I grinned. "Yeah, this one's gonna hurt more than the others. The sting is pretty severe."

He struggled like he wanted to escape.

I checked in. "Do you want to try it? I can hold off on this and the cat for now."

He settled down. I ran the end of the quirt over the line of his body again. He liked that, so I kept doing it until he told me to go ahead.

"Good boy. You're very brave."

He shuddered a breath as I pulled back and brought the tip of the quirt down quite hard on his right buttock.

He howled and jerked. "Fuck! *Fuck.*"

I couldn't help smiling because I was an evil genius and because he looked so fucking good tied down, struggling against the pain. I brought it down twice on his left buttock and he cried out again. I reached underneath. His cock was rock-hard and leaking. He was getting off on this big time. I fucking loved it.

I whipped his ass with the quirt then dropped it to the floor and picked up the cat. I did the same thing and ran the strands of the cat along his back. There were five strands and each one resembled the strand on the quirt. His head jerked up and he cursed.

"Yes, or no? We can stop anytime."

He thrust into the air and I wondered if he was close. His ass was pretty red, he was sweating and panting and the pelvic movements were telling. I waited for his answer.

Finally, he moaned, "Yessss," and I had a feeling he was close.

I would use the cat on him then get him off. He had definitely earned it and the cat was nasty, so I'd just give him a small taste.

He came on the third strike of the cat on his back. I was standing there with my mouth open watching him convulse and his cock spray semen onto the floor of my basement, while I almost had a sympathetic orgasm of my own. It was fucking amazing to watch. And I could barely compute that he'd come without a hand on his cock, only the thin furls of the cat-o-nine tails on his skin. It was a fucking revelation.

And his sounds! He moaned so loudly and long that I wondered if my neighbors would hear. I honestly didn't care, and the cadence of his pleasure was music to my ears.

I dropped the cat and moved forward, sliding on my knees by his head and stroking his hair, making comforting noises as his cries began to dissipate. I reached under the table and gave his cock a comforting stroke, although I knew he would be sensitive.

He sighed and jerked in my grasp, trying to get away.

"Vincent, that was fucking incredible. I should punish you for coming without permission, but I've honestly never seen anything like that."

He panted, his mouth open and slack while I pushed the blindfold off his head. His hair was damp with sweat and his eyes had closed.

"Vincent?" I whispered.

He opened them and gazed at me with something close to awe. I couldn't accept this. It had been him as much as me.

"Thank you," he whispered.

Something inside me broke open and filled with sunshine.

Chapter Nine

I gave Vincent a solid two hours of aftercare that included a cuddle, a warm bath and rubbing his sore spots with arnica cream. He was very quiet while we did this and I wondered if he was experiencing sub drop, but when I asked him questions, his answers reassured me.

Just before he left, as we confirmed he would return the next Saturday at nine and wouldn't get himself off in the meantime, he looked at me with an expression so mournful that I started to think I'd done something wrong.

"What's the matter?"

"I miss you already," he said softly, sincerely, and it was enough to send a small bite of panic through me. I'd thoroughly enjoyed our day but it had affected me deeply, and I needed some time to myself to sort that out. I wondered why Vincent didn't seem to relish the same thing.

But he was so sweet that I couldn't help smiling. "You can text me. And if you ask nicely, I might even call you."

"Yeah?" he said, brightening.

I raised my eyebrows. "Maybe. If you can prove to me what a good boy you're being without me there to watch you."

He grinned.

"And, uh, Vincent?"

"Yeah?"

"You owe me an essay."

"Fuck."

* * * *

Sunday was a complete write off.

I couldn't stop thinking about Vincent. I half expected him to text or call me but he didn't and I felt disappointed. Fuck it, I was crushed, which made me furious at myself and frustrated with him. Why wouldn't he at least touch base?

At least I could go to work on Monday and Tuesday, which helped. The office was as busy as usual. By Wednesday I had to admit it bothered me that he hadn't texted at all. I wondered if he was second-guessing our connection or if he was regretting ever having come over. Then again, there'd been no text saying any of that.

I decided if I didn't hear from him by the time I was done with supper on Wednesday, I would send him a quick text making sure he was okay. He's seemed okay when he'd left but maybe he'd started having regrets?

At five minutes after six I got a message from him. I actually sighed with relief.

Trouble: Hi, Sir. I'm having issues with your request.

My grin almost split my face but I decided to clarify:

Me: The essay or the one where you have to keep your hands off your dick?

Trouble: The essay is done, Sir.

Me: Wow. I'm pleased to hear that.

I quickly changed his contact name from Trouble to SweetH—for Sweetheart—because the essay was done and he deserved it.

SweetH: It's the other thing, Sir.

Me: Which, as I recall, wasn't a request but an order.

SweetH: I believe I was supposed to abstain from having an orgasm, not from keeping my hands off. Is that correct, Sir?

Me: That is correct. Although the other seems like an exercise in frustration.

SweetH: It is. I want to come so bad. This is *hard*. And so am I. Sir.

Me: Then maybe you should keep your hands *off* your dick.

SweetH: I wish they were *your* hands, Sir.

Me: No you don't. If they were my hands, I'd be deliberately teasing you and edging you and not letting you come.

SweetH: It kind of feels like you are, Sir.

Me: Well then, maybe I should call you.

SweetH: *Happy excited faces with hearts*

Oh hell. He had me wrapped around his finger — or his cock. *Whatever*.

"Hi."

"Hello, Vincent."

I heard breathing. Then, "Am I in trouble?"

"Not yet." He sounded really turned on. "How hard *are* you, Vincent?"

"Painfully hard."

"After only two days?" I made a clicking noise.

"Almost three," he said mournfully.

"You should probably have a cold shower."

"I did."

"You did?"

He sighed. "After work…but it's back."

I laughed. "The perils of being twenty-four, I guess."

"And having a dream Dom." His voice was warm and so sweet.

"Flattery is not going to get you an orgasm." I was pretty sure I was blushing, which was fucking ridiculous.

"Fuck. Damn." He sounded genuinely disappointed.

I actually laughed. "Oh, Vincent, you kill me."

His breath hitched. "In a good way?"

"In a very good way. Now listen. Go take another cold shower and watch TV or something. Get your mind off sex."

He laughed. "It's not on *sex*."

"Then what are you thinking about that's making you so hard?"

I heard him swallow thickly. "Your basement. Being tied down. Being whipped."

My mouth dried as I remembered what had happened in my basement on Saturday. "I see."

"Can we do that again?"

Oh, fuck yes. "I think that can be arranged, but only if you fulfill my requirements this week. The essay...and no orgasms. You want to touch your dick, be my guest. But if I find out you climaxed, you are going to have one boring-ass weekend. Do you understand?"

"But I live alone, Sir. If I have an orgasm, who's going to tell you?"

"You are."

He groaned, then laughed. "Yes, Sir."

I hung up the phone with a smile on my face.

I slept well, knowing that Vincent might struggle but that he'd do his very best to obey my orders.

Work on Thursday sucked balls, but when I finally had a chance to relax after supper, I received the following message—

SweetH: I'm still hard, Sir.
Me: That's good to hear. I like your stamina.
SweetH: *Single tear on sad face emoji*
Me: *Sunglasses and grin on face emoji*

On Friday evening, I got this one.

SweetH: I can't take it anymore. I need to come. *Please!*

I smiled at my phone and sat on the sofa, getting comfortable.

Me: You can wait until tomorrow, Vincent.
SweetH: I don't want to, Sir.

Me: Tell you what. If you do as you're told and *don't* come tonight, tomorrow I'll let you have not one, not two, but *three* massive orgasms.

SweetH: Are you screwing with me, Sir?

Me: Not at all.

SweetH: You're screwing with me, Sir.

Me: Well, tomorrow I'll be screwing with you.

SweetH: *Three* orgasms, Sir?

Me: Yep. Massive. Explosive. *Epic*.

SweetH: Fuck. Okay, fine. Then I'll hold off, Sir.

Me: Good boy.

SweetH: *Sobbing face emoji*

* * * *

The kid was practically bouncing in place when I opened the door on Saturday morning, a huge smile on his pretty face. This was my fault and I needed to tone things down.

"Vincent, calm down. You're not getting them right away."

He looked crestfallen. "But…but I've been so good!" He thrust a sheaf of papers at me. "Here's my essay."

"Thank you. Take your clothes off and go sit at the piano. Did you wear the panties?"

"Yes, Sir."

"Leave those on."

"Yes, Sir."

He obediently disrobed except for the panties. I had given him the choice of color and he'd chosen the pink ones. I wasn't at all surprised.

"I want you to practice your scales while I finish in the kitchen. Then you can make us some coffee."

He did what I'd asked, and when I was satisfied with his piano work, I let him get up.

I eyed his erection. "Have you been hard since I talked to you last night?"

He blushed. "No. Luckily it subsided in the night. But it came back as soon as I pulled into your driveway."

"Pavlov was a genius."

"What?"

"You've heard of Pavlov? His dogs salivated at the ring of a bell."

"Oh. Right. So, I'm one of his dogs?"

I blinked, and an idea formulated in my mind. "No. But maybe someday soon you'll be mine." I watched realization dawn on his face and answered it with a grin. "But first, coffee."

I had to say it was awfully nice to have someone make coffee while sporting only pink lace panties and an erection, especially someone like Vincent, who had a natural grace of movement about him. It was like a strange, perverted, breakfast ballet. Should I have gotten him to fry some eggs? I wasn't really hungry but maybe he was?

"Did you eat breakfast, Vincent?"

"Yes, Sir."

"What was it?"

"A banana."

"How interesting. Why don't you fry a couple of eggs?"

"Okay, Sir."

He got what he needed while the coffee spurted and I watched him with much enjoyment. He flipped one of the eggs and some of the grease splashed him on the belly. He hissed in pain. "Ow, shit."

"You okay?"

"Yeah. I'm fine. Just not used to doing this naked."

"Well, I'm really enjoying the show. But you should probably wear this." I grabbed a black apron from the cupboard and got him to step away from the stove for a second so I could slide the neck loop over his head and fasten the strings at his back. I took the opportunity to slide my fingers underneath the fabric of his panties just below and tickled the top of his crack. "There, your bits will be safe now." I sat down again.

"That's good, Sir." He wiggled his ass and I chuckled. *Cheeky boy*.

"You are going to earn yourself a spanking before this day is through," I said.

He glanced at me with a grin. "Promises, promises."

God, there was this lightness that he brought to my home — an optimistic, sensual energy that I loved. The place had been unusually quiet and empty with him gone. Before he'd come over the past weekend, I hadn't thought it was missing anything…hadn't thought *I* was missing anything.

When he'd finished, I had him put the eggs on a plate and bring them to me, along with a knife and fork. "Sit beside me," I told him.

He did.

I picked up the fork and knife, cutting a small piece of fried egg and dipping it in the yolk. Picking it up, I blew on it to cool it. Then I held it out to him. "Open."

His eyebrows lifted in surprise but he opened his mouth and I carefully fed him the egg, watching his tongue lick the yolk off the fork as a jolt of arousal went through me. I hadn't had that tongue on me yet — only his fingers.

I fed him the rest of the egg, slowly, watching him lick and chew and swallow like it was a video I'd bookmarked on Pornhub, because it fucking well could have been. In fact, it was hotter than most of the things I'd seen on that site.

When he finished, he licked his lips, and I pushed down the urge to do it for him. I wouldn't kiss him. That would have taken this thing to another level and I wasn't ready. I might never be ready. I was fully on board with the kink and humiliation, but real, genuine *intimacy*? That still scared the fuck out of me. I didn't even know if *he'd* be on board with a kiss. Although he seemed to be up for whatever I threw at him.

The question was, *what* would I throw at him today? I *had* promised him three orgasms, so I'd better get started. Perhaps some edging was in order. And, since he hadn't had an orgasm since last Sunday, it wouldn't be difficult to get him worked up in a short amount of time.

"Let's go downstairs."

He jumped up from the table as if he'd been waiting for this — which he probably had been.

In the basement I showed him the slide-out panels on the spanking bench, then fastened him on his back with his knees bent and his feet on the padded platforms. It was kind of like a doctor's exam table and I cuffed his ankles to the platforms so that he was spread for me. His wrists were cuffed to the legs of the bench. I didn't blindfold him this time. I wanted him to see me in action.

I picked up the quirt from the table and traced his lips with the end of it. He gazed up at me adoringly and obediently responded when I told him, "Open."

I trailed the end of the quirt into his mouth. "Suck."

He closed his mouth over it and sucked on the leather knot, rolling it in his mouth and biting on it. I saw his cock twitch and my body responded to this sensual image.

"Very good." Then, "Enough."

He parted his lips and I dragged the knot from his tongue, tracing his face and neck with it before gliding it over his chest. He dropped his chin to watch as I traced his nipples then glided it down his belly to drift over his arching cock.

"Oh fuck. Oh God," he panted as I teased him. I tickled his balls and buttocks before I put it down. I picked up the one with the long, flat tip and did the same thing. He sucked on the end of it lovingly, closing his eyes and acting like it was something intimately connected to me.

"That's very good, Vincent. You'd be good at sucking cock."

His eyes flew open and a blush ascended his neck and face.

"Too bad I don't have one of those. Because you'd be down on your knees right now with it deep in your throat."

As if in response, he sucked harder on the crop, making me crazy.

"Fuck," I said. "I want that mouth on *me* by the end of the day."

He moaned as I drew the crop out of his mouth and glided it down his body, the same path I had taken with the quirt. This time, I pulled it over his cock and down his balls and rubbed it over his pink pucker again and again until he groaned and his knees gaped.

"Oh, hell yes," I said. "This is what I'm going to play with today."

He inhaled a shaky breath and let his head fall back.

I put the crop down and picked up a glove, pulling it on and snapping it in place. His whole body jerked at the noise. I watched his pink hole clench then relax. He wanted this badly. But we were going to start small.

I held up a thin black vibe with a flared end. It wasn't wide but it was long and undulated.

"Vincent, look at me."

He lifted his head and his eyes widened when he saw it.

"This is going in your ass."

His lips parted and his breaths came quicker. "Yes, Sir."

I grinned at how precious he looked tied down on my spanking bench, so very hard and excited, awaiting my fancy. I felt so lucky to have such a beautiful boy to play with. And I told him so.

"Thank you, Sir," he said, but I could tell he was desperate for me to begin.

I picked up the bottle of lube and squeezed some onto his balls and perineum, then rubbed it with the tip of the vibe, sliding it up and down his taint to his hole and below his balls while he tensed in preparation for the invasion that was coming. I knew he had had bigger things than this skinny vibe in his hole but sometimes the smaller things felt even more depraved. And since the stretch was mild, the pleasure would be more obvious. It was a good place to start.

I teased his hole with the tip, playing it around and pushing gently to open him. I nubbed it into him again and again as it slid in farther and farther. Eventually I was pushing it all the way in and pulling it out. He groaned and I could tell he loved this so fucking much.

So did I. I loved having him at my mercy, his hole displayed and his body restrained while I had my way.

"Your hole is so pretty, Vincent. Pink and delicate and hungry...so hungry," I crooned as I pushed the vibe in deep again, accompanied by a sweet sound from my *oh-so-willing* sub. This wasn't any different from the way I'd have handled a woman in the same position, but I loved seeing his cock twitch and leak as I pushed the vibe in and out. There was something extra vulnerable about a *guy* on the bench.

Women were fucking *strong*, contrary to stereotypes. They could take a lot of punishment if that were what they were into. I felt at once more dominant and more inclined to be gentle with Vincent, like I had a precious specimen that I had to treat carefully. And I did. He may well have wanted rougher treatment, but we'd start like this.

After a few minutes of this, I pushed the vibe in smoothly all the way and held it deep, as I pressed the button to make it hum. It didn't have much power but the gentle vibration was enough to make him whimper and caused his glans to emerge fully from its foreskin, a sight I found absolutely entrancing. It reminded me of a tulip blooming and, in fact, blushed a beautiful purple color.

"Your cock likes this," I said, reaching over and sliding my other hand over him, stroking gently.

He cursed and pushed into my grip but I let go. "Not yet, sweetheart. We have miles to go."

I left the vibe nestled inside him, the flange peeking from between his pale cheeks, then picked up the standard crop, tapping his lips gently with the tip. "Open."

He did and I pushed it in his mouth as he sucked and licked at it. His gaze locked with mine as he slobbered and sucked on the crop like it was my dick. He knew what he was doing and must have noticed how it affected me. I was barefoot in a pair of leggings and a long black cotton men's shirt with the top two buttons undone and the sleeves rolled up. I started to feel excessively hot as I watched his tongue lave the crop.

"Enough," I said in a gravelly voice. One side of his mouth crooked as I pulled the crop from his lips and I felt the need to chasten that smugness, to stop him from feeling like he could play me—although he totally could. He knew my weakness.

I slid the wet tip of the crop to his nipple, pulled back and slapped it sharply—first on one brown bud then the other. He moaned and writhed on the bench.

I dropped the crop, leaned forward and took one nipple into my gloved hand, the other in my bare hand, and squeezed.

"Shit! Oh God," he said, panting and throwing me a wide-eyed stare.

"How do you like this?" I asked, squeezing harder.

"You're gonna make me come," he grimaced.

I released him and picked up the crop, deliberately showing him my ass as I bent over. "Not yet, sweetheart. Not yet. I want to torture you some more."

"You're such a bastard," he moaned.

I straightened and gave him an evil grin. "Oh, you have no idea, Vincent." Meanwhile, I was so *pleased* he'd called me a bastard rather than a bitch that I almost gave in. But, no. He had expectations for me to fulfill.

I walked back to the business end of the bench where his legs were splayed and I could see the flange of the vibe. I traced the crop up and down the inside of each thigh, then peppered his sensitive skin with delicate but stinging strikes that made him try to close his knees. Such a pretty sight—but the small vibe needed upgrading.

I put aside the crop and ran my hands down his thighs, soothing the heat. And because I couldn't seem to resist, I ran my gloved and lubed hand along his pretty cock, pumping it roughly, making him groan.

"Please make me come!" he begged. "I promise to be so good!"

I tilted my head to the side, considering. If I got him off now, that gave him one of the orgasms I'd promised. And knowing Vincent's recovery time, I could surely get him hard again with the other toys I had in my arsenal. In fact, taking my time playing with his ass while he regrouped would be highly entertaining. And he was just so desperate. He had been such a *good boy* this week.

I let him go and walked around so I was standing beside his hip, gazing down at his exquisitely bound form, throbbing cock and spread knees.

"You want me to get you off?"

"Oh God, please. Please, Sir!"

"If I do, I'm keeping you in this position and playing with your ass until you come a second time."

His eyes widened and he jerked in his restraints. "Is that supposed to scare me?" he panted. "Because it's all I want in the world!"

I actually laughed. I didn't think I'd ever laughed when in Dom mode before. And maybe that was my fault. But something about Vincent brought it out of me.

"Oh, Vincent, you cheeky boy. Let's see how far you can shoot." I squirted some lube into my ungloved left hand and wrapped it around his dick, stroking slowly to prime him, although I knew he was close.

He dropped his head back on the bench, opened his mouth and made stuttering noises of bliss while I moved the skin of his cock back and forth over the glans. I was so glad he had a foreskin, because it made things so much easier. Zane had been cut, and even though I'd loved his cock, I think I liked Vincent's better. *And fuck Zane anyway.*

My right hand moved to the vibe in Vincent's ass. I grabbed the flange and pulled gently, sliding it out of him as he emitted a deep groan and pushed into my hand. I speeded up the strokes on his cock as I slowly pushed the vibe back in and wiggled it.

"No...no..." he stuttered, muscles tensing. He was right on the edge. He was probably scared of the potential power of his orgasm, as he should be.

I pumped the vibe twice, hard, as Vincent yelled and semen arced from his glans to his nipples. His cock spurted again and kept spurting. His shout was so loud that I almost lost my rhythm, but I was experienced so I didn't falter. His body convulsed around the small vibe as his dick jerked and spat onto my hand. And, yeah, I think it was definitely worth waiting a week for.

I kept stroking him, milking him, until his cries quieted and his muscles relaxed. He whimpered and muttered and I couldn't quite make out what he was saying.

"I beg your pardon? Speak up, please," I said in my best Dom voice as I pulled out the vibe and let it fall to the floor then brought my hands together to play with Vincent's slippery emission. I was like a kid with slime, gleefully plying the strands and enjoying the texture. God, but men were *fun*.

Vincent let out a frustrated groan as a remnant shudder took him. "Fuck you and your mad skills," he said with his eyes closed. He opened them and watched me finger the spunk on his chest. "What are you doing?"

I grinned. "Having fun. I don't have a man come on my bench very often, you know — or at least I haven't, only last weekend and today. I'm making the most of it. I didn't realize I liked semen so much." I pulled my hands apart to examine the fine strands.

"You could feed it to me, Sir," he said, shyly now. "If you want."

"It's a little cold," I replied, but suddenly that was all I wanted to do, especially since he'd asked. I stripped off the black glove and scooped up more splooge from his chest and belly — there was a lot — then rubbed it on his lips and pushed my fingers into his open mouth as he gazed at me with that look again.

He sucked my fingers clean while jolts of desire shot through me, as though he were licking my cunt. My mouth opened and I made a small sound. His eyes widened and he sucked harder. I pulled my hand away and stepped back.

Not yet, my pretty.

"All right then. One down, two to go."

He watched me pad over to the cabinet and bring a few things over, then pull another glove from the box.

"Back to business," he murmured. His cock had subsided and leaned to one side, the glans hidden. It looked so vulnerable and sweet, but I was eager to get it excited again.

I put on a glove, showing him the big silicone dildo with the textured surface, then held up the string of medium-sized anal beads.

He made a sound then cursed.

"Okay?" I asked.

"Yes, Sir."

"Good." I put them down and grabbed a glove for my other hand. "But I want to have a little fun first and I need to get you good and horny before we get serious." I lifted my hands and waggled my fingers. "Besides, nothing beats a few fingers in the ass as foreplay." I knew this from personal experience and suddenly I remembered Vincent's long fingers on the piano keys. One day maybe, when I trusted him enough... Meanwhile, I was thrilled to have him at *my* mercy.

Chapter Ten

"God, yes," he said in post-orgasmic tones. "Please."

I made a clicking noise with my tongue. "So very polite. You are such a *good* boy."

I moved to the bottom of the bench. "I'm going to bind you a bit differently for this," I told him. In a few minutes I had his legs bent at the knee and his ankles cuffed to his thighs so Vincent was spread wide and vulnerable to whatever I had in mind.

"Oh God, Sir," he said, "Oh fuck."

"You like that, sweetheart?" I asked, knowing he loved it more than anything. "You like being tied down and spread open for me?"

"Fuck. Oh God." He jerked his wrists against the legs of the bench as if he wanted to sit up and look at himself spread out for me like a pinned butterfly. But he couldn't, so he just let his head fall back and moved it slowly from side to side.

For my own comfort, I asked if he wanted to safeword. I could tell he was completely turned on, although not hard yet, but sometimes a sub needed to safeword because they were overwhelmed, even though it was with good feelings.

He panted. "No. God, no. Nope."

"I'll take the head movements for something positive then. Since you can speak, don't hesitate to safeword if you need to, Vincent. Tell me what your safeword is?"

"Piano," he grunted and his breathing quickened. His cock had begun to wake up, just from the bondage and anticipation. I hadn't even touched his ass yet, but that was about to change.

I walked to the end of the bench and gazed at the pleasing sight of his legs in the air and his ass spread for me, so fucking vulnerable and so fucking pretty.

I held the bottle of lube high and squeezed, dripping it onto his perineum and asshole like chocolate sauce on an ice cream sundae. The cold lube hitting his skin made him gasp. His hole clenched. It was a wonderful view.

"You are so pretty, Vincent, even without your pink lingerie. So sweet." I used a gloved finger to spread the lube on him, tracing his hole and rubbing up and down his perineum. His gasps were lovely to hear, and when I slid my index finger into his hole, he stiffened and cried out softly.

"Oh yes, sweetheart. So delicate and pretty." I touched him gently, moving my finger in and out slowly, swirling it inside him, teasing it over his prostate. His balls tightened and lifted. I peeked over top and saw that his cock was hard again, although the glans was still hidden. I added a second finger, then a third, as he cursed and groaned.

"You like that, sweetheart?"

"Oh yes, Sir. Oh God, yes." It was the same as having one of my girls spread on the bench, his noises so sweet and breathy, his body so responsive. But I enjoyed the sight of his cock as it responded to my touch, more than I had ever thought I would. I wanted to kiss his penis as it grew and showed itself, as my fingers pushed deeper and rougher. I could have made him come just from this, and one day I would. But I was too eager to use the toys I'd selected.

When I withdrew my fingers, he sighed and his cock jerked regretfully. "I think you need something bigger in there, don't you, Vincent?"

He moaned and pulled against his restraints. "Yes!"

"Eager boy. A-plus for enthusiasm."

"Thank you, Sir."

"Thank me after I put this dildo in your ass."

"Yes, Sir. *Always*, Sir."

He was just so sweet and so polite. Daphne knew I'd go nuts for that.

I wasn't fond of brats. They tried my patience, which was pretty limited already. Some Doms liked to rise to that challenge. Not me. I liked my subs to be deferential and polite, eager to please. Good girls and boys who waited patiently for what I decided was best.

Vincent was everything and *more*.

I took my time with the dildo. It was bigger than the vibe and it was fun to go slow, to watch his ass open gradually to accommodate it, to hear his sounds as the dildo went deeper and deeper. When it was finally seated inside him, I held it there and spoke over his soft moans.

"What do you say, Vincent?"

"Thank you. Thank you, Sir. Oh, thank you, Sir."

I looked at his dick, which was fully, painfully hard again. He *definitely* liked ass play. And since it was one of my favorite things to do to a sub, I felt a sense of synergy with him. It wasn't like I thought he was meant for me or anything as dramatic as that, but I thought Daphne had been right to send him here and to convince me to try him out.

"I'm going to fuck you with this now, boy," I said harshly, like a Leather Daddy in one of those porn scenes shot at the distillery in San Fran…because those were the best.

Vincent groaned as I dragged the dildo out and shoved it back in, over and over, as his moans became louder and his hips moved on the bench.

"Oh fuck, oh fuck, *oh fuck,*" he panted. I rocked it against his prostate and his moan became high-pitched and desperate. I could have made him come from *this*. But I pulled the dildo out and threw it to the floor with a loud thump.

"That's enough of that."

Vincent uttered a devastated cry as his gaze followed the dildo then returned to me. He looked so sad but I held up the beads and his eye closed in relief.

"Yessss," he moaned. "Oh please, yes."

His thighs quivered as I added more lube and began to push the first 'bead' against his already-stretched hole. The beads were roughly the same girth as the dildo, but round. The first went in pretty smoothly and Vincent sighed as his ass closed after it. I rubbed the shiny pink skin with the pad of my finger.

"Good?"

"Oh my God. So good. *More.*"

Greedy boy.

I pressed the second ball against his hole as he slowly opened for me, taking it inside his body with a groan. Again, I rubbed his anus and reached over with my other hand, grabbing his cock. "How do you like them apples?"

He laughed, then groaned as he felt their fullness. "You didn't put *apples* in me, did you, Sir?"

I grinned, teasing his hole, poking my finger in to push the balls farther inside him. "Nah. I believe in using appropriately manufactured sex toys. Ready for the rest?"

I inserted the third, fourth and fifth balls. By the time his ass accepted the final one, his cock had leaked vast amounts of pre-cum and his moans were constant. He fucking loved this. It was incredible to witness.

"Dammit," I swore, wishing I could have rubbed myself. I could have totally gotten myself off to this image. "If I were a real *bastard*, as you say, I'd make you get up and walk around the room, keeping those babies inside you."

He whimpered at the thought.

"But I don't think you'd make it off the bench before you shot your second load, would you, Vincent?"

He shook his head, whimpering again. "No, Sir. No, Sir."

I slapped his cock, playing rough now. He cried out and shifted on the bench, feeling the rubber balls inside him. I did it again.

"Oh fuck. Oh fuck!" His voice came out reedy and thin, like he was holding on by a bare thread.

I tickled the bottoms of his feet, making him squirm. Any movements, however slight, that he made just rolled those balls around inside him, forcing him to feel them. His cock surged and more liquid seeped out.

"I'm not going to touch your cock, Vincent. I'm going to pull each of these balls out, one by one, and we'll see how many I can reclaim before you climax. Okay?"

He groaned in anguish.

I began to pull on the cord as his anus stretched around the ball. He made a desperate sound as it slowly emerged, but he didn't come. I was betting he would go off on the third or fourth ball.

I rubbed his anus as I carefully pulled the next ball from him. On a hunch, as it popped out, I flicked my finger against his taint and that was it. He screamed as he came. I kept pulling. His cock jutted in the air, his body jerking as he howled and spurted. I pulled the last ball out. Lube dripped from his ass and the toy fell to the floor as Vincent's scream died away and he gasped for air.

"Oh fuck. Jesus Christ, Jesus *Christ*," he muttered, words slurring, eyes shutting, damp hair stuck to his forehead.

"I think Jesus Christ would be jealous of you, sweetheart," I said, rubbing his anus and taint to sooth him.

He continued to breath heavily for some time, while I removed my gloves and stroked the insides of his thighs until they stopped quivering.

"You okay, sweetheart?"

He didn't answer right away.

"Vincent?"

"Yeah. I mean, I'll recover, Sir. I think." His voice sounded shaky and weak.

I laughed and stood up, looking at him lying there, blissed out, completely spent and stunningly gorgeous.

I cupped his chin in my hand and smiled down at him. "I think you'll be fine."

"Okay. Sure."

I removed the cuffs and helped him stand. He gazed down at his limp dick, the mess of semen on his chest and belly, and swayed.

"You need a drink of water and something to eat. I'll help you upstairs."

He stared at me with a dreamy look, like he just wanted to take a nap.

"You can have a rest after, but then you owe me two more orgasms."

He blinked. "I can barely think right now but didn't I *already* have two? That leaves one."

I smiled. "One's *mine*."

His chin dropped as understanding dawned. "Oh!"

Once we made it upstairs, I ran a bath and helped him clean the lube and semen off his body while the warm water relaxed his muscles. While he was soaking, I dipped into the bedroom and found the pair of boy shorts I had found in the women's department and purchased for him. When I held them up for him, I turned them so he could see that the word 'Princess' was written in large purple letters on the rear.

"I bought three pairs in different colors. They're cotton, so they'll be more comfortable for lounging than the lace ones."

He put the briefs on with his gray T-shirt. I sat him at the kitchen table and fed him leftover tuna salad from a fork. Once he had some food in him, I took him upstairs and we cuddled on my bed until he fell asleep.

I only realized I'd done the same when I woke up an hour later, staring into blue eyes that looked like a summer day on steroids. Why were they so *bright*?

I squinted at him. "Are you on drugs?"

He snorted a laugh. "No. Why?"

"Your eyes are too bright. They are *unnaturally* blue, Vincent."

"Sorry." He didn't look sorry.

I reached out and touched his cheek. "They're beautiful, sweetheart. But why are they so *bright*?"

"Because you said something about *you* having an orgasm. And you have no idea how excited I am to help you with that." His forehead creased and some of the lightness left his eyes. "I mean, if that was the idea? I mean, I assume…"

"Shh-h, don't speak. But, yes. I'm going to demand your assistance, Vincent. Because I can't take it anymore."

He raised his eyebrows, obeying my command to be silent.

"I can't take watching you fucking unravel and blossom under my hand without having a part of you."

A genuine and delighted smile bloomed on his face. "Well then, you'd better tie me down because if you don't, I feel like I might just go airborne."

I grinned at him. "Yeah, that was the plan. Clothes off and lie on your stomach with your arms and legs spread."

He seemed confused. "Stomach, Sir?"

"Yes, Vincent. Do you have a problem with that?"

"No. I just… I kind of imagined you were going to…sit on my face or something."

"Well, we're going to go the *'or something'* route, okay? Just trust me."

"Yes, Sir."

He got into position. By the time I'd finished cuffing and fastening his wrists and ankles to the eye hooks in my bed frame, he was erect. I knew this because he had to shift position and rutted into the mattress in a casual *I don't even realize I'm doing it* kind of way. When he saw me staring, he stopped, looking guilty.

"I feel like I should enroll you in some kind of competition. Is there an Olympics of Tumescence?"

He blushed. "I feel like there should be. I could see Daphne organizing it."

I laughed. "Yeah, me too. I'll suggest it next time I see her."

I produced the cat from behind my back like a circus showman. "Ta-da."

Vincent's eyes widened and he unconsciously ground against the mattress again. "Fuck."

"Now look. I've got plans for your mouth *and* your cock, so don't you dare come until I say it's okay. Got it?"

I ran the strands of the cat down his back and over his buttocks. He shuddered and stiffened.

"Yes, Sir."

A thought occurred to me. "Would you like a blindfold, Vincent?"

"Yes, Sir. Thank you, Sir."

I put down the cat and retrieved a soft piece of black silk from a drawer. So…maybe I had blindfolds stashed all over my house. Sue me.

Blindfolds were a great way to focus a sub and could give them a sense of security and enhance their ability to surrender. When I resumed playing the cat along his back, he moaned with anticipation and balled his hands into fists.

"Please safeword at any point if you need to."

"Yes, Sir."

I took some time trailing the cat tails across his body, down his arms, the backs of his legs, before stepping back and getting down to *business,* as Vincent had called it—the very enjoyable *business* of turning my dear sub into a writhing, panting, moaning mess.

As usual, his responses to this treatment—the sight of his beautiful muscles tensing and relaxing, his pleas to be allowed to climax and just the sounds he made deep in his throat, left me in a state. I dropped the cat, pulled off my leggings then my underpants—a pair of men's tighty-whiteys if I had to say—and unbuttoned my shirt the rest of the way, leaving it on. I felt I must retain some level of dignity, even if it *was* superficial. I moved to the foot of the bed because I couldn't resist diving into him before I did anything else.

He must have felt the mattress shift when I climbed on behind him because his head jerked up, angling toward me, even though he couldn't see. As soon as he felt my hands on his buttocks, spreading him, he dropped his head to the mattress and pulled hard on his wrist cuffs. He knew what was coming and he apparently wanted it, badly.

This time I was not so delicate. I plunged my face into the crack of his ass and ate him out like the pro I was. My tongue had a mind of its own and licked, prodded and invaded Vincent's most sensitive orifice. He cried out and struggled under my assault, but I had a firm grip and he wasn't going anywhere. I rolled my tongue into a tube and started plunging it in and out of him as he went crazy with pleas and curses.

"Oh fuck, please, please, please, *God, Jesus, fuck*, Sir! Sir! *Sir!*"

I paused and lifted my head. "What do you want?"

He whined in desperation. "Oh my God. I can't take it. I'm going to come."

"You'd better not, Vincent. The punishment will be severe. And I don't mean a fun punishment. I'm talking not being allowed to come back tomorrow."

"What? Oh *God*, Sir, really? But...but...I'm so fucking *hard* and I'm *leaking* all over your sheets!"

"Keep it together, Vincent. I promise the reward will be yours soon if you can hold out."

"Yes, Sir. I'll try."

And with that, I parted his ass again and gazed at the saliva-slick skin of his twitching anus, just before I bowed to him again. This time I used my teeth gently — and not so gently — around his rim, slipping my tongue in as far as it would go and slurping it noisily *everyfuckingwhere.*

He tried to stay still, probably because all the writhing was working his cock into a frenzy, and he did a good job. When my mouth and tongue began to tire, I drew back and gave him a resounding slap on his behind that echoed as loud as his howl in the quiet room.

"Good boy. Very, very *good boy*," I said, slapping him hard with each word. He groaned in protest and lay there, subdued and muttering under his breath.

"What's that?" I asked, rubbing my hands over the globes of his ass because they were just so perfect and soft and pink and hot from the abuse.

"You are such a *bastard*," he hissed, but I heard the affection in it too. "*Such* a bastard."

I grinned. "I know. I am, aren't I? Still like me or do you hate me now?"

"I couldn't ever hate you, Sir."

"Do you like me, though?"

What possessed me to continue this line of conversation I didn't know.

"I think I love you."

His words hung between us as all the air left my chest and the room started to spin. But I got myself under control. He was in *subspace* right now. Anything he said was highly influenced by those endorphins shooting through him.

So, I decided to minimize the damage.

"You did not just say that, did you, Vincent? I'm going to pretend you didn't say that, because we are in the middle of an intense scene and it means nothing. And you're very naughty to think that saying something like that is going to make any difference in terms of the way I'm going to treat you right now. Got it?"

He let out a mournful sigh, as if he'd just realized his mistake. My heart hurt for him a little. "I like you *a lot*, Vincent. And I know you like me. And I think that's pretty amazing for the short time we've known each other."

"Yes, Sir."

I moved forward, climbing over his ass and straddling his lower back, leaning forward and putting my mouth by his ear. "Do you feel this, Vincent?" I slid my crotch back and forth over his skin. I was so wet he felt like a waterslide.

He gasped. "Fuck, Sir. You're soaking wet."

"Yes, I am. And it's all your fault. So, I'm going to get you to do something about it, all right?"

He bobbed his head furiously. "Yes, Sir. Oh, please Sir, please! Please let me do *something!*"

I laughed at his desperation but was also getting to a pretty needy place. I placed my hands on his shoulder blades and pushed myself up to a standing position over him. Then I stepped over his arms and maneuvered myself so I was sitting in front of him, propped up by the headboard of my bed, my legs spread, knees bent over his arms, shirt fanning out to either side.

"Can you smell me?" I asked.

He groaned and licked his lips, sniffing the air like a dog after cocaine. I *knew* he could smell me. I could smell *myself*. I scooched forward and placed my hands on his face, guiding him to where I needed him. "Do as you will, sweetheart. Make me come."

He uttered the sweetest sound, then instead of ravaging me like I expected, he tentatively reached his tongue out and licked me delicately from my ass to the top of my clit. He did this again and it was all I could do not to grab his head and press his mouth down onto me.

But I didn't want to do that. I wanted to see what he would do. I wanted to see how he would enjoy me.

I let out a most un-Dom-like whimper and fisted my hands in the bedsheets as he explored me gently, *so* softly with his agile tongue while my soul combusted into flames of frustration. I let my head fall back and stared at the popcorn ceiling, trying to keep breathing as I focused on what his tongue was doing to me.

He took me apart one slow lick at a time until I was the one begging. I mean, I could have just told him what to do and how to do it. But what would have been the fun in that?

"Fuck, Vincent, Jesus! *Jesus*. How is your tongue so fucking *soft*?" I moaned in a most unladylike fashion since I was no lady at all. "Please, please, please, do it harder. Please, please, please just fucking *eat me*." I tried not to squirm as he increased the strength and vigor of his attack.

I sounded like a pouty teenager and I hated it. I started to give in to the feelings of vulnerability and almost stopped him so I could go back to being the top and whipping his ass. But I changed my mind. Instead I put my hand on the black blindfold and pushed it up and off his head.

He didn't even stop what he was doing, except to glance up and dive right back in. I clutched the blindfold in my hand as my head fell back against the headboard. That short glimpse of his bright blue eyes reverberated inside me as the coil tightened and clenched and suddenly let go in a paroxysm of ecstasy.

I keened as my body took over, releasing days of built up tension onto Vincent's handsome face. I bucked up against him as I came and came and came, my breath heaving into my lungs, my legs quaking and my cunt drowning the poor boy while he continued to bite and lick and suck me.

"Oh God," I managed to say finally, then sagged back against the headboard. My hands found Vincent's cheeks and I pushed his face back so I could stare into his eyes. "Okay, okay. You did it, sweetheart. You did it *so* well! That was fucking *amazing*. Thank you."

His face was shiny all over with my juices, his eyes frantic and lit with desire. I realized we weren't done and gathered my resources. I leaned over and unclipped one of his wrists from its cuff.

"Okay. Now use your fingers to work me up again. Then I'm going to flip you over and ride that sexy cock of yours."

He squinted at me as if he couldn't quite believe what I was saying, then grinned wide and brought his hand to my pussy, rubbing his fingers on my slippery skin.

I hissed. "Easy, easy. Put them inside me," I whispered. My clit was sensitive and I didn't want it touched just yet.

He complied and slid two of his long fingers inside me with ease because I was so relaxed and pliable.

I closed my eyes and stroked his stubbled cheeks as he played his fingers in me. My legs splayed wide as I fondled his earlobes, knowing he could go off at any moment but hoping he'd hold off, because I really wanted to ride him.

"Tell me how you want to be fucked, Vincent. How do you want me to ride you? Slow and steady or rough and fast?

He groaned as his fingers pressed deeper, hitting my G-spot, which re-ignited in an instant. "Whatever pleases you, Sir."

"That's not an answer."

"You better start slow or I'll go off like a rocket," he admitted.

I laughed, then groaned as he added a third finger and licked at my pussy lips, nowhere near my clit. He knew to avoid it for now.

"I'll keep that in mind."

I let him finger me until I was squirming with need. I brought my own hand to my clit and rolled the hard nub between my fingers, letting out a gasp.

"Oh, fucking hell," he cursed. I felt his hot breath on me and suddenly I couldn't wait anymore.

I scrambled up and over him, undoing his other wrist cuff then his ankle cuffs, making him roll over. I grabbed a condom out of my bedside table as he pushed up on his elbow and shook his head. "Do we have to use one? Daphne has my paperwork. I should have got her to send it to you."

"She did. I know there's no risk with you. But you don't know the same about me."

He blinked. "I trust you. Have you had a test?"

"A month ago. I haven't been with anyone for a long time. Just you. But I'm still on the pill."

"Then don't, Sir. I don't want it." He pleaded with me. "I want to come *inside you*."

"Fuck it," I said, tossing the condom at the wall and straddling my beautiful boy. "I want that too. Very much." I leaned forward and he dropped from his elbows to his back, staring up at me with half-lidded eyes.

"Vincent, seriously, how are your eyes so fucking *blue*? Are you a witch?" I asked, kissing his cheek and licking the lobe of his ear as I rubbed my clit over his cock.

He whimpered. "Maybe?"

I laughed, rubbing on him back and forth. He felt *so good*. I could have totally come that way. "I could come like this," I said, moving up and down his length.

He groaned. "If you don't stop soon, I *definitely* will."

I shook my head. "Now that would be a shame. Guess I'd better get you inside me."

"Please. Please."

I pinned his eyes with mine and Dommed him good. *"Don't. Move."*

He whimpered as I sat up and grabbed his cock at the base, sliding myself onto it in one fluid motion. His chin dropped, his back arched and his breath rasped.

The sensation of his cock piercing my body shook me to the core. It felt so good and so *right*.

"Vincent," I said, astonished.

I circled his wrists with my hands and held him down as I moved slowly, as per his request.

God, he felt good inside me. He filled me up and hit all the right spots. He was just so *hard*. I didn't think Zane had ever been this hard. Then again, Zane was ten years older than Vincent and smoked weed every weekend.

"God, you're so hard, Vincent...like rock."

"For you. All for you, Sir." He panted heavily as he thrust his hips upward, making his cock hit the right spot. I cursed, swirling my hips, chasing that pressure as he kept thrusting, beyond obeying my order to be still.

But I didn't care because he was hitting my G-spot with his cock and my clit with his pelvis and I was groaning and gasping and convulsing around him, squeezing his wrists in the vise of my hands. He thrust upward again then cursed as he came, bouncing me on his cock as I cried out and collapsed over him, spread out on his chest as my body shuddered and his warm release leaked out of me.

He was still thrusting, as if he didn't want to give up on this pleasure, and I couldn't blame him. He made lovely little noises that warmed me inside. My head rested on his chest and I listened to his quickly beating heart as it slowed and steadied.

After a little while I felt him shrink and slide out of me as a trickle of semen followed.

"Oooh, Vincent. I'm dripping you everywhere."

"Oh fuck, Sir. Fuck."

I looked up and saw him blinking at me. I relaxed my hands on his wrists.

"Can I hold you, Sir? Please?"

I loved so much that he had asked me first. "Yes, Vincent. All right." We fell asleep completely wrapped up with each other.

So much for taking things slow.

Chapter Eleven

I woke up a couple of hours later at half past five. Vincent should have been gone and I should have been making supper.

Instead he lay in my bed, his legs tangled with mine and his face a vision of innocence in his slumber. He looked so very young. He *was* young, especially compared to me. I should have woken him and sent him on his way, but I really couldn't bear to.

His eyelids fluttered and suddenly I was gazing into those bright blue orbs. They seemed less luminescent coming out of sleep than in the throes of passion, but only slightly.

"Hi," he said.

"Hi," I replied. With my hand I pushed a bit of hair from where it had fallen over his eye.

"God, what time is it?" he asked, sitting up.

"Why? You got a hot date?" For a second, I worried he'd say, yeah, actually. But he grinned and shook his head shyly.

"I just had one." His forehead creased. "But I should probably go home now."

"Yeah, probably. I have an essay to read, after all."

He blushed, smiling. "Oh yeah. Hope I get a good mark."

I gave him a wink.

"Uh..." It seemed like he wanted to ask me something.

"What is it?"

He picked at the bedspread, glanced at me with those blue eyes. "I wanted to ask you something but I'm worried you'll say no."

"So, ask me. Maybe I'll say yes."

I started to panic that he was going to ask me to marry him or something crazy like that when he blurted out: "Do you think I could come over tomorrow?"

We stared at each other for a long moment. "You don't want to wait until next Saturday?"

He grinned and shook his head. "No, I don't. I really don't. I *can't*."

He looked so damned anguished at the thought of waiting a whole week to come back here that I took pity on him—and admitted to myself I didn't want to wait that long either.

"Fine. Nine o'clock tomorrow then. How are you getting home?"

He looked relieved and so happy. "I was gonna get an Uber."

"I'll drive you. Why don't you grab a shower then we'll go?"

"Okay."

Ten minutes later I heard the water running and couldn't resist putting the white shirt back on, unbuttoned, because...why not? The guy had been inside me. I guessed he could see me almost naked, especially since I was going into the bathroom to gawk at *his* naked body under all that running water. But, then again, I was the Dom, so I could do what I wanted. Theoretically.

And the vision of Vincent under the running water of my shower was nothing less than magnificent. I leaned against the vanity and gaped, enjoying the view, while he squirted some body wash into his hand and lathered up.

"Don't forget to clean behind your ears," I said loudly.

Vincent spun and fell back against the shower tiles, bracing himself with both hands so he didn't fall.

I lifted up my hands and grinned. "Easy, easy. Don't hurt yourself, sweetheart."

"Jesus!" he said. "You scared me."

"I didn't mean to scare you." Which was kind of a lie.

"What are you doing, Sir?" he asked, straightening up.

"I'm watching you."

"Why?"

"Because you're beautiful."

He looked down at himself. "I'm too skinny."

"Says who?" I asked, wanting to punch anyone who would dare criticize him.

He opened his mouth, then closed it and shrugged. "I don't have much muscle."

Is he fucking with me?

"Are you fucking with me?" I asked, sliding the shower door open and getting in with him.

He looked shocked but pleased and moved back to give me room. "Never, Sir."

"I hope not," I said, and moved in close. The hot water soaked my cotton shirt and I felt the weight drag against my shoulders. But I didn't care. Vincent glanced down to my small breasts and he licked his lips.

"You have gorgeous muscles, Vincent. You have a swimmer's body. Or a dancer's."

"*You're* beautiful," he whispered, glancing at me shyly out of those luminous eyes.

"Ah fuck. Can you just be an adorable sub and not the gorgeous, daring and sexy creature you are, Vincent? I mean, Jesus Christ."

He looked at me with some kind of heady emotion and I just wanted to escape — not from him, but from the deeper emotions he called up in me. So, I did what I always did when that happened.

I held Vincent's gaze with mine and circled my hand around his cock, pulling him close to me and stroking him gently. He was already half-hard and it didn't take a minute to get him to full mast.

He gasped. "Please."

"Please, what?"

"Please, Sir, can I touch your nipples? Please!" It was a desperate plea, and although nothing made me feel more vulnerable than having my nipples touched, I couldn't help but give in to him.

I nodded, not trusting my voice. I knew how I would tame him, but I'd let him have a moment with my tits. It was only fair, after all.

He parted his lips and raised his hands to push aside the wet cotton of my shirt and splay over top of my very flat breasts. I mean, they were bumps at least, and my nipples at that moment were hard and peaked. So, yeah, even *I* had to admit they looked hot, especially with his long fingers on them, touching them so gently, gliding over my nipples, making me gasp. He cupped them oh-so-delicately in his hands and moved his thumbs over them, watching my face.

I closed my eyes and kept moving my hand on his cock as he reached inside me and pulled deep reactions from my body. I felt it deep down, the way he was touching me. But then I was distracted from looking at *him* and I pulled back.

"That's enough now," I said as his hands dropped and hung at his sides. His eyes widened as I went to my knees and took his cock in my mouth, looking up at him to see his expression, which showed nothing short of blissful surprise and pleasure as I swallowed him to the root and pulled back, licked his tip, then swallowed him deep again.

He groaned and braced his hands against the wall. "Oh God, Sir."

I pulled off and stroked him roughly. "He can't help you right now," I said before plunging him into my mouth again. I silently thanked Zane for letting me practice my oral skills on him, because I was so pleased to do this for Vincent, and do it well. And I liked Vincent's cock much, much better than Zane's.

I explored him with my tongue, licking up under his foreskin and swirling his glans, then taking his length in my throat and swallowing, sucking, until he begged to come. Because I didn't want to stop for anything, I gave him a quick thumbs-up and he laughed, then groaned and came hard down my throat as the warm water washed over us. I swallowed everything and wondered why I was down here on my knees when I was supposed to be dominating Vincent.

But I *knew* why. And, honestly, he probably knew it too.

After we dried off and dressed, I drove Vincent home.

He directed me to a neighborhood about ten minutes away. It wasn't far at all, and at least his apartment building was in a good area and looked well-maintained. I didn't know what I'd have done if he'd lived in a shithole, probably turned the car around and brought him back to my place. I almost wanted to do that anyway, but I forced myself to drop him off.

"I'll see you tomorrow at nine."

He smiled. "I'll be there."

"And, Vincent?"

"Yeah?"

"Wear the blue panties."

He blushed. "Yes, Sir."

* * * *

Back home, I put on sweats and streamed some Vivaldi, lying on the sofa and enjoying the memories of that incredible day. The feelings I was starting to have for Vincent scared the fuck out of me, but they also challenged me to let myself enjoy the possibility of something extraordinary. Maybe love was terrifying for everyone. I pretended I hadn't just used the 'L' word in my thoughts.

I made a tuna salad sandwich and got comfortable, picking up Vincent's essay.

He'd titled it 'Exclusive Tales from Daphne's Dungeon', which made me smile. I couldn't wait to find out all the dirty details of their time together.

When I'd finished reading it through the first time, I needed a cold shower.

Holy. Fuck.

If I had ever thought Vincent was an ingenue to the BDSM scene, I had been sorely mistaken. In fact, I almost felt like I'd been treating him with kid gloves compared to Daphne. They'd pretty much done it all. Rope bondage, check. Anal fisting, check. Milking sleeve, check. Some mild breath play and one instance of caning.

He'd told me about that. He hadn't liked it at all, and I totally understood. It wasn't something I'd wanted to do to anyone, although I didn't judge Daphne. People *did* get off on it. The one thing I hadn't seen mentioned in this thoughtfully presented and well-written essay was chastity. I would have thought Daphne would have gone there with him. I didn't recall it being a hard or soft limit for him. And it was something I definitely wanted to explore with him, more than just telling him to hold off. I wanted to make it impossible for him to climax without my cooperation.

I put the essay down and stared at the ceiling, so many images coursing through my brain. I wanted to talk to Vincent *now*.

I picked up my phone and texted him.

Sorry to bother you. Are you up for a quick call? I read your essay.

After a moment, I heard my phone ringing and I swiped my thumb over the face, lifting it to my ear.

"Vincent."

"Sir." His voice sounded breathy and anxious.

"This is the hottest fucking thing I've ever read. I have a little boner right now. Well, it feels like a big boner but, you know, I'm a lot smaller than you."

"Oh God, thank *God*. I was worried you'd think I was a gigantic man-slut."

"Oh, you *are* a gigantic man-slut, Vincent. Don't doubt that for one minute. But you're *my* man-slut. I need to get you a T-shirt with that on it. Or maybe I'll just write it on your chest with indelible marker."

He laughed. "Did you really like it, Sir?"

"Oh yeah," I said, "I really liked it. In fact, I'm giving you an A plus plus."

"Really? *Yes!*" He sounded so thrilled. "Did any of it shock you?" he asked after a pause.

"Shock? No. However, I am surprised by the…variety of things you've done."

"She did get pretty creative," he admitted.

"Holy hell, Vincent."

"It was my fault. I'd get hard easily enough but she had trouble getting me off, so we kept pushing the envelope. And it would help at first but then I'd get bored or something."

"Seriously? Are you fucking kidding me?"

"Because she didn't do it for me. And it didn't matter what she did to me. Eventually, it just wouldn't work because I didn't feel any desire for Daphne herself."

As much as it reassured me to hear that, I couldn't believe my sub with the hair-trigger come-switch had ever had trouble climaxing.

"But when you're here, you can't seem to help yourself."

"I know," he breathed. "It's amazing. *You're* amazing."

"I've barely done *anything* to you, Vincent."

"I know. It's so different. I only have to think of you and I get hard. I only have to remember being dominated by you and I want to come. It's you, Nic. It's all *you.*"

I was stunned at this admission, although it seemed to be true and the only thing that explained his response.

"Well. I don't really know what to say to that."

"Say, 'Don't you dare come without my permission, Vincent.'"

"Don't you dare come without my permission, Vincent."

"See? You just made me hard with that one sentence. Say it again."

"Don't you *dare* come without my permission, Vincent," I repeated, even more sternly.

"God, I want to come right *now.*"

"Two words, Vincent. Cock. Cage."

Silence. Then, "Holy. Fuck. Really?"

"Really. We have a little shopping to do."

"Tomorrow?" he asked breathily. My eager little sub.

"If they're open on Sundays."

"Can you check? Please?"

"Hold on," I said, looking up the sex shop I was familiar with. "They open at eleven. So, we'll have time for some piano practice beforehand."

"Okay. I mean, yes, Sir."

"You realize if we buy one tomorrow, you're going to be in it all week?"

He moaned. "Oh no, Sir."

"Oh yes. Are you touching yourself right now, Vincent?"

He cleared his throat. "Yes."

"Stop it. Hands off."

He sighed with regret. "Yes, Sir."

"See you tomorrow, Vincent."

"See you tomorrow, Sir."

* * * *

Vincent arrived promptly at nine on Sunday and I put him to work at the piano with some simple pieces of music that would challenge him. I think he liked it better than the scales, which he'd mastered.

At five minutes to eleven I walked over and kissed him on the neck, inhaling his scent and trying to keep my head straight. "Want to go shopping?"

"Yes, Sir!"

"Get dressed and meet me at the front door."

Vincent put his clothes on and we headed out. I made him drive and directed him to the sex shop on Gilmour Street. It was called Stuff and No Nonsense.

When we walked in, a woman with crazy red hair saw me and shrieked.

"Nicky!!! I can't believe you're here!" she yelled and ran over, remembering to ask before she grabbed me up in a big bear hug.

I assented to being manhandled, much to Vincent's obvious astonishment. He stepped back and watched closely, almost protectively, as Shanice assaulted me.

"Shanice! How you doin', girl?" I said, delighted to see her working today. It had been a while and I knew she could help me with what we needed.

"Great! Oh, I'm so happy to see you, Nicky!" She turned to gawk at Vincent, who now appeared out of his depth and apprehensive. He had probably expected this to be a covert mission. And, me being me, I decided to exploit his unease because...y'know, *sadist*.

"Shanice, this is Vincent. We're here for a cock cage."

Vincent's mouth opened, then closed. His face went three different shades of pink in five seconds. He looked like he might bolt.

But Shanice, bless her kinky heart, took this in stride.

"Lucky, *lucky* boy," she cooed, taking Vincent's hand and leading him over to the items in question. He glanced back at me with a *Help, save me!* expression on his face, which I ignored. I followed them.

They stopped in front of a glass display case, inside of which lay an array of variously sized and constructed chastity devices for men. Vincent's eyes widened and he seemed even more panicked.

Shanice turned to me. "How are you, darling? You look amazing!"

"Thanks. I'm good."

She nodded at Vincent, who stood gaping at the display case. I could almost see his mind spinning and there was a telltale bulge in the boy's jeans. Because...of course there was. He was a sucker for punishment.

"Keeping busy?" she grinned.

I grinned. "Yeah. Real busy. He's basically in training with me, although he has quite a bit of experience already."

"You don't say?" She eyed Vincent up and down like she wanted to eat him for brunch, which I totally understood.

"Daphne recommended him."

Vincent's head snapped to me and I knew he was wondering why I would reveal all this to Shanice. But he needed to trust me—trust that I wouldn't reveal these things to anyone who would hurt him.

"Daphne? Well, then. I'm sure he's used to being taken in hand." She smiled at Vincent, who seemed mollified and gave her a tentative smile back. "You are a lucky, lucky boy, to be with Nicky. He doesn't do boys often."

"How about at all?" I replied, splaying a hand on the glass of the case and eyeing its contents. Zane hadn't been a *boy*.

"Touché," Shanice replied, then gestured me closer. "What is your pleasure, Sir? Will this be long-term chastity or just a fun afternoon?"

I examined the items in the case. They ranged from simple stainless-steel cages to fancy polycarbonate devices.

"I need something he can wear for a week...maybe longer."

Vincent gaped at me then closed his mouth. He'd gone a bit pale but the bulge seemed to thicken. *Bingo.*

Soon his dick would be trapped. My mouth actually watered at the thought and I wondered how he would like it? *Would* he like it? Or would he hate every moment of it? *Guess we'll find out.*

"Do you have his measurements?" Shanice asked.

"Shit. No," I admitted. An oversight. I knew how big Vincent's dick was when erect, but we'd never measured him flaccid.

Shanice produced a tape measure from her pocket. "No worries. We have a change room where you can do the honors."

Vincent backed up a step, peering around him at the few customers who were browsing in the front of the store.

"Vincent!" I said it in the loudest, most no-nonsense tone I could muster, as if he were a misbehaving child. And it worked. He turned toward me and seemed to immediately calm down now that I was making him do what I wanted.

"Come with me." Again, a firm tone. I turned and walked purposely after Shanice, who led us to the change rooms in the back of the store. She unlocked one and I brought Vincent inside, taking the tape measure from her. "This won't take long," I said and flashed her a smile.

"It better not." She giggled. "Just measure it. That's *all*."

"Got it," I said as Vincent stared at me with a lost look. "Drop 'em." I gestured at his jeans.

"But…"

I raised my eyes, like I couldn't believe he would hesitate to follow my order. And that worked also. He immediately dropped trou. But we had a slight problem. I'd forgotten.

"Shit," I said.

His forehead creased and he looked at his penis, which was not at all flaccid. It was decidedly half-hard and growing. He really did get off on humiliation and shame. Dirty little slut.

"Vincent."

"What?"

"You need to be soft for a correct measurement."

"Oh. Shit. Sorry?"

I glanced at the door of the change room. We didn't have time for a jerk-off, no matter how quick it might have been. Plus, it was messy. I gave him a half smile. "Okay. Sorry for having to do this," I said, moving close and sliding my hand under his balls.

He squeaked as I squeezed them in my fingers, enough to cause pain but not enough that he screamed or fainted.

"Oh, fuck no," he protested, trying to escape, but that only made me hold on tighter.

"Stay still. This won't take long if you work with me."

"Ow. Ow. Fuck, that hurts," he protested, but he forced himself to stay still. His hand was on my forearm but he didn't try to stop me.

"Do you want to safeword?" I asked.

"No. No, just…it *hurts*."

"I know. I'm sorry. But your cock is behaving now. Hold your hands above your head. I'll be quick."

He did as I asked and I let go of his balls then quickly wrapped the tape measure behind them, got the reading and measured his cock before it started to fill again.

"Got it. Good boy."

Out of some grateful and misguided instinct I leaned forward and kissed him on the mouth.

It was quick, perfunctory and chaste but neither of us could process it when I drew back. We stood there gaping at each other — Vincent with his hands in the air, me with the tape measure dangling from one hand.

What the *fuck*?

"I don't know what that was," I said quickly. "I'm sorry."

He licked his lips, looking stunned. He said, "I'm not," as he lowered his arms and pulled his jeans back up. "Thank you, Sir."

My brain was exploding but Shanice was waiting and we were on a mission—an important one. I didn't reply, but once he'd dressed, I pulled open the door and we exited.

I handed Shanice the tape and gave her Vincent's measurements as we walked back to the display case, which she unlocked.

"What's your pleasure, Nicky? Polycarbonate, stainless-steel? Rings or bars? Or do you want Vincent to choose?"

I shook my head. The guy knew nothing about cock cages. Plus, he was probably too flustered to make a reasonable choice.

"I'll choose. What about that one?" I pointed to a simple stainless-steel device with metal rings along a curved metal spine.

Shanice took it out and showed it to us. "A classic. And I have it in various sizes. I'll just have to check my inventory."

I took it from her and handed it to Vincent, who fumbled it and dropped it to the carpeted floor. "Shit," he muttered, looking around, but no one was watching except me and Shanice.

"Pick it up, sweetheart," I said. "I want you to touch it and see if you can imagine having that on your penis."

He frowned as he bent down and retrieved it. He moved so his body would block anyone's view except for mine and Shanice's. Then he gazed reverently at the device and glided his fingers softly over the steel rings. "Yeah," he said breathlessly, "this one."

"We'll take it if you have it in his size," I said, holding out my hand. Vincent reluctantly gave it to me and I handed it to Shanice.

"Back in a flash. Have a look around. See if there's anything else you need while you're here." She took it with her as she ducked into the back room.

I led Vincent past the array of colorful dildos and vibrators, over to the anal beads. They ranged in size from tiny ones for beginners to huge ones for the experienced player.

"Which ones, Vincent?"

"Those," he said softly, nodding at the display.

"Point to the ones you like," I told him, knowing he didn't want to. But I needed to make sure I bought the right ones and I couldn't tell with his vague gesture, although I had a suspicion.

He glanced to the side to make sure the other customers didn't see then pointed to a set of dark purple anal balls on a string. They were definitely larger than the ones I'd put up there the day before but not as big as the hardcore, giant ones I couldn't envision going in anyone's rectum except maybe a really, really big guy.

Anyway, I nodded and he dropped his arm, giving me a look that said, *Can we get out of here now?* I did feel a bit sorry for him. Not much, but a bit.

Shanice brought a boxed version of the metal cage in the right size and I asked her for the anal balls as well.

"Nice choice." She said, bringing a box from under the counter. She leaned toward Vincent. "You're going to love those."

Vincent blanched and stuttered. "I...sure...thanks."

"Oh my, he *is* adorable," she said to me. "If you ever decide you want to share..."

"Nope. No sharing," I said with an icy smile, although I winked at her to lessen the blow.

"Oh. Oh, I see. Well, that's wonderful."

I paid her for the toys and she gave me a hug goodbye. "Hope to see you back soon, Nicky. We have some nice anal hooks in stock. They train up a boy real nice."

"Thanks, Shanice, but I have that covered."

Vincent made a small noise in his throat but followed me obediently out of the door. Once we were out on the street, he turned and folded into me, so that I instinctively wrapped my arms around him.

"Can we go back to your place now?" he asked tremulously into my hair.

"I was planning to take you to lunch."

"Oh."

"Can you make it for another hour? I know that was difficult, but you did great."

He thought for a moment, holding me tightly then releasing me and standing straight. "I can make it."

"Good boy. We can plan our afternoon." I lifted the bag of goodies and shook it gently. "But let's put these in the car for now."

Chapter Twelve

Over lunch in the back corner of a little bistro, I told him in great detail what I was going to do to him before sending him home in chastity for the week. By the time I'd finished, he was squirming and sweating with anticipation and some fear. If Shanice hadn't reminded me of the hook, I might not have thought of it. But now it seemed the perfect distraction and was something else Daphne had overlooked.

Back in my basement, I made him strip out of his clothes and kneel up on the spanking bench. With a length of soft red rope I bound his wrists and fastened them to a grid in the ceiling, to put him into a praying position, although his arms were lifted high. He could twist his torso but I cuffed his calves to the bench so he would stay in position when I started to do things to him.

I brought out the stainless-steel anal hook with the medium-sized ball on the end to show him.

His lips parted as he sighed. "Oh, Sir."

"Yes, sweetheart, this is going inside you."

He struggled, his eyes locked on the shiny ball. "Fuck."

"Mmm-hmm-m. You are going to be fucked by this steel ball on the end of this long hook, while I crop your backside and do other unmentionable things to you. If you move, the ball will move and the steel of the hook will stretch you open, so you'll want to stay still as much as you can." I took his chin in my fingers and turned his head so he focused on me instead of the toy. "I'm going to take my time. We have all afternoon."

He shuddered and moaned, his cock hard and bobbing in front of him.

"It seems only fair to get you off one last time before you have to refrain from orgasming all week."

"Yes, Sir."

"I'm going to make you come like gangbusters before I lock your pretty cock away in that cage."

He moaned, the organ in question twitching. "Yes, Sir. Please, Sir."

"So fucking *polite*," I muttered, putting the nitrile gloves on and lubing up his rear. We'd need a lot of it.

I used my fingers to loosen him up and turn him on so he wouldn't care what I put in there. By the time I was ready to use the hook, he felt as supple as wet clay.

"I'm going to press this ball against your hole, Vincent. I want you to relax and try to open for me."

I covered it with copious amounts of lube and pressed it against his wrinkled skin, pushing carefully and steadily. Vincent's breaths quickened. He made a small squeak as the muscle stretched. The ball began to sink as I kept up a consistent pressure. With a stuttering moan Vincent accommodated it, his anus clamping tight around the steel bar.

"Oh God...oh God..." he panted as his body got used to this intrusion.

I used the bar to nudge the ball in farther, as Vincent gasped and sighed.

"Oh, sweetheart, that looks so fucking good."

"Feels good, Sir. Feels *so* good."

"I'm glad you like it. It's one of my favorite things."

"Oh..."

I grabbed another length of rope and tied one end to the top of the hook and the other end to the leather collar Vincent was wearing. This meant he had to keep his head at a certain angle or the rope would pull on the bar and stretch him open, also shifting the big metal ball inside him.

"Now just relax while I have some fun back here, okay, sweetheart?"

"Oh yes, Sir. Do whatever you want, Sir."

I chuckled, then slid my gloved finger along his anus where the steel penetrated him. I circled it with the lightest pressure, knowing it would drive him crazy.

"Oh fuck, oh *fuck,* Sir."

"Shh-h."

I teased him with my finger, circling the steel bar several times, sliding it down his taint and back, then pushed the very tip of my finger in him alongside the steel.

Vincent twisted on the ropes, an action that jostled the steel ball and caused the bar to spread him so I was able to push my entire finger inside.

"Oh, that is lovely," I said, with admiration. "You are quite pinioned, my sweet fellow." I pushed in as far as I could then withdrew and watched his anus close around the bar. There was nothing quite like that sight.

Then I used two fingers and did the same thing. I played with Vincent this way for a long time, working up to three, then four fingers. His cock was ridiculously hard by the time I started using the black dildo. It was barely bigger than my three fingers, but when I slid it in alongside the steel bar, he cried out and stiffened, then jerked and gasped. For a moment I thought I'd hurt him and my heart stopped. Then I realized he was actually coming, his cock spurting into the air as his ass clenched hard around the steel and vinyl.

Naughty, naughty boy.

I was impressed and not really that disappointed. Sure, he'd come without my permission but *holy hell*. This was when my acting chops came into play.

"Oh, Vincent. *Really?* You've come *already?* Just from *that?*" I made myself sound profoundly disappointed and displeased.

"I'm sorry," he gasped, wrung out and shaking. "I'm so sorry, Sir. It just... I just... I'm sorry."

He sounded as though he might cry, so I moved around and wrapped my hand around his spent cock, shiny with slick and still weeping for me. I stroked him roughly as he tried to get away, and saw the conflict on his face, because he was still pinioned by the hook. I knew his cock was sensitive at the moment. I rubbed my hand roughly over the head, causing Vincent to shudder and complain with a cry.

"Well. I think this deserves a sound spanking. Since you can't escape me right now, I'll just take care of that for you."

His eyes flew open as he realized I was going to spank him with the hook still imbedded inside him.

"Yes, Vincent. *That* is your punishment. I'm only going to use my hand, so it should be quite safe but hard not to move."

He moaned then grunted as I slapped him on one buttock.

"Count, Vincent. There will be ten to start."

"One," he said, then "*Two!*" As I slapped his other cheek. After each one he whimpered and groaned. "Three! Four! Five!"

I took my time, making each one count. After the fifth slap, I grabbed the steel bar and rocked the ball inside him, back and forth, back and forth, as he moaned and struggled. His cock had hardened again.

"Six! Seven! Eight!"

I rocked the hook again and he stuttered. "Oh! Oh! Oh!"

Two more slaps. "Nine! Ten!"

My hand was throbbing by then, so I stopped and moved forward, bending to take his cock into my mouth. Vincent cried out as I rocked the hook while sucking him aggressively.

"Oh fuck, fuck, *Fuck!*" he yelled as he came down my throat, pinioned and unable to move. I'd made him curse and forget every polite thing he'd ever learned, and I loved it.

For kicks I let his spunk dribble out of my mouth as I pulled off, gazing up at his wild eyes that watched me with awe and gratitude — and maybe a little fear. I had just forced two violent orgasms from him and he seemed shook, not to mention exhausted.

Impulsively I climbed onto the spanking bench in front of him, sliding my hands around his back and pressing against him, thrilled when he opened his mouth to mine so I could push the remnants of his seed onto his searching tongue. He moaned and so did I.

It took me apart, this connection, our mouths wide open, tongues touching and teasing, while Vincent hung on his ropes and tried to recover from what I'd done. What *we'd* done.

When we pulled apart, I felt dazed and confused. "Sorry."

"Don't be sorry. Please don't be sorry," Vincent said.

"But I'm supposed to be the *Dom*. I'm not supposed to love on you."

He smiled then, so sweet and blissful in his post-orgasmic state that I had to return it. "Fuck being the Dom. Just be Nic. And I'll just be Vincent. And we'll just do what we do."

"Because we do it so well."

"Exactly."

I sent him up to shower while I made a snack for us. When he was done, he came down in the Princess shorts and his T-shirt.

"How does your ass feel, Princess?" I asked, putting a plate of bacon and eggs in front of him.

"Like you stuffed a stainless-steel ball and hook up it, Sir."

"Oooh, you sweet talker. That was very enjoyable on my end." I brought a plate for myself and sat down opposite him.

"My end too, Sir," he said, glancing at his rear. "But I *am* a little sore."

"Well, you've seen a lot of action. Luckily you will be out of my evil clutches for an entire week." I lifted my fork and pointed it at him. "And yet, *still* under my control."

His forehead creased. "How exactly does that work, anyway?"

"Well, you see, I put this metal contraption on your penis and you can't come," I said smugly.

"No, I mean, I *get* that, but when I'm at home and you're here or at work. What happens if I need to take it off? I mean, am I supposed to sleep with it on?"

"Vincent, I get that you have a lot of questions. Let's have our meal and I'll go over everything, okay?"

"Okay."

He held his fork loosely and watched me eat for a little bit.

"What?" I said finally.

"Umm-m. That time when you fed me. I really liked that."

A slow smile spread over my face. "Would you like me to feed you when I'm done with mine?"

He smiled and it was the sweetest thing in the world. "Yes, please. Sir."

I winked at him and continued to eat, taking my time while he waited patiently. When I was done, I put down my fork and knife and moved to the chair beside him.

"Fork, please."

He handed it to me. I picked up the knife and proceeded to feed my sweet sub, trying not to get turned on watching his mouth in action, especially now that I knew what it could do to me directly. But our sexcapades were over for now, and we needed to seriously discuss the idea of his being in chastity all week, because I would make allowances for his inexperience. Enforced chastity was a very particular form of torture which wasn't usually torture at all. Most men found it extremely enjoyable, since they were able to build up to a level of arousal normally beyond their self-control. At least, that was what Zane had told me.

I got a very pure form of enjoyment from feeding Vincent, making sure he was getting nutrition and knowing I was taking care of my boy. I was feeding him more than eggs at the moment. This was a form of aftercare too.

When we were done, I had him load the dishwasher and wipe up the kitchen. Then we went into the living room and talked about male chastity. My weekends had gone from fucking boring and useless to incredibly interesting and fun in a very short amount of time. I probably owed Daphne a phone call.

I sat on the sofa and directed Vincent to the comfy armchair across from it when he asked to sit beside me. I was trying to stay focused and he was a terrible distraction.

"So, my expectations for the week are the following," I said.

He leaned in, his forehead creased in concentration. He was a good student. Maybe we should do some formal teacher-student role-play next weekend. That might be fun.

"I'll put the cage on you before you leave today. There are two keys to the lock. I will have one and you will have one. Yours will be in a sealed envelope so I'll know if you use it."

He opened his mouth, then closed it.

"Do you have a question? Feel free to ask me anything. And I will be available for you by text or phone call, whenever you need to speak to me, at any time during the week."

"Okay, good. What if I *do* have to unlock it? Will you be mad?"

"Jesus, Vincent, I'll never be *mad* at you. I'm so pleased you want to do this with me. If you feel you have to take it off, call or text me first, unless it's an emergency. I'll most likely give you permission and that still leaves me in control, right? Which is mainly what we want from this experience. Although, I also want you to get used to denying yourself, which you did *very* well last week. The cage just makes it easier."

"Okay."

"That being said, sleeping with a cock cage on can be uncomfortable, because guys tend to get multiple erections during their sleep. So that's going to wake you up. It's going to be painful."

"Oh. Yeah. I didn't think about that."

"Don't just lie there waiting for your erection to go away because it probably won't. You'll have to get up and walk around, do some boring shit until it subsides and you can go back to bed. If it turns out to be a problem and you aren't getting enough sleep to function during the day, we can reassess the situation. I may give you permission to leave it off at night."

He frowned. "Okay. So…I don't need to take it off to go the bathroom or anything?"

I shook my head. "Nope. The one we got can be worn long-term. It's easy to wash when you're having your shower. Just make sure you have a shower at least once a day. Twice a day might be better while you're wearing it. Or just use soap and water and a cloth on it before you go to bed."

He glanced at me shyly. "What if I'm losing my mind and I want to masturbate, like, desperately?"

"Then you call me and we figure it out. I'll either talk you down from the ledge or I'll take care of it somehow.

But I don't want you to do anything without talking to me first."

"Yes, Sir."

"Does that sound okay?"

"Yes, Sir. It sounds awesome. I'm excited to try it."

"I'm excited for you to try it, too. From the research I've done, most guys with inclinations like yours enjoy the feeling of being controlled this way, and the build-up of desire can be intoxicating."

Vincent nodded. "Yeah, I can see that. I mean, last week was pretty awesome, even though it was difficult. I'm glad I held off."

"I'm so proud of you. That's why I'm rewarding you by putting you into enforced chastity this week. In a lot of ways, it will be easier, like I said."

His forehead creased again. "Will it be visible under my clothes?"

"No. Do you normally wear snug briefs?" I asked. "I mean, when you don't dress in the lingerie for me?"

He blushed in such a pretty way that I wanted to go over there and kiss his cheek. "Boxer briefs. Yeah."

"Then it shouldn't be a problem."

He looked worried about it. I stood up and walked over to stand in front of him.

"Vincent."

He regarded me with a vulnerability that fueled my soul. "Yes, Sir?"

"Nobody is going to know you're wearing a chastity cage except me and you. That's another thing that's amusing about this sort of thing. It's a delicious kinky little secret between the two of us, like a joke we're playing on the mostly vanilla world. Right?" I cupped his stubbled chin in my hand, stroking his lower lip with my thumb.

When he opened his mouth, I pushed my thumb inside, holding his brilliant blue gaze. His tongue swirled around it then he sucked, causing a jolt of desire deep inside me.

"Fuck," I whispered.

He moaned softly and it was all I could do not to climb on his lap and kiss him. Instead, I withdrew my thumb and held out my hand.

"Come on."

We went upstairs and I had him strip and sit on a plastic chair in my en suite bathroom. I had him hold his hands together behind it while I trimmed his pubic hairs shorter.

"You did a good job, but it's best to get them as short as possible if you're wearing a cage."

"Yes, Sir."

Of course, I should have anticipated this would give my responsive sub a boner, and it did. "How are we going to put that cage on you now, Vincent? You have to be flaccid."

He gazed at me hopefully.

"Fuck that, Vincent. I am not sucking you off right now. You are pretty fucking lucky I've done that at all. *That* is a special treat. I'm the Dom, remember?" I was half-joking because I loved sucking him off, and my being the *Dom* wasn't a valid reason to avoid it. I'd do what I wanted and I didn't stand on ceremony.

He looked chastened and amused at once. "I can take care of it myself?"

"You can and you will, while I stand here and watch you."

Because, hello, huge voyeur here. Obviously. And I loved stuff like this—punishment and reward at the same time. Because even though it was hot masturbating in front of someone you knew enjoyed it, it was also a little embarrassing.

Since Vincent was prone to embarrassment, he blushed and protested. "I, uh, I can just do it in here by myself."

I grinned. "I'm sure you can, but I want to watch."

He blinked. I noticed his dick was still hard, so it wasn't upsetting him much.

"And I want to control it. So just do whatever I say, all right?" That would make it easier for him.

He nodded. "Okay. Okay." I thought he liked that idea.

"There's a bottle of lube in the drawer." I pointed to it.

"You have lube stashed in a lot of places, Sir."

I raised my eyebrows at him. "You got a problem with that?"

He was right, though. You never knew when a little bit of lube would come in handy. I'd used it on door hinges.

He tried not to smile and shook his head. "Nope."

"Then get it out and put it on your dick, Vincent. *Now.*" *Ooooh, big Dom voice.*

He took a shaky breath and his cock twitched. He did what I'd told him.

I leaned against the vanity and watched him slick up his cock, his eyes on the floor but glancing up at me now and then.

"Slowly. Slowly stroke yourself, Vincent. Enjoy it, sweetheart. We're not going to rush."

I watched as he fisted his erection and stroked it leisurely, as I'd instructed. His erection grew, the glans poking out of his foreskin on the downslide. Whenever he started to speed up, I reminded him to go slow. This happened again and again, until it was obvious it was killing him not to move his hand faster.

"Please, let me go faster, Sir," he begged.

"No."

He blinked and forced himself to slow down. I could see it was really difficult. *Too bad*. Yet again, he unconsciously sped up.

"Slow, Vincent. *Go. Slow*."

He obeyed me with a huff but his ass shifted in the chair and he moaned desperately. He tried again. "Please, Sir. I need to come."

"No. You don't. You need to do as you're told."

He whimpered and his hand stilled. It was probably easier for him to leave it alone at that point. But fuck easy.

"Keep *going*, but go *slow*, Vincent."

"Yes, Sir," he whispered, lifting his chin defiantly but doing as I'd asked. His cock was getting bigger and his glans had completely emerged from the foreskin, shiny with moisture. It glistened in the fluorescent lighting.

"Oh...Sir," he said, trying to obey but it was so difficult for him.

He might even come from this. It was turning him on — the control, the slow, languorous strokes.

"Keep it slow, Vincent. But you may come whenever you want." I felt very magnanimous as I watched him keep up the torturous stroking, his cock leaking precum, his arm muscles straining with the control.

He was unable to stop himself from speeding up, but each time I saw his hand go faster I said, "No," in a loud voice, and he slowed it down.

I made a sound of disapproval in my throat. "Vincent, grab the legs of the chair with both hands. Now."

He seemed surprised but did as I'd asked. His abandoned cock swayed and pulsed in front of him as his chest rose and fell with quick breaths.

"I'll have to show you what I mean," I said, moving in close and kneeling beside the chair. He gaped at me, his lips slack and wet with moisture from his tongue. "Don't you dare move and you keep those hands together."

"Yes, Sir," he said breathily.

I poured some lube into my hand and wrapped it around him, giving his dick the long, slow strokes that he couldn't seem to maintain. I kept the pressure light and gave him just enough to drive him mad but keep him from going over. I didn't care how much he begged me. I was not going to move my hand any faster.

"Oh...oh, Sir...*Sir*..." he groaned, grimacing and starting to thrust into my grip.

"Stay the fuck still, Vincent."

He struggled but complied. His sounds grew more and more desperate as I kept up my very steady and leisurely movements. He glared at my hand as if he could visually make me go faster. He gave me a pleading look, but I was merciless. I turned my head and stared at the wall as if I were bored by all of it.

But I could feel his dick swelling and straining and I knew he was close. I slowed my hand down even more but increased the strength of my grip. Vincent wriggled and whined, the strain of it causing sweat to break on his forehead and making his arms and thighs tremble.

Oh, *fuck yes*.

He moaned long and low, stamped his foot on the floor but forced himself to be still as I teased his cock, taking my time, on and on, like I could do it for hours.

"Sir...Sir..." he begged.

"Yes, Vincent?"

"Please go faster. I'm so close, Sir. I want to come. I need to come, please, please, please."

"I'm not rushing this."

He whined and gripped the chair so hard that it shifted against the floor.

I glanced at his cock. The glans was shiny and purple, his foreskin barely covering it on the upstroke now. He panted and stared down at himself with wide eyes as a glob of pre-ejaculate gathered and spilled over.

"Fuuuuuck..." he groaned. "Oh fuck."

"This is fun. I could do this all day."

He whimpered.

"You know what, Vincent?"

He groaned and his eyes rolled back. "Wh-what, S-sir?"

"One of these days I'm going to strap on a cock and fuck your ass so hard you won't even understand what's happening."

"F-fuck, fuck, fuuuuuuck," Vincent groaned. He stiffened, his knuckles white where he gripped the chair, and started to come as I kept up my lackadaisical rhythm. The jizz spat out of his cock as it jerked in my light grip and Vincent groaned and cried out and whimpered with relief as his dick kept spurting. I took my hand off him and we both watched him finish, the desperate quivering arch of his cock a testament to his pleasure.

Chapter Thirteen

These were our text and phone exchanges after I'd sent him on his merry way with his cock caged and locked.

Monday, seven-thirty a.m.

Wow. I barely slept. Like, at all. Never realized how many times I popped wood in my sleep.

Well, then. Is it still on, at least?

Yes, Sir. I just cleaned it in the shower.

Good boy.

This is alot harder than I thought it would be.

Do you want to stop?

No, Sir. I want to be good for you.

Twelve-thirty p.m.

I feel like I have a dirty little secret in my pants.

You do. But it's only little at the moment. I've seen it get pretty big. *happy face*

blushing face Thank you. But I also feel like everyone knows it.

That's because your face probably gives it away. You're kind of easy to read.

Fuck.

But you're so cute!

I feel a bit perverted.

In a good way?

Yeah. *Big teeth smiley face*

Five p.m.

I shouldn't have texted you from work. My dick tried to get hard all afternoon.

Poor baby.

It hurts.

I'll consider kissing it better on Saturday. If you're a very good boy.

Stop! Please stop.

I'll never stop.

Good.

Eight-ten p.m.

Good night, Sir.

Good night, lovely boy. I hope you sleep better this time.

Me too!

Tuesday, six-thirty a.m.

I need to call you. Can I call you?

Yes.

Soon my ringtone for Vincent started playing. It was
I Feel Pretty from *West Side Story*.

He was right. I was officially a bastard.

"Hey. Everything okay?"

"Oh, Sir!"

He sounded so devastated that a jolt of alarm shot
through me.

"What's wrong? Tell me."

"I didn't mean to, Sir. I didn't know it was *possible*. I
don't know how it *happened*!"

"*What* happened, Vincent? Tell me what happened."

He said something I couldn't hear.

"What? Speak up, boy!" The anger came from being
worried.

"I just woke up, and I was coming...*somehow*. There's cum all over the sheets. I'm so sorry, Sir. I'm *so, so* sorry!" He was almost crying because he was so upset.

I felt a great wave of relief passed over me. "Vincent," I said calmly.

"I'm *so* sorry!"

"Vincent, it's all right."

"How did that happen? You didn't tell me that could happen." He wasn't accusing me, just explaining his distress.

"Sorry? I didn't realize it could. But, yeah, I guess it's possible."

"I'm *so* sorry!"

"If you don't stop apologizing, I'm going to come over there and take that cage back. Is that what you want?"

"No. No, Sir."

"Are you still wearing it?"

"Yes, Sir. Yes. It's...a bit of a mess right now."

"You didn't do anything wrong, Vincent. If the cage is still on, you're still keeping to your part of the bargain."

"But I *came*!" He sounded so endearingly frustrated about it.

"I know that. And it's impressive that you did. I'm in shock and awe at the moment."

"Really? I thought I was going to be in *so* much trouble."

"Nope. Just go have your shower and clean yourself up. I don't count nocturnal emissions as proper orgasms. They are out of your control."

He let out a long breath. "Thank you, Sir."

"I think you're doing great so far." I really did.

"Thank you, Sir." He sounded so relieved.

"I mean, if you had a wet dream, you must have been asleep?"

"Yeah. Yeah, I was," he said with relief.

"Do you remember your dream, Vincent?"

He hesitated. Then, "Kind of. I mean, bits of it."

"Tell me."

"There were anal balls involved."

"Dark purple ones?"

"Yep."

"I see."

"I've got to go shower, Sir, or I'll be late for work."

"Well, we can't have that. Text me later."

"Okay. Bye."

Seven-twenty p.m.

I can't stop thinking about those balls, Sir.

The ones from your dream?

Yeah. The ones sitting in your cabinet right this minute. Are we going to try them this weekend?

I haven't decided yet.

Oh, please! Please, Sir! Please…

Begging won't work.

Really?

Not over text anyway. Maybe when you're here, if you beg properly, I'll consider it.

I'll do anything for those balls, Sir. Anything.

I'll keep that in mind. Good night, Vincent.

Good night, Sir.

Wednesday passed with only good morning and good night texts from Vincent. He seemed to be getting used to the cage. I'd asked if he'd had another wet dream and he'd said no.

I still couldn't believe he'd come in the cage, however, it was something I wanted to explore when he was here. Some men could orgasm when confined, depending on the circumstance, and the emotions they experienced when forced to come in chastity could be interesting. The key seemed to be anal stimulation, so I figured we were golden.

Again, on Thursday, only a good morning and a good night text.

Friday, six-o-five a.m.

*It happened again! *sobbing emoji**

What did?

*I came in the cage! *multiple sobbing emojis**

Do you usually have wet dreams, Vincent, when you aren't wearing a cock cage?

No! Not since I was twelve!

Interesting. What was the dream about, Vincent? Those balls again?

No. You were in it.

Really. What was I doing?

You were behind me.

Naturally.

But you had a cock, Sir.

Oh?

And you were fucking me with it. Hard.

I grinned when I read this. *Well, now, isn't that interesting?* And that was the thought that had pushed him over the edge Sunday afternoon.

You know we can make that happen.

Yes, Sir. Please, Sir. Pretty, pretty, please...

You'll have to be a very, very good boy for me.

I promise. I promise I will be.

Eight-ten p.m.

I can't wait until tomorrow. I miss you so much.

I miss you too, Vincent. Wear the pink panties. Good night.

On Saturday, Vincent texted me five minutes before he was supposed to arrive.

Sir? My ride bailed. I'm so sorry. I'll order an Uber now but I'm going to be way late.

Don't be silly. I'll come get you. Wait for me out front.

I don't want you to go to any trouble, Sir. I'll just order an Uber.

Don't *order an Uber. I will be there in ten minutes.*

Yes, Sir. *heart emoji*

It had rained all morning and was coming down hard now. It drummed on the roof of my car as I pulled into the curved drive at Vincent's apartment complex, wipers going at top speed.

Instead of standing underneath the shelter of the front entrance, he was on the sidewalk, completely drenched, in just a hoodie, sweatpants and sneakers. He saw my car and waved, clutching a rucksack to his chest. At least the rucksack looked waterproof.

I pulled up and pressed the button to slide down the passenger window. "Get in the car, Vincent."

He immediately complied, throwing his rucksack into the back and sliding into the passenger seat with an apologetic grin on his water-streaked face. His soaked hair stuck to his forehead.

I pulled away from the curb, radiating disapproval.

"Thanks for picking me up, Sir," he said.

"Don't you own a raincoat, Vincent?" I asked. "Why didn't you stand under the roof?"

"It's just a little rain. I wanted to make sure I saw your car pull up."

I couldn't help a laugh escaping, even though I was still pissed off. "A *little* rain! You're soaked. And I'm thinking of googling flash flood warnings."

"Okay, *Mom*," he said, but when my head snapped around he backpedaled. "I'm sorry. God, I'm sorry. I shouldn't call you that."

I stared at the road, gripping the steering wheel. "Show me your cock in that cage, Vincent. Right now."

He laughed, then realized I wasn't joking. His face paled. "What?"

"Pull the front of your sweats and the panties down so I can see it."

"Oh God, really? *Really*?"

"Yes, Vincent."

His hands shook as he complied with my order. His face went completely red. His cock looked sweet and innocent in its cage.

I licked my lips then met his gaze.

His eyebrows were raised in silent inquiry.

"Good boy. Everything looks as it should. You can cover yourself now."

He seemed relieved as he readjusted his clothing, but I wasn't finished with him.

"Put your middle finger in your mouth."

He gaped at me but did what I asked.

"Now suck it. Make it nice and *wet*." His eyes widened but he sucked and slurped on his finger. I gave him bonus points for the sounds.

"Now put it in *my* mouth."

He made a small noise as he pulled the finger from his mouth and reached it toward me.

It proved tricky to drive while sucking on another person's finger, I discovered, although as far as kinky stuff to do while driving, it was fairly benign. I worked his finger as if it were his uncaged cock as he moaned and shifted in his seat. I continued for a couple of blocks then bit down so he pulled his finger out of my mouth.

"Ow."

"Sorry. I couldn't really tell you to take it out of my mouth."

"Yes, Sir," he breathed, staring at me with anticipation and agitation. "Now what do I do?"

"Put it in your mouth again. Make it even wetter."

He did. When he spoke, his words were garbled. "Um, isn't this your street?"

I smiled as I drove past. "Yes, it is. But I'm going to drive around the block."

"Oh."

"And you are going to slide your hand down the back of your pretty pink panties and play with your hole."

He blinked. "*What?*"

"You heard me."

"What if…what if someone *sees* me?" He peered out of the car window. Because it was pouring with rain there were few people about and those seemed intent on their business.

"Do it. *Now.*"

"But, Sir…"

"Vincent. I want you to sit on that finger and I want you to do it *now.*"

He gave me a shaky and sullen, "Yes, Sir," and proceeded to push his hand down the back of his sweatpants and under the waistband of his panties.

"Safewording is always an option," I reminded him.

"I know that, Sir."

It turned out it was even harder to drive when your very cute passenger was fingering himself beside you, at your order. I tried to keep my eyes on the road but I was able to get glimpses of him and watch from my periphery. He leaned forward, pushing his ass out against the seat, and I saw his hand moving under the fabric.

"Are you touching your asshole, Vincent?" I said very quietly.

"Yeah," he said. "Fuck, yeah."

"Good boy. Rub your finger over it slowly," I whispered, even though nobody could hear me. It made it seem even more depraved and naughty.

He closed his eyes and made a sound.

"Is the cage getting tight right now?"

"Yeah," he moaned.

"Then you're doing it right."

"Yes, Sir."

"Okay. Now slide that finger inside your ass. Right now."

He let out a long groan as he obeyed my order. "Oh fuck, Sir. Fuck."

"Is it all the way up there?"

"Yeah," he grunted.

"Good boy. Now wiggle it."

He did, making breathless little noises as he worked himself up.

"If you can make yourself come in that cage, I'll give you a very fun reward."

I tossed it out there, not expecting it but thinking I'd enjoy watching him try.

His movements became rougher, more frantic. He was all twisted up trying to finger-fuck himself and I was loving every minute of it. Thankfully, the streets were almost empty of other cars.

He made stuttering sounds of pleasure and I thought he might actually come. He was pumping himself pretty good.

"Pull down the front of your pants, Vincent. *Now.*" My voice sounded ragged and excited.

He grabbed at his waistband with his left hand and pulled the rain-wet cloth from over his caged prick.

"Oh fuck. I'm going to pull over, but you're going to keep at it. I mean what I say. If you can make yourself come in that thing, I will be so impressed, and I will do something very special for you, even though you've been a very naughty boy, standing in the pouring rain. You're going to catch your death!" I made myself sound like the world's sternest parent as I pulled to a stop by the curb where there was a grassy space between the last house and a wooded area.

Vincent seemed oblivious as he groaned and rocked his hips, his arm stretched behind him, wrist disappearing down the back of his pants.

I sat there with my hands on the steering wheel, my mouth open, breaths coming fast as he reamed himself viciously. His cock bulged through the metal rings of the cage, leaking so much pre-cum that I wondered how I'd tell when he actually climaxed, *if* he climaxed.

Then he uttered a soft moan and stiffened. Spunk oozed out his glans and spilled over the steel bar at the tip of the device. Most of it soaked into his sweatpants but I didn't give a fuck about the leather seat at the moment.

Vincent shuddered and jerked as more fluid pulsed out of him, like milk from a frother. His eyes were squeezed shut and he continued to moan quietly. It was seriously one of the hottest things I'd ever seen. He kept fucking himself until it ended then pulled his hand out of his pants and sagged back against the passenger seat, his eyes closed, face flushed, mouth open.

"Bravo," I whispered, truly awed. "Bravo, my beautiful boy."

He turned his head and opened his eyes, gazing at me sleepily. I wanted to applaud but that would have been crass. Instead I offered him a sincere smile, which he returned. Then I pulled a wet wipe from the package in the console and held it out to him, my eyebrows raised.

He shook his head and rolled his eyes, but took it from me and cleaned his hand. "Can we go to your place now?"

I took him upstairs and put him in the bath, washing him with a soft cloth. I was unbelievably impressed and so horny after that performance that I could barely contain myself.

When we'd finished and he was drying off, I said, "That display in the car made me really horny, Vincent. Just looking at your cock in that steel cage turns me right the fuck on."

"I'm glad, Sir."

"But when I saw you standing out in the rain, getting soaked to the skin in the cold, I was furious. I need you to take better care of yourself."

He blinked, maybe wondering if I was joking.

"I'm serious, Vincent."

"Yes, Sir," he said, seeming chastened.

"And if you want to call me anything other than 'Sir' it had better be my name or 'Daddy' and not that other thing. Got it?"

His head bobbed frantically. "Yes, Sir, sorry, Sir. I won't call you that again."

"Because, Vincent, if I have to go all *Daddy* on you, I won't hesitate. If you're going to act like a child, I'm going to treat you like one."

He gaped at me, and I saw the wheels turning as he wondered what 'going all Daddy on him' meant.

I sat on the edge of the bed and beckoned him over. He was dry but still naked, which suited me just fine.

"Kneel."

He went down on his knees in front of me.

I leaned back and spread my legs. I was wearing a pair of stretchy jeans and his eyes flew to my crotch.

"Take off my jeans," I said, my voice deep and husky.

He glanced up at me with excitement.

"Do it."

He reached toward the fly of my jeans then pulled the zipper down with his long fingers. I could hardly wait to get them off.

He slid his fingers under the waistband and tugged as I leaned back on my hands and lifted my ass to assist him. He drew them down to my thighs as his mouth dropped open.

"Oh fuck. You're not wearing underwear," he breathed, his eyes flitting up to mine briefly.

He breathed deep and I knew he smelled me. The sex smell wafted up from my bare crotch and the soaked denim he was holding. I liked it as much as he did.

"All the way off."

He pulled them past my ankles and off my feet and tossed them to the side. I was still leaning back on my hands. Now I stared at him as I slowly, *slowly*, spread my legs wide.

He closed his eyes, then opened them. They burned blue fire as he stared at my crotch like he wanted to have me for breakfast. He glanced at me with a question, his trembling hands gripping his naked thighs.

Because I was a bastard, I stared at him silently, not giving him any orders but letting the suspense and his barely controlled desire build. He remained obediently as he was while I bought a hand forward to play with myself.

He opened his mouth. His gaze followed my hand as I rubbed myself for several moments, then lifted my fingers to my mouth and sucked noisily.

He moaned and trembled like a puppy being denied its dinner. If I hadn't been so fucking horny, I'd have laughed. But this was no laughing matter.

I played my fingers in my folds again, as Vincent's eyes widened and he looked like he might explode. Then I held them out and said one word.

"Lick."

He grabbed my wrist and guided my fingers into his mouth where he held me, licking and sucking the juices off me, moaning and slurping while I tried not to writhe with the need that suddenly jolted in my groin, my belly and up my spine.

"Stop!" I said, pulling my hand from him because it was too much and not enough at the same time.

I needed *more*. I spread my legs wider, pointed at my crotch and leaned back. "Make me come, boy."

I didn't give him anything more specific, and he surprised me by grabbing my thighs and spreading me before diving into my cunt, face first. I cried out and cursed involuntarily as he went at me frantically, nosing into me and using his tongue like the dick I had trapped, poking it around my clit then plunging it inside me as he elbowed me apart and spread me with his long fingers.

He was a whirlwind of desire. I had to stop myself from telling him to back off because, even though it was overwhelming and not the actions of a well-trained sub, it felt so fucking *good!* I threw my head back and concentrated on the pulses of delight his attack elicited.

After what seemed like about three seconds, I came so hard that I thought I would drown him. My groan sounded loud and primal as my body jerked and shuddered, my thighs pushing against his strong arms that kept me spread. He kept licking me, plunging a finger, then two, inside me, pressing my G-spot until I came loudly a second time, harder than the first. All I could do was give in to it and make ridiculous, undignified noises. God, he would fucking pay for this with his ass, but at that moment, I was loving every second of it, except the helplessness I felt as he made me come a *third* time.

"Vincent. Stop. *Stop!*" I finally had to say, for fear I'd pass out from the bliss and exhaustion of it. He gave my cunt one last long lick as he pulled his fingers from me and sat back on his heels obediently, his face shiny with my juices, his eyes wild with his own desire.

I stared at him with half-closed eyes and a blissed-out and confused expression as he regarded me with, yes, smugness. I wanted to slap that expression off his face at the same time that I wanted to uncage him, swallow his cock and do to *him* what he'd done to *me*.

Chapter Fourteen

"Stand up."

He blinked then stood and I remembered how tall he was.

"Run me a bath."

He smiled, although I saw him bring his hand down to rub at his caged cock for a second. "Yes, Sir," he said and left me.

I fell back on the coverlet, staring at the ceiling while the aftershocks of my three orgasms assaulted me. I had never come so quickly or so thoroughly from a man's assault like that. There had been women who had reduced me to the same quivering shell, but they had been few and far between. I didn't understand how Vincent had accomplished this.

My hand found my poor wet cunt and I soothed it gently while I thought about what I would to do to both punish and reward him that afternoon. Should I use the anal balls he was so obsessed with or deny him and take him apart with a small vibrating plug? Or should

I harness on one of my rubber cocks and fuck him until he begged to be allowed to come?

The way I felt that moment, like I'd just been thoroughly vanquished by my own sub despite myself, made me opt for the latter. I wanted to fucking *destroy* him the way he'd destroyed me. *Figuratively*, of course. But the thought of fucking him hard with one of my strap-ons while his cock was restrained was too delicious to forgo.

And watching him come inside the cage had been something I was dying to see again. If I kept him caged all weekend, I would remove it before he left on Sunday. He'd just have to obey my rules without the aid of a restraint. It seemed the cage turned him on so much that it was more of a handicap anyway.

I listened to the tub filling and pictured Vincent doing my bidding with his cock pushing at the metal bars. I'm sure he was on edge from what had just happened and ready to come again. But I'd settle him by sending him downstairs to practice his piano lessons while I planned out his afternoon.

I took a long, luxurious soak while I listened to Vincent's piano practice. I had made him put on the Princess shorts and a T-shirt so he wouldn't get cold, and told him to be a good boy and keep his hands off his asshole. Now that we both knew he could finger himself to orgasm in that cage, he would have to practice some *actual* restraint when I couldn't physically restrain him.

I pulled on a short cotton bathrobe in navy that I usually wore over a pair of sweats and padded downstairs, the ends of my spiky hair damp, my skin humming with energy.

Vincent at the piano obediently concentrating on his practice was one of my favorite things to see. He was progressing well, considering that he only got a few sessions on weekends. His fingers were perfect for it, and he seemed to have the brain for it as well.

"You're doing great at that," I said as I slid in beside him. He flashed me a smile while he continued his finger work.

"I really like it. I wish I had a piano in my apartment."

"Is there room for one?"

He shook his head. "Not really. It's a one-bedroom but it's small. I have a lot crammed in there." He glanced at me. "You should come over sometime."

I found his invitation startling, even though it shouldn't have been. We had an arrangement. It wasn't like we were in love or anything.

Except for that kiss. We hadn't really discussed that kiss.

"Sure. Sometime." I left it open, feeling like a dick but unable to commit to more than the vague possibility.

"Anytime you want," he said.

"Vincent," I muttered. "Are you just, like, generally accommodating? It's not just your rear-end?"

He laughed and shrugged, continuing to play. "I guess. I really like you," he said.

I was quiet for a long time, listening to him play my piano like he had always meant to. "I really like you, too."

I saw him smile, but he kept his eyes on the keys and his agile fingers.

Those fingers. I knew what those fingers could do. He wasn't just a natural born *piano* player.

"Vincent, do you know what 'pegging' is?"

His hands froze. He stared at the piano keys. After a moment he whispered, "Yes."

"Did Daphne ever do that? I don't recall it being in your essay."

"No," he said, breathing more quickly, still staring at the keys. "We talked about it, but she never actually did it."

"I see."

"Sir?" he said after a moment.

"Yes, Vincent?"

He closed his eyes and swallowed. When he looked at me, his expression was pleading and vulnerable and beautiful. "Are you… Are you going to do that, Sir?"

I smiled slowly at him. "I think I might. What equipment I'm lacking in my pants, I have in my basement." Namely, a harness and a varied selection of silicone and rubber cocks.

He inhaled and closed his eyes.

"I'll even let you choose."

His eyes flew open. "Oh God." He swallowed thickly. "Really?"

My smile widened. "For you, Vincent, *anything*."

He smiled his sweet smile and I told him his piano lesson was over.

It didn't take me long to get things ready downstairs. I was looking as forward to this as he was.

I laid my dildos out on the spanking bench, which I had made sure to wipe down with disinfectant after our last session.

"Wow, I do have quite a few."

I was very impressed with myself. Some people collected stamps. I collected cocks.

He looked them over with growing excitement. "Can I pick them up?"

"Sure."

He lifted up a fairly sizeable rubber model in a bronze color, checked it out then put it back down. Picked up a longer black one that wasn't as girthy. Put it down. Looked over all of them again.

"This one," he said, choosing a flesh-colored dildo that was shorter but thick. It was natural-looking with bulging veins and a defined, uncircumcised head. The pretend foreskin sheathed most of the glans and would provide a delicious bump when inserted. It was one of only three I had with that feature.

"*Nice*. That's one of my favorites."

Now, where to place Vincent for the fucking of his life?

I could do it there, which might be more practical, or take him to the bedroom. *Decisions, decisions.* I gave it to him, because I was in a very good mood and feeling magnanimous.

"Where do you want to do this, Vincent?"

He blinked. "Pardon, Sir?"

I put my hands on my hips and tilted my head. "Where do you want me to fuck you? Here or in my bedroom?"

He looked at the spanking bench, which I hadn't moved from the middle of the room since the first time we'd used it. "Here. Definitely. I want to be restrained, Sir."

"I can restrain you in my bedroom."

"I like the bench, Sir."

"Fair enough."

I thought he might have chosen the more intimate and personal space of my bedroom, but I honestly didn't care where we did it. I could make him scream down here as well as I could upstairs. But perhaps the acoustics were better in the basement? And the sound-proofing.

The only issue was that he was taller than me. His thighs were longer. I would have to make some adjustments. I wanted to be standing, so he needed to be bent at my waist height.

"I'm going to have to raise the bench so it's more of a table," I said. "Can you give me a hand?"

"Yes, Sir."

He helped me raise the bench to a workable height. I had him bend over it a number of times to check and took each opportunity to slap his ass in the Princess shorts and thrust my pelvis against him to make sure the height was right. He groaned and wiggled then complained that the cage was hurting.

"That's because you keep trying to get hard."

"*That's* because you keep teasing me, Sir."

"Yeah, I know. Sucks to be you."

He laughed. "Don't say *sucks*, Sir. *Please!*"

Now *I* laughed. "Okay my little comedian, strip off and get on the bench with your ass where I need it."

He gave me a heated stare and did as I asked, his caged cock just below the seat and his knees bent to bring him to my level.

I bound his wrists and his upper arms this time. I also placed a thick leather collar around his neck and fastened it with a clip to the bench. He blinked at me. *Probably didn't realized I would up the ante.*

"I want you motionless for this. I want to have *my* way with you, Vincent," I said, ruffling his hair. "Your safeword is always available, though, and I'm not going to gag you. Since you can't turn your head, I don't need to blindfold you, unless you'd rather."

His "No, Sir" came out harsh, and he humped the bench with his useless dick.

Excellent.

I bound his ankles and placed a leather band around his waist, clipping it to the bench on both sides.

"Oh fuck, yes," I said, loving the sight of him fastened down like he was. I ran my fingers from his shoulder blades to his lower back, then over one flank. "You look *stunning*."

"Thank you, Sir," he said, the pitch of his voice high. His breathing was ragged and we hadn't even started.

I grabbed the bottle of lube from the cabinet. "I'm going to finger you to get you ready, okay?"

He moaned. "Yes, Sir."

"Good boy."

I dribbled a ton of lube onto his lower back and pushed it down his crack with my fingers. He gasped and made an excited sound, feeling my skin instead of a glove.

"I know the gloves give an added component of objectification during a scene, but I'm not using them for this."

He remained silent like the good sub he was and I smoothed my finger over his hole, teasing him gently. "I am going to fuck this hole so good," I said, rubbing harder then pushing my finger in deep.

He groaned.

I pumped him with it a few times, then added another and did the same. He made such wonderful, vulnerable sounds.

That was something I really liked about Vincent. He didn't hold his vocalizations back unless I forced him to. He was so unrestrained verbally, when usually very much physically restrained. And I loved it.

"I love the sounds you make, Vincent. Give me all the groans and moans and huffs and whimpers. I love it. And it tells me how you're doing without you saying a word, although I'll still check in here and there."

In answer, as I added a third finger, he whined and whimpered.

"I know... I know that was a lot all of a sudden," I said, sliding them out and going in more gently. "But you're doing fantastic, sweetheart."

His answering groan was modulated and calm.

Good boy.

"Let's take this to the next level." My voice betrayed my excitement.

I knew he could hear me as I stripped and grabbed the harness I'd already fitted with the dildo, but he couldn't turn his head to see. He tried, then growled with frustration and pulled at his wrist bindings.

"Nope. Not gonna show you. Maybe next time. For now, you'll just have to imagine it."

He whined and huffed.

"Sorry, baby. That's the deal. Take it or leave it."

"Fine, I'll take it."

"Oh, you sure *will* take it." I was so hyped that I sounded like a teenager heading to prom.

"May I ask a question, Sir?"

"Yes, of course."

"Have you done this before? With women, I mean?" He was adorably hesitant to ask this, like it was none of his business. But it was. Finding out if I'd had experience with something I was going to do to him was completely relevant.

"Oh, Vincent. If I had a dollar for every time I've put this on and fucked a girl silly, well, I'd be pretty rich."

"In the ass?"

"Oh yeah. In the pussy, in the ass, in the mouth for the debasement of it. Yeah."

"Okay." He sounded relieved.

"That make you feel better?"

"I mean, I figured you had since you've got all the stuff. You've got *a lot* of stuff."

I chuckled. "Yeah, well. I have had a lot of practice with this. I don't think you have anything to worry about."

Nervous laughter. "I'm a little worried about *my* reaction, Sir," he said.

This surprised me because I had no doubt he'd enjoy it. "That you won't like it?"

"That I'll love it and I won't want to do anything else."

"Uh, you're forgetting about those purple balls."

"Oh. Never mind."

I adjusted the harness and the dildo so they were comfortable. "And anyway, there's still a *ton* of stuff I want to do with you, Vincent. So, don't worry about always wanting to do *this*, because I won't allow it. *I* will control your impulses so you don't have to worry about anything."

He sighed. "Thank you, Sir."

"You're welcome, Vincent. Hey, guess what?" I said as I made the final adjustments to the harness straps.

"What, Sir?"

"This harness even has an attachment for a dildo that goes *inside me*, so I'll get something out of this over and above reducing *your* ass to a quivering, pulsing, pleasure conduit."

He made a surprised noise, then, "Oh fuck. Oh fuck."

"I'm only using a small one so it isn't too distracting. But, yeah. Fun, huh?"

"Oh *fuck.*"

I let the fake cock slap against his ass as I added more lube and coated his crack with it. "We'll go slow at first, like we did with the black dildo." I slid the silicone implement along his crack so he got a sense of the size of it. Then I slipped it underneath him and thrust it beside his caged cock. "When you're used to the size, I'm going to fuck you like you won't believe."

"Yes, Sir," he gasped, then moaned. "*Please.*"

"Please, what?"

"Please put your cock inside me, Sir. Please!"

Well, then.

I glided the head down his crack and bumped his hole—not to get in yet, just to let him know what was coming. I slid it over his sensitive skin, teasing him, getting him to relax. Finally, I held the head against him and pushed firmly with my pelvis.

Vincent groaned as the head slowly sank in. I stopped, letting him get used to the invasion. He gripped the metal legs of the bench.

"How does that feel, sweetheart?"

"Good. So good," he said.

"Fuck, you should see how it *looks.*"

He made a desperate sound.

"Yeah. It looks so hot, Vincent. Ready for more?"

"Yes, Sir," he moaned.

I fucked him then...slowly and carefully at first. When he seemed to like that, I went more quickly and aggressively. I kept one hand on the base of the realistic dildo, and one on his hip, holding him steady, even though he couldn't move much. His cries went from soft moans and whimpers to deep low groans, grunts and growls as I plowed his ass.

He was definitely enjoying it and so was I. The dildo inside me rocked to my thrusts. I had chosen a short one because if it had been long enough to rub my G-spot, I'd have come three times already. As it was, I was close.

I reached beneath to his cock in its cruel cage. It bulged through the metal bars, slippery from all the pre-ejaculate. I wanted to make him come. I thought I could make it happen.

I angled the dildo so it hit his prostate every time I pushed into him. His cries went back to soft moans and whimpers, then to high-pitched gasps as I worked him and rubbed that spot. On a hunch, I slid my hand over the cock cage again, touching as much of his flesh as I could, teasing it.

I thrust hard against his prostate and felt hot fluid gush over my fingers as Vincent groaned from the depths of his being. His sphincter contracted around the dildo as the anal orgasm rocketed through him. He whimpered as more and more liquid oozed out. His body shuddered its torturous release.

My cunt spasmed violently around the small dildo and I came *hard*. The sound that came out of my mouth sounded vulnerable and primal. I clutched Vincent's hip with my spunk-coated fingers and rocked against him, prolonging the pleasure and celebrating my accomplishment.

Finally, we were both quiet.

I stayed deep inside him as my orgasm subsided.

"Oh, Vincent."

"Thank you, Sir." His voice cracked with exhaustion.

"You were magnificent," I said, easing out carefully.

The dildo slid out of him as he whined with regret. I quickly divested myself of my gear and let it fall to the floor.

I considered putting my clothes back on but I didn't want to. Instead, I unfastened Vincent's bonds and helped him stand.

"You okay?" I said as I let go of his arm.

Instead of answering, he fell to his knees so quickly that I reached for him because I thought he'd collapsed. But he bowed his head and began to kiss and lick my naked feet, cupping each heel with a hand as he did so.

I stared at the top of his head, stunned but inordinately pleased.

"Vincent," I whispered, his lips on my skin like the wings of a butterfly — so gentle and fleeting. Tiny grateful kisses along my arch and on my toes.

He looked up and those bright blue eyes were my undoing.

"Fuck it, Vincent," I whispered. "I think I might love you."

His eyes widened as he smiled. He didn't say a thing, just moved his worshipping kisses up my calves slowly, sliding his hands up behind my knees.

I dropped to the floor, tilting his chin so he looked at me. "Vincent, I *love* you."

He nodded. "I know."

I laughed and my eyes tingled, more from the fact it was a *Star Wars* reference than for any other reason. At least, that was what I told myself.

"You asshole," I muttered.

His lip quirked. "Not *just* an asshole, apparently."

"Never," I said as I guided his face close and pressed my lips to his.

Our lips parted and we kissed hungrily, desperately. All protocols were abandoned as his hand came up behind my head and pulled me into him, his mouth devouring mine the same way mine grasped at his. The only thing that separated us finally was the need for air.

"Fuck. Holy shit," he said.

"Ditto. Let's go upstairs, Vincent."

"Yeah, okay."

He stood, his poor cock still in its confinement. There would have been a mess on the floor under the bench but I didn't care. I'd have him clean it up before he left.

In my bedroom I got the key and released him from his imprisonment. He leaned back on his elbows and watched me clean him with a warm wet cloth. While I was doing so, he found my nipple with his fingers and stroked it gently.

I gazed at him with a small smile. It was hard to believe we'd only known each other a few weeks and I already trusted him with my body. I trusted Vincent more than I'd trusted anyone before him. I wasn't sure why. I just knew I felt safe and that he'd shown me such deference and respect I wasn't nervous being naked with him at all.

When I'd cleaned him off, I climbed on top of him, straddling his hips and pushing his shoulders back against the pillows.

"You took that very well."

He blushed. "Getting fucked in the ass, you mean?"

"That's exactly what I mean."

"You *did* it very well. Mad skills, Nic. You've got *mad skills.*"

"Well, I do when it comes to asses. Not much else…like emotions or anything like that." I felt the heat in my face at this brave admission.

He laughed quietly. "You're a pretty good piano teacher."

I raised my eyebrows. "*Pretty* good?"

"Exceptional. You're an *exceptional* piano teacher."

"Thank you, Vincent. You are a wonderful student."

He found my hands with his and entwined our fingers. "I like learning the piano in my pretty underwear."

I growled and kissed him, hard this time. He responded and we went at it again like teenagers. I writhed on top of him, feeling his cock swell beneath me.

"Hello, what's *this*?" I asked, glancing down. "That didn't take long."

"Not when you're around, Sir."

I frowned. "Don't call me Sir right now…just Nic. Call me Nic."

"Not when you're around, *Nic*."

I couldn't believe how much I enjoyed hearing my name from his sweet lips. I ground myself on his hard cock. "Say it again."

He grinned. "Not when *you're* around, *Nic*."

I let my eyes roll back as if I were in Heaven and groaned. "Oh yeah. *So* hot."

"What's your *full* name?" He frowned. "Never mind. You don't have to tell me."

And I loved him even more for that. "Nicole. But please don't use it. I gave it up a long time ago. It's not who I am." I gazed at him steadily and seriously.

"I won't. I like 'Nic' better anyway."

He guided my face to his and we kissed again. He was so hard now and I was dripping wet. Without saying a word, I spread my legs and guided his cock into me, sitting on him with little-to-no preamble.

He threw his head back and gasped, then pierced me with those blue *blue* eyes and grabbed my hips, moving me on him, making *me* cry out.

I pushed back and forth, riding his dick until he gasped my name. "Nic…Nic…oh fuck, Nic! Nic!"

And I came, groaning into his neck, jerking my hips. When I'd finished, I told him to pound me, fuck me, hard, Vincent, so *hard*. And he did. He held me steady and thrust until he came, his cock shooting thickly inside me as I rocked myself on him and felt like I'd come home.

Chapter Fifteen

On Wednesday, Vincent begged me to come to *his* place.

"Please, Nic. I need to see you."

"You just want me to let you off the hook." We had agreed he wouldn't have another orgasm until the weekend.

"No, I swear. You don't have to make me come. You can just tie me up and tease me. I really miss you."

"It's been three days, Vincent." But, honestly, I missed him too.

So, I agreed to go to his apartment. I packed up some bits of soft rope, a blindfold and a ball gag, in case I did decide to play with him. I mean, who was I kidding? If he was up for a bit of tease and denial, who was I to argue?

I headed over there in the early dusk, driving my car slowly as if I were savoring the fact that I'd been invited over to my...*submissive's* place, *boyfriend's* place? I wasn't a huge fan of labels and I couldn't pick which one fit more accurately. So, I didn't worry about it. We weren't at the point of introducing each other around our social circles yet.

Even after a few days I was stunned at the way this, well, *relationship* — for lack of a better word — was progressing. It still scared me, but everything with Vincent felt so right that I couldn't fight it. I was going with it and trusting everything would be fine. *Great*, in fact.

But a part of me felt like it could crash and burn at any moment.

I parked the car in a Visitors spot and pressed the buzzer for his apartment.

"Hello?"

"Hi."

"Who is it?" he said, baiting me.

Since there wasn't anybody near me, I replied, "It's *Sir*. And you'd better buzz me up right now because I don't like waiting, Vincent."

I heard his sweet chuckle. "Of course, *Sir.*"

The sound of the buzzer filled the small space. I pulled open the door, grinning and eager to put my sub in his place. I was beginning to realize it might take some willpower to not fuck him again. *I must be strong.* He expected me to be the Dom most of the time.

I rode the elevator up to the fifth floor with my satchel of goodies, wondering what secrets his apartment would divulge. I was incredibly curious to see his living space.

He responded to my curt knock with promptness, opening the door wide with a smile and beckoning me in. He wore black skinny jeans and a red cotton tee that said *Slave to Love* on it.

On a hunch I asked, "Have you been shopping, sweetheart?" touching the words on the shirt.

He blushed. "Yeah. I got the jeans on Monday and the shirt yesterday. I wanted you to see it." He twirled in front of me as the door closed, flourishing his hand at the way his ass looked in the jeans.

"Love the jeans, Vincent. And the shirt? Well. It's perfect." I grabbed his chin when he stopped turning and brought him in for a kiss. His lips felt familiar and his scent made my heart happy. He smiled against my mouth, kissing me sweetly before pulling back.

"I'm *so* glad you came over. Let me show you around."

I lifted up the satchel and raised my eyes. "Where should I put *this*?"

"Ooh, what's in there?" he asked, leaning toward it.

"It's a secret for now," I said, tousling his hair. "Give me the tour and I'll show you."

"Just leave it on the sofa. Anyway, this is the living room. It's not that big but I've tried to make the best of the space."

The only place I'd seen more IKEA furniture was at IKEA, but everything looked cozy and comfortable. The room was tidy and relatively uncluttered. There was a tall bookcase and a small entertainment unit with a large flatscreen TV on it, a low wood coffee table with a few neat piles of books and a model sailboat. I glanced around the room, becoming aware of some other coastal-themed decor objects—a framed print of a lighthouse on some unknown shore and more boat models on the shelves of the bookcase.

"Did you make these?" I asked Vincent as I examined one. "May I touch it?"

"Yes, and yes. Just be gentle. It's very delicate," he said, moving closer.

I side-eyed him. "It's okay. I'm used to handling delicate things."

He blushed and I wanted to kiss him, only I was holding a model boat in my hand. "That's one of the first ones I did," he said.

I turned the blue-and-white object in my hands, noticing the fine workmanship. "It's beautiful, Vincent."

He shrugged. "I mean, they're all from kits."

"You've done a beautiful job." I replaced the sailboat and checked out some of his books. "You like to read. That's good."

"I get that from my mom. She loved to read. In fact, quite a few of these are hers," he said. "Dad didn't know what to do with all of them after she died. He gave most of them to me."

I glanced at him. "I'm sorry. It's tough to lose a parent. I lost my dad a few years ago."

"Yeah. It sucks."

"Majorly," I said. "Oooh, I really like this one," I told him, holding up a red schooner with white sails. The name *Evelyn* was painted in pretty white letters on the bow.

"I named that one after her."

"God, you're sweet," I said, lifting my hand to his face.

He lowered his eyes and grinned. "I don't feel very sweet right now. My dick is so fucking hard. And I'm trying to figure out where you're going to tie me up in this place." His voice was soft and breathy.

"Well, there are different ways to be sweet, you know. It looks like you have a *sweet* hard-on at the moment, right?" I glanced at his skinny jeans where the bulge of his cock was obvious.

He blushed. "Pretty fucking sweet, yeah."

"Uh huh. Maybe you should take off your jeans and lean over the couch for me, Vincent. We can do the tour after."

His breaths came heavier. "After what?"

"After I do a little examination to make sure my boy is still in proper working order."

He groaned. "Okay. Yeah." He looked at the sofa. "Where?"

"Take off your pants, Vincent," I said, replacing the sailboat he'd named after his late mother on the shelf. I sent a prayer apologizing for defiling her son like this. Still, I was making him happy in so many ways and what mother wouldn't want that?

Maybe I should stop thinking about his mom. I turned around.

"Oh, Vincent, fuck." It came out of my mouth before I could think, because all I could see was Vincent sitting on the edge of his IKEA sofa in a pair of white satin panties with pink polka dots on them, trying without much success to pull the jeans off his bare feet. A raging erection pushed at the top of his panties as he leaned over.

He glanced at me with a frustrated grimace because he was *literally* stuck in his skinny jeans. But I didn't laugh because nothing about this was humorous. He looked *hot as fuck* and so sinfully sweet in these new panties that he must have picked out himself, that my mouth went dry. I had to clear my throat to get the next words out.

"Hold on," I said, walking over and falling to my knees. I lifted his feet into my lap and gently pulled at one pant leg where it was bunched at his ankle. "These are *very* tight, Vincent."

"I thought you'd like them. I got the panties, too."

I held up my hand without looking at him. "Don't even *talk* to me about the panties until I can properly examine them. I love the panties," I said, still trying to get even one of his sexy feet out of the jeans. "The panties are *exquisite*. They are rocking my fucking world right now."

"Oh good," he said. "They were ninety bucks plus tax."

My head snapped up. "*Ninety* bucks? For a pair of satin panties? You got taken, dear boy. Although they *are* lovely." I tried not to look at his cock in those polka dot panties because I literally *could not even*. "I like the jeans, too. They just might not be very practical for my purposes."

"I don't know. I think these panties are worth ninety bucks," Vincent said, smoothing his palm down his cock over the satin and closing his eyes wantonly. "They're just so *soft*."

I pulled his foot out of his jeans with a vicious tug and growled at him. "I said don't *talk* about the panties, Vincent." I tugged the other side off with the same aggression, almost pulling him from the couch. "And keep your fucking hand off that cock. That cock is *mine*."

I stood and leaned over him, my face inches from his, and glanced down at his cock as I trailed a finger over the panties where it pushed at the delicate satin in a most profane way. I drew a quick breath at just how soft the satin was, and cursed. "Oh hell. It *is* very soft."

I trailed my finger back and forth over his cock and he puffed out small breaths as he gazed at me with wide, excited eyes.

"You like that?" I said, feathering my finger back and forth while his cock swelled under the fabric.

"Yeah," he said breathily.

"I beg your pardon?"

He let his head fall back as his eyes fluttered shut and whispered, "Yes, Sir," then groaned.

I slid my fingers under the waistband of his panties and touched the warm flesh where it was swollen. I was fascinated by this feeling of softness and hardness — the skin was silky smooth but his dick was rock-hard.

"Kiss me," I said as I leaned forward and wrapped my hand around him, stroking slowly, languorously, as our mouths met and opened to each other. I drowned in his taste and texture as Vincent gasped and moaned, his tongue frantically exploring me.

But I had to shut it down because we were both getting too excited too quickly. I didn't want him to climax until the weekend but, at this rate, we both would — and *soon*.

I wrenched my hand off him, pulled my face away and stood up, stepping back and giving him a nod. "Shirt off and stand up, please."

He blinked, trying to recover himself, and did as I asked, peeling the red shirt off and tossing it to the floor.

"I'm very sorry to say these panties have to come off, Vincent. But I'll do it. You just stand there and don't move until I tell you to."

He dipped his head obediently as I moved close and slipped my thumbs under the silk waistband. With practiced calculation, I lifted the waistband over the top of his arching cock and slid the panties down his legs, keeping my eyes on his as I crouched down and touched his right calf. "Lift."

He did and I pulled one side off.

"Now this one." I touched his other calf and he accommodated me.

I stood up, clutching the soft satin in my hand, rubbing my thumb and finger over it gently. Maintaining his gaze, I lifted the fabric to my nose and inhaled deeply. "Mm-m."

Vincent watched me with wide eyes and moaned.

I balled them up and tossed them aside like they were nothing. His gaze followed as they arced through the air. Ninety dollars of overpriced panties on the floor.

"I want you to turn around and kneel on the sofa cushions with your elbows on the back of the sofa and your ass pushed out toward me."

"Yes, Sir," he said and moved his lithe body into place as I watched.

When he was ready, he glanced behind him with raised eyebrows and I wanted to take a photo of him displayed like that. He looked delectable. But I knew a way to make him look even better.

"Good boy," I said, moving to my bag of tricks and tossing the ball gag and blindfold on the sofa. I pulled out a length of soft rope.

He quivered with excitement as I moved behind him. "Now lower your chest to the back of the sofa and cross your wrists at your back."

He did this as his cock bobbed gracefully.

I wrapped the black rope around his wrists and knotted it tight, getting him to test it.

"Good?"

"Yes, Sir."

A slap on his ass made him hiss in surprise. "Louder."

"Yes, Sir."

I moved around him and took the ball gag from the cushion. I looked at it for a second, then tossed it back in the bag. I wanted to be able to ask him questions.

I adjusted him higher on the sofa so he was more evenly balanced, pinching a nipple hard in the process and giving his cock a little slap.

He groaned.

I tied the blindfold and grabbed a pair of blue nitrile gloves from my bag, making sure he heard me putting them on. He'd said he was *kind of* into medical play, *so let's find out.*

"So, Mr...."

And *that* was when I realized I didn't know Vincent's last name. While I was hesitating and trying to figure out how to ask something so obvious and embarrassing, he told me.

"Blake."

"I can't believe I didn't know your last name."

"You never asked."

"Well, now I feel like a shit."

"You're not a shit. It doesn't matter."

"Mr. Blake," I said, clearing my throat in embarrassment and trying to get back in the game, "I hear you've been having a sexual issue that you wanted to discuss with me? I believe when you called my receptionist you said that you have trouble concentrating without something in your rectum?" It was a statement out of an amateur porn video, but I made it work.

I ran my gloved finger down his crack and over his hole. "As a medical doctor, I can tell you that everything looks normal back here. But it's always best to do an internal examination to rule out a less-obvious problem."

Vincent moaned and pushed his ass against my hand. "Yes, Doctor."

"You may be wondering why I asked my assistant to truss you up in this manner. It's de rigueur in my practice to have my patients silent and obedient during their examinations. My examinations get quite personal, and some patients have trouble staying still and being sensible."

As I said these words, I moved my finger back and forth over his hole—a light, tickling pressure that was already driving him crazy.

"Now, Mr. Blake, please don't hesitate to be vocal during the examination. I like to hear my patients have a healthy set of lungs and that they are responding properly to what I'm doing."

Vincent emitted a loud groan as I pushed my finger into him.

"Mm-hmm, yes, I see," I murmured, trying to sound cold and professional as I prodded Vincent's ass. He swayed and moaned and whimpered. I placed a hand on his hip to steady him as I pushed my finger as deep as I could get it, twisting my hand and applying pressure at various angles. It was a very *thorough* exam.

Vincent turned his head, even though he couldn't see. He held his lip in his teeth and moaned.

"I'm afraid I will need to use two fingers to check you properly, Mr. Blake."

"O-okay," he stuttered. "I mean, yes, Doctor."

As I inserted two gloved fingers and palpated the walls of his rectum, brushing them over his prostate, my other hand went underneath to check his penis.

Vincent made a soft "Ohh-h" sound.

"Mr. Blake, I seem to have located the cause of your distress. You seem to have an amplified response to anal stimulation."

"I know. I do." Vincent moaned.

I rubbed his passage more virulently and stroked his dick. "Please refrain from ejaculating, Mr. Blake. I'm trying to conduct a professional medical exam."

"I'll try...not to," he said tremulously.

I let go of his cock and pumped my fingers before relinquishing him and snapping off my gloves.

"We'll take a little break. I need a glass of water," I said, patting him on the rump as he trembled with the effort of obeying my order not to climax. "Don't go anywhere, Mr. Blake. My time is valuable and I'd like you to be ready for further examination when I return."

"Yes, Doctor."

With that, I left him to go into the kitchen. It was around the corner from where Vincent lay draped over his sofa in a state of desperation. It must have been quite something to be dominated like this in your own space. He seemed to like it.

While I found my way around Vincent's small but neatly decorated kitchen space, finding a glass and turning on the tap, my eyes caught on a black-and-white photo in a small frame on a corner unit with open shelves.

Strangely, it wasn't *Vincent* I recognized first.

A strange out-of-body sensation passed through me, along with a sharp shock as I leaned closer to see the photo more clearly.

As the recognition of Zane's familiar, laughing profile solidified itself in my brain, I looked at the other two men in the photo. One of them was unknown to me, but the other was definitely Vincent, although his hair looked longer and he was sporting more stubble than I was used to.

It was a good thing the glass I had hold of was plastic, because if it hadn't been, I'd probably have shattered it with my grip.

What. The. Fuck.

I realized I was holding my breath. I let it out slowly while I tried to process my thoughts. I had so many *questions.*

Why does Vincent have a photo with Zane in it?

What is their relationship?

Does Daphne know that Vincent knows Zane?

Does Vincent know that Zane is my ex?

What has Zane got to do with the fact that Daphne recommended Vincent to me?

My brain spun around and around. I was in shock. I rested my elbows on the counter and closed my eyes, to force myself not to stand and stare at the photo. I had to go back to Vincent, and I couldn't let him see how angry and upset I was.

I had to put an immediate end to this scene, but I could not confront him at that moment. I needed to leave. I needed to leave *now.*

I opened my eyes and stood up straight. Taking a couple of steadying breaths, I summoned my 'in control Dom' mode and strode back into the living room. I walked over and began to unbind Vincent's wrists. As I removed the blindfold, I tried to smile.

"We have to end this scene, Vincent. I'm really sorry but I'm suddenly not feeling well."

It was a terrible excuse, but I needed something realistic that would get me out of here before I caved and let him see my anger.

He blinked at me but pushed up from the sofa and sat down, his dick still astonishingly hard. I mean, he had been ready to come a few minutes before.

"Oh. Okay," he said. "You can lie down in my room for a bit if you want? Do we really have to stop?"

"Yeah, I'm so sorry. It's just that I'm having stomach cramps and I feel like I might throw up." This, at least, was the truth. "I'd rather be at home and I don't want *you* to get sick."

He stared at me. I think he knew I was lying. He didn't know why, but he didn't challenge me.

He searched my face for the truth. "Okay."

"I'm really sorry," I said, gathering my stuff, throwing it into my satchel. "I'll text you later to check on you."

"Okay."

I looked up, feeling terrible about the lie but not about leaving, because it was a necessity at this point. So, I said, "You can come if you want. I don't care."

Which was, of course, the very *worst* thing to say. I realized it as I watched his face fall. He looked away. He didn't know what he'd done wrong.

He hadn't done anything wrong except to *not* tell me he knew Zane. And I didn't know if I could forgive that.

I didn't say anything else because it would just make the situation worse. I walked out of Vincent's apartment, with his model sailboats and IKEA furniture, and got into my car.

Chapter Sixteen

I blinked back angry tears as I drove. I had to pull over to the side of the road because I couldn't fucking see. I was so, *so* mad. I was fucking *crying* over this.

Honestly, I felt *so* betrayed—like the literal rug had been pulled from under me and I was falling, falling to the dark ground. Soon I'd smash into it and nothing would be the same.

I thought we had something, Vincent and I. Over four measly weeks he'd gotten under all my defenses, the ones I had put up so carefully after the whole Zane-thing had ended. I'd been ready, despite my better judgment, to try again.

Now it turned out I should have kept those fucking walls up, should have built them even higher so maybe no-one could've gotten in, not even Daphne.

I needed to call her but I didn't even want to think about her. Had she *known*? Had she realized Vincent knew Zane when she'd offered him to me? I would fucking *kill her* if she had. Or just never talk to her again.

I gripped the steering wheel in tight fists, my forehead pressed against it, while these thoughts raced through me. But I needed to pull myself together and get myself home.

With much concentration and an iron will, I did.

I stripped off all my clothes and stumbled into the shower, letting the hot water calm and soothe me. I tried not to think about *anything* but images of Vincent kept taunting me. I didn't want to ever see him again but I knew I had to check on him later. It was my duty as a Dom.

I shouldn't have left him so abruptly in the middle of a scene but I couldn't see any alternative. If I hadn't left right away I might have, I don't know, broken down in tears — *the horror* — or given in to the urge to punch him. I didn't feel out of control like that very often and I hadn't trusted myself in the room with him.

But I already fucking missed him.

After I got into a T-shirt and a comfortable pair of pj pants, I sat on the sofa staring at the wall for a very long time. Then I messaged Vincent, but not before changing his contact name to something more impersonal. VB for Vincent Blake, now that I knew his last name.

Me: Hi. Sorry about rushing off.

VB: Hi. Are you okay?

Me: Still feeling off. How about you? You don't have sub drop or anything?

VB: I don't know.

ME: What do you mean?

VB: I feel like you're lying to me right now.

ME: I'm sorry. I just need some time. I'll text you tomorrow.

VB: What's wrong, Nic? Why did you leave? Did I do something?

I ignored his last text and clicked out of my message app. I wasn't getting into an argument. I couldn't do this right now. Besides, I needed to call Daphne.

But I was scared to call her, because I felt in my gut that she knew all about Zane being friends with Vincent — or related to him or something. It was just too big of a coincidence.

I texted her instead.

Hi. I need to talk to you. Are you available for a phone call right now?

Instead of a text back, my ringtone for Daphne went off after a minute or two — The Rolling Stones' *Sympathy for the Devil* had never seemed so accurate. Except I had no sympathy for her right now.

I hit the Answer button.

"Hi." My tone was curt, cold.

"Hey," Daphne said cheerfully. "What's up?"

I didn't beat about the bush. I wasn't that kind of guy. "How do Zane and Vincent know each other?"

She hesitated. And that was when I knew for sure that she was aware they did.

"Daphne, what the fuck? Tell me how they know each other."

"They're barely friends, Nic," she said, her voice regretful.

I put my hand to my closed eyes. "I just saw a photo of them together with another guy."

"Then Zane must have been friends with the *other* guy. Zane told me Vincent was an acquaintance."

"You…you *sent* me Vincent, knowing he had ties to *Zane?* What is *wrong* with you?"

"Nic, calm down. Shit, I *told* Vincent not to mention Zane. I knew you'd be mad." She sounded pissed off now.

I tried to keep my breathing calm. "*Mad*, Daphne? Mad doesn't even *begin* to touch what I'm feeling right now."

Vincent, always the good, polite, obedient sub, hadn't mentioned Zane. But he must have forgotten about the photo in his kitchen.

"Nic, look. Zane sent Vincent to me because he wasn't responding to him the way they thought he should. He was into the dominance thing, but either not the *Zane* thing or not the cis-male-Dom thing. He likes *women*, but not stereotypical women. He likes women like *you*."

There was silence while I processed this and maybe Daphne realized her mistake. "Vincent's been *Dommed* by Zane? Jeez, this just gets better and better."

"Briefly. It didn't work for him. So, Zane brought him to me. And it didn't really work with me either."

Then I asked the question that was picking at my brain. "Whose idea was it to send him to me? Yours? Or Zane's?"

She hesitated and I really, *really* wanted to scream.

"Zane's. He thought it might make up for the way things ended between you two. It was kind of an apology, Nic."

I was starting to get a headache from all this. "Why didn't you tell me?"

"Because you would never have agreed to even meet Vincent if I'd told you."

That was true. But it still didn't excuse her — *their* — behavior. I was silent, because if I had opened my mouth, I would have cursed her forever.

"Is it working between you and Vincent?" she asked carefully.

I hit End Call and threw my phone across the room.

* * * *

Two hours later I picked it up off the floor and examined it for damage. There was none. However, there were multiple messages from Vincent and Daphne. I had blocked Zane's number a long time ago or there would have been some from him, too, I was sure.

Vincent was losing his shit. He'd tried to call me too, but I'd had my phone on silent mode for our scene and hadn't changed it.

Daphne must have spoken to him.

Nine-o-five p.m.

VB: Nic, I'm so sorry. Daphne told me not to mention Zane but I didn't really know why. I wish I'd told you.

Nine-ten p.m.

VB: I don't even know why I framed that photo. I hardly know Zane at all.

VB: Please text me back. I'm so sorry. It doesn't mean anything. But you mean everything.

It means you lied to me.

My heart felt like it had been flattened under someone's foot—Zane's foot actually. He was the one I was *really* mad at. The other two were just stupid, but I couldn't deal with it.

I left my phone on silent and didn't listen to any of Vincent's voicemails because I couldn't handle it. After placing it face-down on the kitchen counter, I went to bed.

I slept like shit, tossing and turning, dreaming of knives and brutal attacks. I wasn't sure if they represented what I felt Vincent and Daphne had done to me or if that was what I wanted to do to them. But the nightmares left me with a bitter taste in my mouth when I woke.

I wasn't hungry and could barely eat. I got ready and went to work like an automaton, but my entire staff knew something was wrong. I fielded probing questions with vague answers and attempts to comfort me with a cold look. I just couldn't deal with people right now.

I missed Vincent so *much* but only because I'd gotten so used to him over the course of four weeks. These feelings would go away and we were better off apart. I didn't think I could ever trust him again. I wasn't sure I could trust anyone again.

I'd had to use my phone for general things like banking and looking up the weather, but I wasn't even opening my message app and I hadn't listened to any of my voicemails.

They could all just fuck right *off*.

* * * *

At nine o'clock on Saturday morning, the doorbell rang. I was sitting on the sofa in a pair of old sweats and a T-shirt that had seen better days, listening to the pounding of rain on my roof. I hadn't showered for forty-six hours. I probably stank but I couldn't care less.

I knew it was him. It *had* to be him because this was when he usually came over on the weekend. It was pouring rain outside but I didn't even get up.

Five minutes passed and the doorbell rang again.

Ten minutes later, I heard knocking and another ring.

Then, nothing. He'd finally given up and left. I waited another ten minutes until curiosity got the better of me. When I peeked out of the front window, I was startled to see Vincent sitting on my doorstep in the rain, huddled against the bricks of my uncovered front porch, staring at his wet Chucks.

Something in me started to break but I locked it down, turned away and went upstairs. He'd always been an idiot about the rain. It wasn't my fault he hadn't worn a proper jacket or brought an umbrella.

Fuck him.

I forced my thoughts away from the image of him, soaking wet and shivering, waiting for some kind of acknowledgment that wasn't coming.

I'm done.

I got undressed and stepped into the shower, savoring the warmth of the water as a form of revenge on the man outside my door.

See? I know how to take care of myself. You're so pathetic that you can't even function without someone telling you what to do.

Then I started to cry — enormous, racking bursts that threatened to break me apart — as I recalled our time together.

Our shopping trips. Vincent practicing his scales at the piano. Taking him apart on the spanking bench. His soft butterfly kisses on my feet.

I fell to my knees and sobbed on the tiled floor of my shower, because I knew he'd gone. I was utterly convinced that the *best* thing in my life was over.

When I couldn't cry anymore, I climbed to my feet and perfunctorily cleaned myself up. I dried off and dressed in different clothes then went downstairs. I paused on the last step, wondering if, by some miracle, Vincent was still on my doorstep.

But there was no way. It had been over an hour since the last knock. I walked to the front door and peeked out.

And my fucking lunatic of a submissive was *still* there, shivering wet, clothes absolutely soaked, water sliding down his face over his closed eyes and sweet lips and dripping from his chin.

For fuck's sake!

Furious, relieved anger filled me like a sudden storm. I flung open the door and crossed my arms over my chest.

"I *fucking* told you to dress for the weather, Vincent!"

He snapped up his head as his eyes flew open. He scrambled to stand but he was shivering so hard and he'd probably been in his hunched position for too long.

Part of me wanted to help him but I kept my hands to myself. He was lucky I was even talking to him right now.

He shook the water off his head and he looked so fucking miserable. "I'm sorry. I'm so sorry, Sir."

"God, you can't even take care of yourself, can you?" It was cruel and inaccurate but my anger needed someplace to go.

He bobbed his head up and down as he whispered, looking contrite. "I know. I know. I just needed to see you."

"And you're a fucking liar." I was so, *so* angry. And *he* was the one brave enough to face it.

He peered at the ground and muttered something.

"Pardon?"

"I never lied," he said, slightly louder, raising those sad blue eyes to mine. "I *never* lied, Nic."

He was right, but I wasn't ready to forgive him.

"Get in here," I said, shoving the door wide and stepping back. "Get your ass in here and close the door."

He stepped inside, his runners squelching on the mat, and gently closed the door behind him. While he toed them off and stood there in his sock feet, I ran my gaze over his familiar form and tried not to faint with relief. Instead, I backed away and stood by the entrance to the kitchen, still hugging my chest.

"Now take off those wet clothes and go have a shower. You need to learn to take proper care of yourself."

He blinked at me as water dripped down his face. I knew there were tears there as well—maybe from earlier, maybe more recent.

"Yes, Sir." He moved to obey.

As he passed me, I reached out and grabbed his arm. My voice was softer now as some of the rage had dissipated in the face of his obedience. "I'm still *really* angry with you. And I'm furious with Daphne and apoplectic at Zane. But when you're done, put on my blue robe and come down to the living room. We can talk, but I'm not promising anything. I don't know if I can forgive any of you."

He nodded without looking at me and, when I released him, moved quickly through the living room and up the stairs.

I'd already forgiven him and I couldn't deny it to myself as I sat on the stairs, my heart flipping, breaths quick with emotion. I lasted about five excruciating minutes then followed his path, clicking my tongue at the wet sock prints on my wood floors.

By the time I reached the upper floor, I wasn't strong enough to resist him or what we had together. I stripped off my clothes and walked quietly into the en suite.

Vincent was shivering, even though he was under the hot water. He leaned against the tiles, his head on his arms, the reflection of my posture from a few days ago. His chest heaved and I realized he was sobbing.

I moved forward, slid open the stall door and stepped under the water, guiding him into my embrace as he wrapped his arms instinctively around my waist like a small, lost child — which he was right now, at least emotionally. He dipped his forehead into the hollow between my shoulder and neck and clutched me like I was his rock.

"Nic, I'm so, *so* sorry."

"It's okay, sweetheart. It's okay. It wasn't your fault."

"I didn't know why I was supposed to keep quiet. Daphne explained everything the other day and now I wish you'd known the whole time." His voice broke with emotion.

I sighed. "There wouldn't have been a *whole time* if I'd known. I wouldn't have gone anywhere near you. She's right about that."

"Still, it wasn't fair to not tell you."

"I know but it's okay. We're not going to let this tear us apart."

He drew a sudden, violent breath and shuddered. "Oh, God, thank God. I thought we were done. I thought you'd never open that door."

"Then why did you sit out there so long?" I asked, kissing his hair, moving it out of the way so I could kiss his skin.

"Because if you did open the door, I'd be there, and if you didn't, nothing mattered anyway."

"Oh, Vincent." I pulled him close, chafing his arms and shoulders with my hands to bring the blood back to them. I adjusted the temperature of the water even hotter and made sure he was under most of it. "I'm *so* sorry. I was just…so mad. I'd had initial trepidations about getting involved with you and this just brought all my insecurities to the surface."

"You're the best thing in my life right now," he said.

Afterward, I dried him and found a fleece robe that mostly fit. I made us some tea and we sat together on the sofa to drink it.

"Zane and I had a weird relationship," I told Vincent. "It was mostly him teaching me the ropes of being a Dominant. But then it seemed like he was using me as a circus performer to impress his many subs. You know, *come see the non-binary Domme I'm training to whip you silly*. It was a gimmick. I thought he actually cared about me. But when I expressed my growing feelings for him, he dropped me like a hot coal, came up with a stupid excuse and refused to have anything to do with me."

Vincent stared at me, his eyes wide. "Are you serious?"

"Deadly. I swore I'd never fall for anyone again because it's better to be alone than to give yourself to someone who doesn't give a fuck." I gestured vaguely his way. "Then, you came along."

Vincent blushed and sipped his tea. "Me?"

"Yes, *you*. I told Daphne I didn't want to meet you but she insisted — and the rest is history. Now I find out it was all an orchestration of Zane's. Do you understand why I reacted the way I did?"

He nodded. He'd finally stopped shivering and looked lovely with his damp hair and flushed skin, holding his teacup to warm his hands and taking small sips like he was in the Queen's parlor.

I continued. "But, I've decided, thanks to you being a complete idiot and risking hypothermia to get to me, that I *can't* give you up. I can't give up what we have, Vincent, because I think it's extraordinary." I said the last part softly, because it was true and I didn't want to jinx it.

He stared at me over his cup for a long moment, not saying anything. Then he put his tea on the coffee table and slid to the floor, resting his head in my lap.

"Thank you, Sir. Thank you, Nic. Thank you, thank you, *thank you*."

I took him upstairs and we made love under the covers so Vincent stayed warm. I sucked his cock into my mouth and stroked his balls until he begged me to mount him. When I did, he guided himself into me and sighed as my body enveloped him.

I leaned forward, kissing him deeply while I rocked on top of him, fucking him softly and slowly until he begged permission to come.

When I gave it, he gripped my hips and thrust, pumping me with his cock and filling me with his seed while I exploded into a million loud pieces.

He stayed at my place all day and we spent our time watching crap TV and cuddling in bed. He asked if he could stay the night.

I said *yes*.

Later I woke up in the darkness, terror in my heart. I glanced at the bed beside me, relieved to see Vincent's form stretched out beneath the blankets, his face on the pillow beside mine.

He was still here. He was *mine*. He was all mine and I'd be damned if I'd let either Daphne or Zane or my own fucking pride ruin this.

Chapter Seventeen

I called Daphne first thing on Sunday morning and let her know I was still mad but felt sorry for the way I'd been on the phone the last time we'd spoken.

"Nic, I am so, *so* sorry. I shouldn't have let Zane convince me this was a good idea."

"Well it was a good idea. It was a *great* idea, and that's what pisses me off more than anything else. Why did it have to be his idea? Of all people?"

"What? You mean, you and Vincent are still — ?"

"Daphne, he is the fucking *perfect* sub for me and I'm the perfect Dom for him and it's already gone way beyond that."

She squealed. "Really? Oh, Nic, that's fantastic! He seems like such a sweetheart. I knew he'd be perfect for you!"

"I'm teaching him to play the piano."

"No way."

"Yeah. Who knew you could make piano practice into a form of service?"

"You devil. I have to admit that I always thought he had a great mouth on him. Eats pussy like a champ. And he knows what to do with his fingers when he's *not* playing piano."

"Daphne. If you ever touch Vincent again, I will destroy you."

"Fine, fine. He's yours. I get it. I can't help appreciating him."

"Yeah, yeah, just appreciate him from a distance."

"Awe, Nic, I'm so glad you called. And I'm glad it's working out with Vincent. You deserve each other, you know. You're both sweet as fuck."

I laughed. "Seriously? I'm *sweet*?"

"Yeah, Nic, you're fucking adorable. I know you want to be the big bad Dom, but you're a romantic at heart."

I chuckled. She was right. "Well, don't tell anyone. Only you and Vincent know."

After I hung up, I found Zane's number in my contacts and unblocked it temporarily.

I shot him a text.

Hi, Zane. It's Nic. Are you going to be home this afternoon? There's something we need to discuss.

After about ten minutes I got a reply.

Hey, kid. Glad to hear from you. Sure, come on by. *happy face emoji*

I sent him a thumbs-up and told Vincent we were going to see Zane. He didn't look thrilled about it.

"Sure."

Vincent's clothes from the day before were clean and dry from the laundry, so he got dressed before we headed out. I was wearing my usual jeans and T-shirt with my leather jacket. I wore my shit-kicker boots and decided to drive, since both those things make me feel in control of the situation.

"Remember the last time I drove us somewhere?" I asked Vincent with a smirk.

"Oh fuck," he said, squirming in his seat. "Yeah."

"Me too."

We shared a glance and I focused on the road. "Let's get this little errand done so we can go back to my place and *play*."

"Yes, Sir."

Zane opened the door wearing a pair of sweatpants and some kind of old-fashioned smoking jacket. It was a typical outfit for him and I rolled my eyes as I remembered some of the things I'd seen him in. He wasn't as handsome as I remembered, perhaps because I had the most beautiful man in the world at my heel.

"Nic. Hey, Vince! Glad you two are getting along." He held the door open for us as we stepped inside.

"Yeah, that's what I wanted to talk to you about, Zane," I said, glancing about his well-appointed townhome and trying not to remember spending time there.

He spread his arms as if he were the Pope and bowed his head. "You're *so* welcome."

The anger rose in me like a swarm of hornets.

When he looked up, he saw my glare and frowned. "What's the matter?"

"Vincent, sit down," I said, gesturing to the sofa and not caring a whit that it was Zane's house.

Vincent did as he was told because he knew *I* was in charge. He was probably happy to be left out of this exchange except as a bystander and, well, the subject of it.

I turned to Zane. "What's the matter, Zane? Besides the fact that you went behind my back and manipulated Daphne into sending me Vincent? As, what, a *gift*? An *apology*?"

Zane shrugged, giving me his standard shit-eating grin. "A little of both, I guess. Why? Don't you like him?"

I closed my eyes to keep my anger in check. "That's not the point. The point is you used this exquisite boy for your own ends. How dare you?"

Zane shook his head like I was making too much of this. "Hey, it seems like it worked out fine. How are you liking Nicole, Vince? She's got a firm hand and a creative mind, doesn't she?"

I gritted my teeth. "Leave him out of it. And I told you not to call me that."

"Oh shit, I forgot. Sorry."

Vincent stood and moved closer. "And I told you I didn't like being called Vince."

Zane raised his hands and backed up a step. "Jeez, you two are made for each other. You're both so particular."

I shook my head, not even sure why I had ever had a thing for this guy. "Fuck you, Zane. Apologize to my face like a human being."

He crossed his arms over his chest. He did seem a bit chastened. God knew why. Was it my anger? My disapproval of his actions?

"Fine. I'm sorry for the way things ended, Nic. I didn't think you'd be that upset about it."

I pressed my lips together. "Yeah? Well, now I'm wondering why I was. I actually think I dodged a bullet."

"Now, that's not fair."

"Don't talk to me about what's fair, Zane. And stop interfering in my life. You blithely divested yourself of any involvement with me months ago, so just stay the fuck out of my business."

He seemed taken aback by my demeanor. "Fine."

"Come on. We're going."

Vincent glared at Zane as he walked past silently.

Zane laughed. "Wow. That boy needs a firecracker up his ass. Ask him how he likes *electro*."

I froze as Vincent turned back to Zane, his face flushing furiously. "You *fucker*! I fucking safeworded and you kept going. You're a fucking *asshole*."

I was shocked by the vehemence of Vincent's assertion but not surprised by this revelation, although it disturbed me greatly. Zane's methods had always been a bit questionable, but finding out he did something to Vincent against Vincent's wishes tripped something in me.

I took Vincent's hand and placed him firmly behind me. Then I was all up in Zane's face before he knew what was happening.

"If you ever even think about contacting either of us or interfering in our lives in any way, I will personally call the cops and charge you with assault on Vincent's behalf."

Zane shrugged. "It wouldn't hold, Nic. The cops see BDSM and they think everything's on the table."

"*Fuck you*, Zane. Fuck you and your self-serving philosophies." I took Vincent's hand and led him out of there and back to my car.

Zane stared out of his open door as if we'd just had a lovely afternoon tea together. He lifted his hand in a casual wave before he closed his front door.

"Fucking *prick*!" I exclaimed as we got in my car. I looked at Vincent as we put on our seatbelts. "Did he really ignore your safeword while he was doing electro with you?"

Vincent sighed and frowned. "Yep. Twice. I thought maybe he didn't hear me the first time. He definitely heard me the second time because I fucking yelled it at the top of my lungs."

I pulled out of Zane's driveway, glad to see the last of him. "Then what did he do?"

"He told me I was acting like a wimp and I could take more. But I didn't want to. He kept it at that high level and made me come against my wishes. I mean, I know forced orgasm is a thing but not when someone safewords." He glanced at me. "Am I right about that?"

"You're absolutely right about that. He was way out of line and that is actually assault, not BDSM. It's guys like him who give kink a bad rep."

"I didn't even want to do electro, but he was convinced I'd love it. Yeah, I didn't love it."

"Ah fuck. I'm so sorry, Vincent."

"For what?"

"For Zane, for what he did, for this whole thing. I need to make it up to you, show you how a real man treats his sub." I winked at him.

"Yes, Sir. Please, Sir. You are ten times the man Zane is."

And that was better than anything I'd heard in a very long time.

When we got back to my place, I asked him if he wanted to do a scene or just chill. I was honestly up for either.

He bowed his head and looked at the floor. "I, uh, I really liked that examination you did at my apartment, Dr. Walker, before everything went bad. I kind of want to finish that scene."

"I can certainly oblige you, Mr. Blake. We must address the problem you are having, after all."

"Fuck. You talk Doctor very well, Sir."

"I know. I've played this game before."

* * * *

Thirty minutes later we were at the point where we'd stopped back at his apartment. He was arrayed profanely on *my* sofa this time, ball gag in, hands bound with red rope, ass in the air — no blindfold. I was pumping him with two gloved fingers and stroking his cock with my other gloved hand. He was so close that he was going to blow any minute.

"Mr. Blake, your penis has gotten very large from the rectal exam I'm giving you."

Vincent groaned, pushing against my hand.

"Do you think you can have an orgasm from this?"

He thrust harder, nodding vigorously.

I took my hand off his cock. "I mean, of course, *just* from the anal exam?"

Vincent whimpered, thrusting against the empty air. I was pretty sure he could come just from having my fingers in his ass, though.

"I'm going to add another finger, Mr. Blake."

I pushed three fingers into Vincent's ass as he emitted a high-pitched whine. As I pumped them in and out, deliberately rubbing his prostate, I continued my clinical diagnosis.

"I believe your problem is a hypersensitive rectum and anal region. You seem to respond very readily to sexual *and* non-sexual stimulation of this area."

Vincent struggled, desperate now. He huffed and moaned and gave a deep grunt.

"I have a sneaking suspicion that if I keep doing *this*," I said, stroking his prostate rhythmically with a gentle pressure, "and just give your penis a little rub right here" — I massaged his frenulum with the pad of my thumb in a circular motion — "you're going to — "

Vincent shouted and shot, his anus spasming around my fingers, cock spurting jizz into the air in epic quantities as I pumped him through it.

Wow. I mean, *wow!*

He kept coming. I kept pumping him with my fingers. He kept yelling.

Finally, his contortions weakened and ceased. He lay there, quivering, sagging against my sofa as I pulled my fingers from him.

"Oh, *fuck* yeah," I said. "That was awesome, Vincent. Are you okay?"

He whimpered but his head bobbed. I stripped off the gloves and smoothed my hand over his rump. "Tomorrow I'm spanking the shit out of you, though. I want to see if you can come from *that.* Maybe if you're over my knee?"

Vincent whimpered, pressing into my touch.

I took him out of his restraints and removed the gag.

He licked his lips and said, "Tomorrow's Monday," with a questioning look.

"Oh, so it is," I replied with a cheeky grin. "Would you like to come over for a spanking before you make me supper?"

Vincent grinned. "Yeah, I would."

Chapter Eighteen

Vincent arrived just before five.

"I wore the polka dot panties for you, Sir," he said as I opened the door for him.

"Oh, Vincent. Then you'll have to strip down right now because I want to watch you walk around in them all evening."

He visibly shuddered as he started to strip in my entryway. I leaned back against the wall and observed him closely. He folded and piled his clothes on the small bench then straightened and looked at me for approval.

"Very nice."

And he did look nice. The small pair of overpriced satin panties looked pretty fucking spectacular with his cock outlined in the front, erect and angled to one side. He'd trimmed his pubes again, so everything looked neat and tidy but still extremely manly.

"Turn around. Hands on the wall." I pointed to where I wanted him.

He licked his lips and turned for me, presenting his gorgeous ass. I admired the polka dot satin then stroked my hand over it.

"So smooth. Maybe these were worth the price after all." I pulled my hand back and spanked him over the soft satin...once, twice.

Vincent groaned and pushed his ass toward me. With a quick movement, I pulled the panties down and laid two more slaps on him.

He cursed. I pulled the panties back up, made sure they were neatly in place before directing him to the kitchen and sitting at the table. "You see all that stuff on the counter?"

"Yes, Sir."

"You're going to make us something with that, and when you're not working on our supper, you're going to clean my counters and sink and sweep the floor. Got it?"

"Yes, Sir. Thank you, Sir."

"You're very welcome, Vincent."

I watched closely as he went about his tasks with a graceful competence. By the time supper was ready, I was fighting my arousal from the sight of his ass in those satin panties, his arm and back muscles rippling as he worked, and the vision of his cock straining against the soft cloth.

He'd made a simple meal of sauce and pasta with garlic bread, but my kitchen shone sparkling clean and the food was perfectly cooked and delicious. When we were finished, I directed Vincent to the piano.

"I want you to practice your scales for fifteen minutes, then work on this piece from last weekend, please."

He placed his fingers on the keys. "Will you be watching, Sir?"

"I have to get some things ready upstairs. I'll come down when it's time for you to stop."

"Yes, Sir."

"And I want to hear you working hard, Vincent."

"Of course, Sir."

Ah, so obedient.

I ruffled his hair. "You are such a *good boy*, Vincent. You're *my* good boy. Supper was delicious. Thank you."

"You're welcome, Sir. And thank *you*."

I left him to it, walking upstairs and heading into my bedroom where I had a surprise waiting for my delicate-not-delicate boy. I grabbed the bag of things I had purchased at the mall during my lunch hour and dumped them on the bed.

With a growing excitement to see Vincent all decked out in pretty things, I sifted through the items. There was a black lace garter belt, smooth black stockings and a purple basque with dainty trim and lacing up the back. I had wanted to keep the outfit a *little* masculine because Vincent was gender-fluid like me, so I had bought a pair of purple Doc Martens that he could wear in public and remember wearing in private with this outfit when he did.

I could hardly wait to dress him up but sat and listened to his talented fingers playing the song I'd assigned him. It was a simple one but he'd mastered it already. He had a knack for the piano and I planned to exploit that. He was now my little project, above and beyond teaching him discipline and service and showing him how much fun two people who understood each other could have together.

I was wearing my comfiest pair of faded jeans and a white button-down, untucked, with the sleeves rolled up. I'd gelled my hair into random spikes and even put on some eyeliner for him. When I went down and told him to stop playing and come with me, he obediently followed me upstairs.

Once he saw the items laid out on the bed, he gasped.

"Oh, fuck, Sir. Is all this for me?"

I laughed. "Well, it sure as hell isn't for me, Vincent."

"May I?" he asked, reaching his hand toward the basque.

"Yes, of course."

He picked up the dark purple corset and turned it over, examining the lace-up back. He ran his long fingers over the satin and lace trim. "This is so beautiful."

"It'll look even more lovely on you, sweetheart."

His eyes shone when he met my gaze. "I want to see how I look in this. Like, *now*," he said, eagerly eyeing the rest of my purchases. He saw the purple Docs. He looked at me, gobsmacked. "Did you buy those for me?"

I smiled. "They just screamed 'Vincent' to me. And you can wear them as regular footwear whenever you want. But they'll look great with this outfit."

"Thank you, Sir. I love them."

I picked up the garter belt and held it in one hand with my eyebrows raised. "May I dress you, sweet boy?"

Vincent blushed so adorably that I wanted to kiss him from head to foot but we didn't have time for that. "Of course, Sir. *Yes*, please."

So, I did. I put the garter belt on him first, then the stockings while he sat and offered me a leg at a time. I had him stand so I could fasten the clips to their tops.

We were both breathing fast as I brushed his thighs with my fingers and smoothed the stockings. I couldn't help feathering my palm over his erection under the polka dot satin and he gasped when I did, his eyes going wide. He parted his lips and the tip of his tongue touched his bottom lip.

"Fuck, Vincent. This is already too much and not nearly enough. You look fucking stunning."

"Thank you, Sir." His voice trembled as he let me place the basque around his waist.

"Turn around. Hands on your head. I need to lace you up."

"Yes, Sir."

"Those Victorians were certainly into bondage," I said as I pulled the laces tight. The silk hugged his torso in a most alluring way. I worked quickly to bind him into the ultra-feminine garment as my breathing quickened.

When I'd finished I turned him around. "Jesus fucking Christ."

He blinked at me, unable to see how fucking incredible he looked. But he had to have realized it from my expression.

"Rocky Horror, eat your heart out," I said, eyes running over his lanky form and defined muscles encased in such feminine clothing, not to mention his sizeable cock pressing against the panties.

My androgynous prince.

The basque pushed his pectorals up ever so slightly, the lace trim tickling his nipples.

I moved forward, settling my hands on the fine silk just above his waist as I impulsively bent my lips to a pinkish brown bud.

Vincent groaned as I licked at him, keeping his hands up obediently, but I could tell it was a struggle. I moved to the other nipple, using my fingers on the first, squeezing and pinching him.

"Sir," he panted. "Oh, Sir. Oh fuck!"

I gave his nipple a final lick with the flat of my tongue and stepped back, giving him a wicked grin and a rub on his restrained dick that made him close his eyes and whimper.

"Now the boots."

I knelt down, had him step into one and laced it tight while he looked down at me, breathing hard. Then the other.

When I stood up and stepped back, I shook my head and crossed my arms definitively over my chest. "If you aren't Victoria's Secret cover material, I'll eat my fucking hat."

He laughed. "Hmm-m… I don't know if they'd approve of *this*." He gestured to his dick, which looked obscenely delicious in the polka dot panties.

"Fuck 'em."

"Yes, Sir."

"Here… Look at yourself." I guided him to my full-length mirror. "What do *you* think?"

His eyes widened and he touched the silk of the basque then smoothed his hands over the lace of the garter belt. "Oh, Sir, I love it. I love it all."

"Oh, I almost forgot." I grabbed a black bag from the dresser and opened it, fishing out an eyeliner pencil. "Hold still."

I traced his beautiful eyes with the black liner, then his lips with a dark burgundy matte stick, just enough to make him look like he was about to head out to the clubs.

"You look fucking stunning. I'm going to be masturbating to this image for weeks...maybe months."

He pursed his red lips at his reflection then reached his fingers to his chest and pinched his own nipple above the lace, closing his eyes and making a soft noise.

And I could *not* wait any longer.

"That's it, you saucy tart. It's over my lap with you. *Now*." I sat on the edge of the bed, patting my thigh as I devoured his reflection. He lifted his chin and met my gaze in the mirror with the sultriest look he'd ever given me. He *was* a saucy tart.

I crooked my finger as I gave his reflection a stern look. "Get your delicious ass over here, Vincent."

He smiled and turned, moving toward me with the sexiest sway to his hips, working the androgynous thing like he'd been born to it.

And perhaps he had been.

He stood obediently by my knee, his arms hanging loosely, but he didn't seem to know what to do or how to place himself comfortably across my lap. It was going to be tricky, because he was so much bigger than me. In fact, I'd probably misjudged this.

"Hold on." I pushed myself back on the mattress until I was propped against the pillows and headboard with my legs out straight and room on either side. "This might work better. But I want you to get me something before you climb on the bed."

"Okay, Sir."

"Go over to my closet and look on the right-hand side, by my shirts. There's a hanger with a number of leather belts. Bring me the brown braided one, please."

He stared at me, his lips parting as he processed this request. He closed his mouth, turned and walked to my closet. His hands trembled as he fingered through the belts to find the one I'd asked for. I noticed his breathing had ramped up considerably. My boy really liked this idea—or else he was terrified. It was one or the other.

When he turned, his face was flushed and the bulge in his panties seemed larger. He walked carefully to the bed and handed me the belt.

"There you go, Sir."

It was a whisper as he stared at the leather of the belt when I took it from him and folded it, placing it beside me.

"Okay, up you get. Over my lap, if you please."

"Should I take the boots off, Sir?"

"Oh, absolutely not."

Vincent climbed up onto the bed with a sheepish smile and plopped down over my spread thighs with a happy grunt. I marveled at the sight of him draped over me in the fancy lingerie, his ass in those satin panties right where I needed it.

"Now that is a delicious sight indeed," I said, smoothing my hand over him. I slid my thumb under the straps of the garter that extended to the tops of his stockings, pulling them taut then letting them slap back against his skin. He gasped and turned his head, gazing at me with his cheek pressed to the mattress.

I lifted my chin and pursed my lips in a kiss as I slid my fingers under his panties and into the crack of his ass. Vincent squirmed, grunting, as I tickled his hole with my finger then pulled it back and smoothed the panties into place.

"Hands stretched out in front, please. I want to make sure they are well out of the way."

He obeyed promptly. As he stretched out, his cock rubbed against my thigh. He whimpered.

"Naughty boy. Don't you rut against my leg while I'm spanking you. I'll know if that's what you're doing and I'll go even harder."

"Yes, Sir. I mean, no, Sir," he said, voice breathy with anticipation.

Let's get started.

"I'll begin with my hand over the panties, then I'll pull them down for a real warm-up on your bare skin. I'll see how you're doing and we'll move on to the belt."

Vincent made a noise.

"Do you like that idea or hate it?" I asked.

"Like, Sir. *Love*, actually."

I had thought so. "Oh good. I'm dying to strap you while you're over my lap. I've always had good results before."

"Yes, Sir." His voice was barely a whisper, his eyes wide as he looked at me from the bed. It was too distracting.

"Close your eyes, Vincent. Keep them closed." Because I just couldn't stay focused with that blue fire directed at me.

He obeyed and I rubbed my hand over his bottom again, smoothing the soft satin in circles over his buttocks. I pulled my hand back and brought it down.

Vincent gasped as the sound echoed through the room.

"*One.* Let's go for ten."

I did the same thing on the other side. "*Two.*"

He grunted and squirmed. His dick bumped my leg but I knew he wasn't doing it on purpose. Not yet, anyway.

"*Three.*" I spanked each side, going back and forth, then the middle of his ass, then up underneath.

"How do you feel, Vincent?"

"Good, Sir."

We were both breathing hard—me from exertion and excitement and Vincent from pain and anticipation.

"Now I'm going to pull the panties down."

"Yes, Sir. Please, Sir."

I reached under the edge of the garter belt and slid my fingertips under the waistband of the panties, pulling them down slowly to reveal Vincent's naked flesh, pink from the spanking it had already received.

"Mm-m. So pretty."

Vincent groaned and pressed his cock against my leg then froze. "Sorry. Sorry, Sir."

"Good boy. Now quiet and keep still."

I started slow again, nice and easy. He liked it. I could tell. He moaned and gasped and tried really hard not to rut on me when I could tell he wanted to.

So, I went a little harder.

He was still into it, but his sounds were more desperate and I could tell it was really starting to hurt. I took breaks here and there to bring him back to the moment. I tickled the base of his buttocks where they met the tops of his thighs. I ran my finger down his spine to his lower back. I parted his cheeks and played with his hole while he made lovely, beautiful sounds.

After I'd spanked him as well as I could with my bare hand, we took an official break.

I kept him where he was but grabbed some lube from the side table and squeezed it into his crack. Then I took my sweet time playing very thoroughly with his ass, sliding my fingers in there, pumping him deep while I rubbed the hot skin of his spanked ass with my other hand.

Above and beyond the deliciousness of fingering him, I was totally getting off on the purple basque and garters, stockings and boots. It was like having an eighteenth-century molly-boy on my lap.

I felt his cock pressing down on my leg and it was *rock*-hard. He desperately tried to keep still but he would lose this battle eventually.

"Vincent."

"Yeah?" he breathed. He was in a dreamy subspace now, I could tell. I didn't remind him to call me 'Sir'.

"Does this feel good?" I asked, pushing my finger in him roughly and pulling it out, then doing it again, the sight of it breaching his ass over and over doing wonderful things to me.

"Oh God. Yes. *Yes.*"

"I love treating you this way, like my personal plaything. My sex toy. My boy toy. *A sex object.*" I jabbed him in time to my words.

He made the most beautiful sounds and I knew he loved it, too.

"I love doing what I want and having you lie there and take it. One finger? Two fingers? Three? It's *my* decision." I wanted him to feel truly objectified, because that was what got him off.

He groaned as I thrust three fingers inside him.

"Ah, fuck!" I said, drawing a breath between my teeth. "You look so dirty and slutty like this."

I pulled them out and flicked his balls with my finger, making him gasp and jerk.

His cock rubbed my leg. "S-sorry! Sorry… Oh…"

"It's okay, Vincent. All bets are off now. I'm going to try the belt on you and I'll let you rut against my leg if you want to. I want to see if I can make you come."

He moaned gratefully and pressed his forehead into his arm, whispering, "Thank you, Sir. Oh, thank you."

I picked up the folded belt, running it over his shoulders where they emerged from the basque and across his buttocks so he could prepare for what was about to happen.

When I brought it down on his ass the first time, he stiffened and cursed.

"You can take it. I won't hurt you for real, Vincent. But safeword if it gets to be too much."

"Yes, Sir." He held his breath.

"Breathe, Vincent."

The second time I hit him, he moaned long and hard. I brought it down a third time and he cried out, pushing his cock into my leg.

"You okay?"

"Yeah," he said, high-pitched. "I'm close. I'm *so* close."

"Oh. *Perfect.*"

I strapped him twice more, his skin flashing white where the belt touched.

He came on the third strike.

A wet warmth bloomed across my jeans as Vincent groaned, his body stiffening as the climax took him, his ass rocking on my lap.

"Fuck, fuck, fuck," I said, soothing him, stroking a finger over his hole as he shuddered through it. "So good, baby, so good. You did so good."

He pumped my leg until the last of his pleasure waned then he collapsed over my lap. The sagging weight of him comforted me, thrilled me. He was mine and I was so, so lucky.

Once he'd had time to rest, I stripped and had him fuck me with a dildo until I came like crazy, clutching his beribboned waist and kissing his rouged lips.

Afterward, he let me take his accoutrements off and accepted my apologetic kisses.

"We will save these things, and I will dress you in them whenever I please."

He smiled shyly, his face a mess of smudged lipstick, and sighed happily. "Yes, Sir."

Chapter Nineteen

Vincent arrived on Saturday morning with a bag of clothes and his toothbrush. We'd decided he'd sleep over for the time being, so we could be together as much as possible.

For whatever reason—maybe because I'd almost lost him—I wasn't frightened in the least by this prospect, only excited to share my space with him and have him serve me as much as he wanted. He could return to his apartment for brief periods when he needed to pick up more clothes or other items. But he was to stay with me otherwise.

He liked this idea and arrived in a great mood on Saturday.

"Vincent, good to see you."

"Sir. I brought my stuff."

"I see that. Why don't you put your bag upstairs?"

"Yes, Sir." He smiled, taking his bag with him.

I followed him to see what he thought of the changes I'd made to my room. I'd cleared a space on the bedside table so he could use it. I'd emptied the drawers as well.

Half of the closet had been cleared so he could hang his stuff up if he wanted to. I had found some well-made models of sailboats at my local thrift store that I'd placed around the room.

When he noticed them, he stopped and glanced behind him. "Did you get those for me?"

I shrugged. "For both of us. I love the ones at your place, and if you end up spending all your time here, you're welcome to bring them over and put them out downstairs…if you want."

"Thank you."

"You're welcome."

We went downstairs for a piano practice, after which Vincent made us lunch. While we were eating, there was a knock on my door. We looked at each other.

"I'm not expecting anyone," I said, standing up and walking to the door. I peeked out.

It was Daphne and, of all people, Zane.

"Oh, for Christ's sake. Why has she brought *him* here?" I said, more to myself than anything. I didn't want to open the door except I hadn't seen Daphne in ages and she saw me looking and raised her eyebrows with her hands on her hips.

"Open the door, Nic. Zane has something he wants to say to you," she said loudly.

"I don't think I want to talk to him."

Vincent came over to stand with me.

"Open the door, Nic," Daphne said again.

And because Daphne was literally the *only* person, besides maybe Vincent, who could tell me what to do, I opened the door.

"Hey."

"Hi," Daphne said, glancing at Vincent. "Vincent. I'm glad you're here. This won't take a moment. Zane?"

Daphne looked glorious in a beautiful camel-colored wool coat and knee-high leather boots, her long hair in an artfully messy updo, face made up expertly.

She pushed Zane forward. He crossed his arms like a spoiled child.

"Daphne wants me to apologize for sending Vincent to you, even though it looks like it's worked out great for you."

I crossed my arms too. It was a stand-off. "It has. But it doesn't count as an apology, Zane. And it was a sneaky and infantile thing to do."

"Fine. I'm very sorry about everything. I'm sorry for making you feel used and like a freak." He stared at me and I realized he was actually being sincere. "You're not a freak and I never thought of you that way. You're pretty fucking amazing, Nic. Just because I didn't reciprocate your feelings for me doesn't mean I don't think you're a goddamn kickass girl."

Daphne kicked him in the shin.

"Ow. I mean, guy. You're a kickass *guy*, Nic."

"Whatever. You need to apologize to Vincent." I felt nothing except disgust for Zane, after hearing what he'd done to Vincent.

He blinked. "I'm sorry for using you to my own ends, Vincent. I'm glad it worked out, though."

"No, not for that. For the other thing."

"What?"

"For ignoring his safeword during an electro session." I enunciated this clearly so Daphne heard every word.

She stepped back from Zane and gave him a scathing look, like she'd just discovered a piece of stinky shit on the bottom of her boot. "What the *fuck*? Is that true?"

Zane looked genuinely scared of Daphne—and he should be.

"He was having lots of fun. Weren't you, Vincent?"

Vincent shook his head. "I safeworded, Sir."

"Don't call that fucker 'Sir'," I said quickly.

"Nic, shut up," Daphne said. "Zane, is that true? Did you ignore Vincent's safeword?"

Zane shrugged. "Look… He seemed to be enjoying it. He came like gangbusters pretty soon after."

"Soon. After. *What*?" Daphne's voice sent shivers down my spine and hopefully turned Zane's bowels to water.

"Fine. After he'd said his safeword. Yeah, he said it and I ignored it and it was only a few minutes before he came hard. Like, *really* hard. What is the problem?"

"Wow. You're an even bigger asshole than I thought," Daphne said. "Get your ass out of here."

"You're the one who brought me!"

"So? Call an Uber. I'm done with you." She turned to me. "Can I come in, Nic?"

"Absolutely," I said, holding the door for her while Zane's mouth opened as if to protest. "Don't come back here," I told him as I slammed the door shut behind her. "What the fuck, Daphne?"

Daphne shook her head with regret. "I'm sorry, Nic. I thought if he apologized in person, things would be okay between you. I see now that I way overestimated his importance to either of us. What a knob."

Vincent cleared his throat. "May I say something?"

"Yes," we both said. Daphne took off her coat and handed it to me, revealing a pretty blue cotton dress that accentuated all her curves.

My sweet boy gazed down at the floor as he spoke. "I just wanted to say that when he had that fucking evil electro plug up my ass, I *did* come but I didn't get any fucking pleasure out of it. I hated it and I didn't trust him after that. If he hadn't sent me to Daphne, I wouldn't have kept going to him."

I moved toward him and tipped his chin to make him look at me then took his hands, staring into his beautiful blue eyes and raining silent curses on Zane and anyone else who would blithely hurt my boy. "You don't have to defend yourself, sweetheart. What Zane did was wrong…on so many levels."

Daphne nodded. "You just can't ignore a safeword in this lifestyle. You just fucking *can't*. Believe me, I'll be letting the community know Zane doesn't follow proper protocols. He'll be blacklisted by tomorrow."

"Okay. Good," Vincent said, not breaking eye contact with me. A silent promise flowed between us. He could trust me to never ignore his wishes and I could trust him to tell me when he needed a break.

Finally, I let go of his hands and straightened. "You want a cup of tea, Daphne?" I asked, hoping to save her visit. And it was really, really awesome to see her. I pulled her into a hug.

"It's wonderful to see you," I said out loud because, hey, maybe I'd matured a little.

She squeezed me tight. "Oh, Nic, I've missed you. We have to get together more often. And, yes, I'd love a cup of tea."

"Awesome. I'll have Vincent make us some."

Daphne grinned. "Can you tell him to take off his shirt, at least?"

I looked at Vincent, who rolled his eyes but smiled.

"I can do even better," I told her. "Vincent, Daphne is my guest, and as such, she is allowed to make requests of you." I snapped my head around and shot

Daphne a death glare while I continued speaking to Vincent. "Not anything personal and she can't touch you. But you have to listen to her unless I say otherwise."

"Sure. I mean, yes, Sir."

"Good boy."

Daphne pulled out a chair and sat down. "Vincent, please make us a pot of tea. I want you to strip to your underwear, if that's okay with you. If not, I will allow you to simply remove your shirt."

"Yes, Mistress." He peeled off his shirt, then undid the zipper and buttons of his jeans and pushed them down, revealing another surprise.

"Oh, hell," I said.

"Well, well, well," Daphne said, eyeing him eagerly. "Seems I missed an interesting opportunity."

Vincent was wearing a new pair of panties. These were black with a cross-hatched design and striping along the waistband. They looked virtually transparent and Vincent's cock was perfectly visible under the material, swollen and arching toward his right hip.

"Are those new, Vincent?" I asked, because I'd never seen them before.

"Yes, Sir."

I clicked my tongue and walked up to him, holding his gaze as I reached out and cupped his balls then stroked my hand along his dick. He closed his eyes and whimpered.

"They are very, very nice. I'm so glad you're able to show them off for Daphne."

"Yes, Sir. Thank you, Sir."

"Perhaps a little twirl is in order. Vincent, turn around, please. I'd like to see you from behind," Daphne said.

Vincent blushed and flashed me a questioning look. I inclined my head.

"Yes, Mistress," he said, slowly turning around in a full circle.

Daphne whistled. "My goodness. He looks gorgeous in those. Well done, Nic."

"That was all Vincent," I said proudly. "He likes to be pretty for me."

Vincent made a pot of tea and the three of us sat around my table and chatted and shot the shit. Daphne and I took turns teasing Vincent until his cock was so hard that I thought he might come right there in the middle of the kitchen. But Daphne noticed and decided to make her exit.

"Looks like he has something else for you, Nic. And, anyway, I must go. But it was fantastic to see you. I'm just sorry I brought that loser with me."

"He's long gone, I'm sure. And he won't be back."

We made plans to meet for coffee at her place the following week after she made Vincent promise to wear something sexy under his jeans again, which he did.

After showing her out, I turned to Vincent. "Okay, you saucy minx. Come here."

He moved close and I grabbed his ass, pulling him into me, rubbing myself against his dick in those see-through panties. "That was one hell of an unveiling, I must say." I fingered the waistband. "I love these."

"Thank you, Sir."

"No. Call me Nic. Daphne's gone and I want to be Vincent and Nic."

I took his hand and led him upstairs.

I laid my prince down on the clean sheets of my king bed and peeled the panties off him. I took his cock into my mouth, sucking and licking him and showing how much I appreciated his little gift. He sat up on his elbows and watched me, occasionally closing his eyes and letting his head fall back, then watching me again like he couldn't get enough of it.

"Stop. Stop, I don't want to come yet," he said.

I did stop but stared at him in surprise. This was so unlike Vincent that I was perplexed until he said, "I want to go down on *you*, Nic."

I smiled. "Okay. Sure."

Then I stripped and I didn't even mind that he was watching me, his eyes roaming freely over my nakedness that some days didn't match the way I thought of myself.

At that moment I didn't care. I lay back and watched as Vincent nosed into my crotch with the excitement of a teenager at his first hook-up. Soon, I couldn't keep my eyes open because I wanted to concentrate fully on the sensations of his tongue, his lips — *God* — his fingers as they pushed into me and stoked my desire.

"Ah, Vincent, Oh," I groaned as he made me come multiple times then climbed over top and pushed his cock deep inside me, making me come again as he came with a deep, long groan.

We lay there afterward, breathing hard and exhausted, our sweaty bodies entwined and wet.

When Vincent pulled out of me and rolled me over into his embrace, he kissed the top of my head like I was a cherished pet.

"I love you, Nic."

Instead of saying it back, because he knew I fucking did and it just sounded so cheesy, I kissed him softly, pulled back and stared my truth into his eyes.

"I know, sweetheart. I know."

Want to see more like this?
Here's a taster for you to enjoy!

Starting Over: The Divorce
Matthew J. Metzger

Excerpt

"Tinder or Grindr?"

For a long minute, Aled's brain refused to understand the words. He stared blankly. He'd only been home for ten minutes and was still in his suit. Words like budget, memo, marketing directive — those words he could understand. Tinder and Grindr meant nothing.

"What?"

His best friend's boyfriend huffed an enormously annoyed sigh and Aled frowned.

"I don't usually get people knocking on the door asking about dating apps," he said defensively. "Not even you're that weird."

Tom just rolled his eyes. "Tinder" — he wiggled the phone in his left hand — "or Grindr?" He wiggled the phone in his right.

"Why do you have Grindr?" Aled asked slowly, then backtracked. "Why are you on my doorstep asking me about hook-up sites? With two phones? Who needs two phones? Why are you even *here*?"

"Er, fourth of January? You, me, Suze, drinks at The Mason's Arms? Any of this ringing any bells?"

"Not in the mood? Don't feel like celebrating? Thirty-three isn't an important number? Any of that ringing any bells?" Aled asked sarcastically and closed the front door.

Or tried to. Tom shoved his size twelve boot in the way and impeded matters somewhat.

"Tom, seriously, I don't feel like —"

"Tough," Tom said. "It's your birthday and we're not having no for an answer this time. And Suze is too soft to say no to you, so she sent me."

Typical.

"I don't want anything except a pizza in front of the telly. Now go away."

Tom snorted. "Is there someone sharing your pizza?"

"What? No."

"Then find one — Tinder or Grindr?"

"You're not going to leave, are you?" Aled asked, pointedly eyeing Tom's boot.

"No."

"Fine. I'll get my bloody coat. And put those phones away. *Why* do you have Grindr?"

Tom made an excuse about a spare phone borrowed from his younger brother and shoved his way into the hall. He even followed Aled upstairs to keep chatting outside his bedroom door while Aled found some jeans and a decent shirt. Aled tuned him out. Tom was a talker and always had been.

"That'll do," Tom said when Aled re-emerged. "Put the good coat on. We're going to get you laid."

Aled narrowed his eyes. "No chance. One drink. That's it. I don't feel like going out in the first place."

Tom stopped dead at the top of the stairs. He was a big lad, built for rugby and about as fluid as a brick wall. Aled, at five seven, had no choice but to wait for him to move.

"You haven't felt like doing anything for a year."

Aled's temper sparked. "That's none of your—"

"Knock it off," Tom said sharply. His usually jovial voice had dropped to a grave timbre. "It's been a year and all you've done is work mad hours. And when you do come home, you drink yourself into a stupor and go through all your pictures. Enough's enough. You've got to stop wallowing and start living again."

"She's my *wife*—"

"And she's gone."

Aled swallowed thickly, shaking his head.

"She's gone, mate. She's not dead—she left. She's moved on. Time for you to do the same."

The words were soft, but they felt sharp. Aled's heart tightened and he jumped when Tom's heavy hand landed on his shoulder and squeezed.

"Come on," he coaxed. "Come out for a few pints and a curry with me and Suze. Like we used to. If you don't want to hook up with someone, then fine. But let's have a laugh and go through some profiles anyway, yeah?"

Aled laughed bitterly. "You call that moving on?"

"I call it better than sitting here in the dark with your wedding photos."

"She's my wife. What else am I supposed to do? I love her. I still love her. I'm always going to love her."

"I know. And I'm not arguing with that. But you're heading right for a breakdown, mate, and you're a better man than that. You think me and Suze are just going to watch you chuck in the towel for Melissa?"

Aled blinked, startled. "Chuck in the—I'm not bloody suicidal."

"Don't have to be to train-wreck your life."

Aled worked his jaw but said nothing. Christ, no wonder Suze had sent Tom round if that was what they thought. The anger ebbed and was replaced with a sickly sort of guilt. He didn't see nearly enough of either of them these days — no pub quiz, no pint and pie on Friday evenings, not even swimming with Suze after work. He never left on time. Or he just didn't feel like it.

Tom was right.

He hadn't felt like doing much of anything.

"So your solution is to find me another wife?" he joked weakly.

Tom snorted with laughter and finally moved. The stairs creaked under their combined weight and he threw Aled's leather jacket at him from the hooks in the hall.

"I'm not talking love, you daft berk. No fucker finds love on Tinder and Grindr. I'm talking about sex."

Stooping to lace his boots, Aled laughed. "You what?"

"Sex? You know, clothes off, penis in vagina? Or in arse, whatever takes your fancy."

"You think having a shag will snap me out of it?"

"Might remind you there's better things to do than sit around waiting for things to change," Tom said flatly. "Might kick-start a bit of the bloody fun meter that's been sorely lacking lately. And I've got a couple of suggestions."

Aled smirked. "No offence, but we're not exactly into the same things."

"Understatement of the century, you kinky, queer bastard." Tom grinned then towed Aled out of the door and barely let him lock up. They walked to the main road in a companionable silence, then Tom hailed a taxi and told Aled to shut up and put up when he moaned about going farther than the local round the corner.

"Suze gave you plenty of chances to pick a place."

Aled grimaced. "I've got some making up to do, don't I?"

"No shit, Sherlock."

They talked Suze—Tom's girlfriend, Aled's best friend—and some new yoga class she was trying to get Tom involved in. Aled's throat felt rusty and his jaw ached, like he hadn't just *chatted* for an age. But his shoulders eased and the vague headache he'd been nursing all day at the office dissipated in Tom's relaxed company.

So when they got to the pub, Aled held up a credit card between finger and thumb and offered to get the first couple of drinks in.

"Not going to catch me arguing," Tom agreed.

When he came back from the bar, both phones were on the table. Tom was tapping out a text to Suze on his personal mobile, but Grindr was still open on his other one and Aled raised his eyebrows.

"Better not let her catch you with that."

"She uses it," Tom said. "Likes to check out the competition."

"*What* competition? They're all gay on there."

"Fine by me!" he said cheerfully. "She's on her way. Game of pool before she shows up and thrashes us both?"

"Yeah, okay."

Aled liked Tom. It had been a bit of an unusual change—Suze's taste in boys all through school had been god-awful and Aled had been almost on an autopilot of immediately hating her boyfriends just because they were the type of shit boy that Suze had fancied back then. But then she'd met Tom and everything had turned around. Tom was just...nice. Laid-back. Genial. Well-meaning. Had a habit of putting his foot in it right up to his backside, but he never meant anything by it. He was easy company and — despite his sharp tone at the house — rarely got involved in other people's business. If Tom wanted to play pool, they'd just play pool. They'd not talk or go hunting on dating apps. They'd just play.

They had a few frames in the quiet, pre-piss-up half-hour before the pub started to fill, and moved on to a better drinking hole when it got too busy. The night was cold, the pubs were warm and Aled slowly relaxed as the lager eased into his system. Tom had a point. This was better than sitting at home, mourning Melissa.

Suze joined them after the fourth pint, a flurry of platinum-blonde hair and kisses, shrieking "Happy birthday!" so loudly that half the pub started singing and Aled grumpily downed his fifth pint with the savage urge to make it all go away. At the same time, though, he did feel a bit guilty. Suze had been his best friend for thirty years, ever since they'd both attended the same nursery. He'd even married her when they were five, playing dress-up in his parents' back garden. He was an only child, but it had never felt like it with Suze there all the time. She had always been on his side, throughout everything — and there'd been a lot of everything throughout their collective sixty-six years — and Tom's blunt words in the hall had jarred Aled a little.

He'd neglected her. In a year of wallowing with his photographs and empty house, Aled had forgotten to lean on her the way he always had. So after necking the pint, he leaned sideways and hugged her on a whim.

"Aw, sweetie, is Tom getting you plastered?" she enthused and kissed his cheek. "Good, you need a celebration. Thirty-three!"

"Don't remind me," Aled grumbled.

"Thirty-three and breaking a dry spell," Tom said, beaming. He had a huge grin that could swallow his whole face and Aled narrowed his eyes at it, sensing further traps.

"Breaking a dry spell?" Suze asked.

"Your boyfriend," Aled said, taking care not to start slurring, "is on Grindr."

"Your boyfriend has a brother on Grindr," Tom corrected.

"Mm, I'm sure it's just Daz," Suze said suspiciously. "Why are you on Grindr? And why does Aled know you're on Grindr?"

"Because it's hilarious, and because I told him," Tom said promptly and slid the phones across the table again. "So, Aled? Made your choice?"

Aled shrugged, draining the pint glass. "Fuck it, whatever."

"Grindr," Tom decided. "Women have screwed you around too much already."

"Excuse me! This woman has been amazing for him!"

"You're not shagging him, though."

"Is this what this is about?"

Aled left them to their minor domestic, dragging himself up to go to the bar and rubbing a hand over his face whilst waiting to be served. In truth, he didn't want to bother with any of it. But if letting Tom make him an account on Grindr and showing a bit of paltry interest would get them off his back, Aled would do it. He didn't want to sleep with anyone. He'd not so much as wanked since Melissa had left him, all interest killed by — by —

He blinked at the bar.

Fuck.

A year without so much as a wank? His whole marriage, they'd screwed two or three times a week. He'd lost his virginity when he was thirteen. Hell, he and Melissa had had an open marriage purely *because* they both had such high sex drives.

And yet he'd not so much as had a quick one off the wrist in a *year*?

Christ, maybe Tom was right. Maybe he was heading for a self-destruct.

"Another round, mate?"

"Yeah, yeah, thanks…"

"On the house. Heard the yelling it's your birthday and all. How young?"

Aled blinked. The barman was grinning at him, all gap teeth and eyebrow piercings. "Thirty-three," he said and the man guffawed.

"I bloody wish! Thirty-three, Christ, still got your life ahead of you! What you doing drinking it away in 'ere?"

Aled tuned out the cheery chatter, frowning at the bar. The guy was right. He was only thirty-three. And maybe if he did what Tom said, jump-started everything out of this rut, then he would get the impetus and the drive back to go after Melissa and talk to her about it properly. Maybe that was all she'd wanted, him to chase after her, like he had when they were teenagers.

He collected the round and lurched back to the table, banging them down, and said, "Right. Laid. Let's do it."

"No thanks, mate, you're a bit too furry for me," Tom quipped, but was grinning and tapping away. "Just setting you up now. Tell you what, I'll text Daz. He was going on and on about this guy he hooked up with when he was over, caused a right domestic, do you remember, Suze?"

"Oh, the repeat offender?"

Tom laughed. Aled frowned. "You what?"

"Yeah, Ryan said the guy was a repeat offender. Daz shagged him about four times, I think. Said he was brilliant. And Ryan didn't like that and they had a right barney about it. I'll text Daz and ask what he was called, see if he's still got his number or something. Sounds like just what you need."

"Not a *literal* repeat offender, I hope," Suze said snottily, then seized Aled's elbow. "You know what we need to do? Lose this dead weight and go clubbing again."

"Thirty-three, Suze. Not twenty-three."

"Thirty-three and doing good!"

"Thirty-three and getting fat," Aled corrected. "If I get my top off in a club like I did at your twenty-first, people'll be sick."

"With jealousy that you're not interested in them!" Suze sang, as Tom pushed the phone across the table.

"There. Start hunting."

Aled rolled his eyes and tentatively flicked through the offerings. Of which there were a lot. Seemed like West Yorkshire was a hive of guys who liked a bit of dick in their lives. But it was a bit depressing, too. Profile after profile detailing sexual positions, measurements, deciding that kinky meant the odd plug and a bit of whipped cream — Aled wanted to laugh. These people weren't kinky. They were just young, horny and thought vanilla meant the missionary position through a hole in the sheets. What the hell was he supposed to say to any of them? Do with any of them? They'd look at him and just see a thirty-three-year-old ginger shortarse with glasses, and assume he was as harmless and boring as he looked.

The phone buzzed, Daz's name flashing up along with the first four words of a message, and Aled pushed it back to Tom with an outstretched finger. "Text for you."

Tom buried himself in some frantic texting and Aled sat back, nursing his pint and scowling at it. Maybe he needed to get back into the scene. Or into it in the first place—he and Melissa had never really been into the actual BDSM scene. They'd more or less figured out what they liked on their own, but if Aled could...well, borrow someone for a bit, maybe, scout out a few other dominant types in the area and make use of a couple of their subs, perhaps.

"Oh, fuck me," Tom said and whistled. "Mate, *I'd* go gay for this one."

He pushed the phone back to Aled and a face stared up at him. Some summer snap, just a casual photo, sunglasses propped up on ink-black hair and even darker eyes almost smirking up at him. But it was the smile that got Aled's attention—perfect lips, flushed like he'd been giving head not five minutes before the picture was taken. He was shockingly attractive, so good-looking that Aled suspected it might be faked, or a photo of some random model, but—

God, that *mouth*.

His cock stirred, for the first time in a year, and Aled swallowed.

"Nice, right?" Tom said, grinning.

"Nice," Aled agreed, "but he's hardly going to want to go for someone like me."

"Daz is an ugly fucker and he banged him four times. Says he's sex mad. Just tell him you'll fuck his brains out and he'll probably pop right down here and join us," Tom said, grinning broadly.

angel23.

"What's his name?"

"Dunno, Daz didn't say. Says he's hot as fuck and a great shag, though. Leeds lad. Message him!"

Aled scanned the description. It wasn't much unlike the others—he bottomed, he wasn't interested in relationships, he—

What the—

I'm trans. Got a V and an A. Feel free to try either, or both if you're that good ;)

"He's trans," Aled said.

"You what?" Suze said, leaning over to look.

"He's transgender."

"What, he wants to be a girl?"

"Other way around," Aled said.

"Huh, maybe I wouldn't have to go gay for him…" Tom said thoughtfully and Suze smacked him. "Ow! What?"

"You're being an arse," she said loftily.

Aled hesitated, then opened a message tab. Why not? He'd done men and women. *angel23* couldn't have anything Aled hadn't seen before and he was fucking gorgeous, whatever he was packing. And that mouth would definitely help rattle Aled right out of this rut.

I'm that good, he sent. *Want to let me prove it?*

Sign up for our newsletter and find out about all our romance book releases, eBook sales and promotions, sneak peeks and FREE romance books!

About the Author

AE Lister/Elizabeth Lister is a Canadian non-binary author with a vivid imagination and a head full of unique and interesting characters. They have published 10 books, one of which received an Honorable Mention from the National Leather Association – International for excellence in SM/Leather/Fetish writing.

"Sensual and visceral BDSM." – Amazon.ca

AE Lister loves to hear from readers. You can find their contact information, website details and author profile page at https://www.pride-publishing.com